Who Bombed the Train?

A Skeeter Hughes, News Reporter, Mystery

Judith Yates Borger

This book is a work of fiction. The names, characters, places and incidents are products of the writer's imagination or have been used fictitiously and are not to be construed as real. Any resemblance to persons, living or dead, actualevents, locales or organizations is entirely coincidental.

First Forty Press Edition,
May 2014.

 Forty Press, LLC, 427 Van Buren Street, Anoka, MN 55303, fortypress.com

Who Bombed the Train

A Skeeter Hughes, News Reporter, Mystery

Judith Yates Borger

For Chris and Nick

PRESS

CHAPTER ONE

March 1

It was just like the good ol' days, slogging down beers and debating politics at happy hour with my best friends, Rachel Rand James and Fred Brewster. Fred and I are still journalists, but Rachel has gone to the other side. Now she's mayor of Minneapolis. Because it was Rachel's birthday, we chose the Loon, a watering hole with history for us, kitty corner from the First Avenue light-rail stop. Our server had just brought us another pitcher of beer.

"As usual, Skeeter, you are a raging liberal," Rachel said to me. "You might want to nail your left boot to the floor to stop your knee-jerk reaction."

"And you are so far to the right of Attila the Hun you're almost left yourself, Rachel," I said.

Fred took a position between us. The debate went on until we had drained half the pitcher.

"Fun as always, guys, but I gotta go," Rachel said.

"Already?" I said. "Come on. One more beer. It's your birthday, for crying out loud."

"I'm up for reelection, remember? Don't want one of you guys writing a story about how the mayor was arrested for public drunkenness."

"On one beer?" Fred asked.

"It was two, and I'm not taking any chances," she said as she dropped some bills on the table. "We politicians know that journalists are always working, even if they're sitting in a bar in downtown Minneapolis."

"Okay, be like that," I said with a smile, sending an air-kiss in her direction. She waved and headed out. I turned to Fred, "Do you think she'll take a cab or the lightrail home?"

"There's no predicting Rachel," Fred said.

* * *

After exiting the crowded bar, Rachel headed toward the lightrail stop. She walked smartly, waving to constituents as she went along. When she arrived at the stop, she stepped across the threshold of the Blue Line train and took a seat in back, a perch that gave her an opportunity to watch the other travelers unnoticed. She loved watching people because it gave her a feel for the voters. She prided herself on knowing what constituents needed before they had figured it out themselves. Sometimes she even took pictures to remind her of what she'd seen.

The train, half-full with folks leaving the bar and restaurant area of downtown Minneapolis, glided to the stop at the Hennepin County Government Center. Rachel watched the crowd, imagining their lives. The woman with the baby is tired after a long day's work and eager to get home to make dinner. The fellow pulling a large, apparently heavy suitcase? He's a little nervous because he needs to catch his flight at the airport and the train is running a few minutes late. The young man with the long ponytail wearing the messenger bag and biking shorts is looking forward to taking his new bike for a spin when the train stops at Minnehaha Park, even though March snow still covers patches of the trails.

When the packed Blue Line Light Rail train pulled into the Cedar-Riverside stop, Rachel pulled her iPhone from her purse. As people disembarked, she grabbed a shot of a chunky someone in a gold and maroon University of Minnesota hoodie and jeans, a couple of giggling Somali girls with their heads covered by red, purple and orange hijabs, and an older white man in a blazer talking to a young Somali in black pants and a tan zipped jacket. A picture of diversity, she thought. Then she sent a quick email to her best friend, Skeeter Hughes, ending it with "Love ya."

CHAPTER TWO

After Rachel left, Fred and I swapped newspaper gossip while we nursed our third beers. We had just ordered a pizza when our cell phones sounded simultaneously.

"This can't be good, Skeeter," Fred said.

The message went to all staff: "Blue Line bombed. All to newsroom."

Oh my God, another disaster. The last time we got a message like that the bridge had collapsed.

"I'm heading in." Fred stood, gave me a quick nod, threw money on the table and left. I did the same.

"I'm going straight to the scene," I said as we walked out the door together.

I ran to my red Honda Civic del Sol, which was parked at a meter, and roared away until I was within a quarter mile of the Blue Line. Road construction had traffic backed up, so I ditched my car in a no-parking zone. I grabbed my personal iPhone, the newspaper-issued piece-of-crap cell phone, and my notebook and pen and took off running. I ran up a pile of dirt, then did a face plant running down the other side. I was feeling that third beer. *Damn, I wish I were in better shape.* I wiped grit from my nose and mouth. Nearby construction workers were so busy watching the smoke billowing to the sky that no one noticed as I pulled myself up and brushed off.

I took off running again, albeit a little slower. Falling and getting up again took time I didn't have to get to the scene. I figured it would be thirty minutes before the police set up a perimeter impervious to everyone, especially reporters like me. I had to get as close as possible to see what was going on before the boundary went up.

If I moved fast enough I might land a spot inside the enclosure—I hoped. But if the cops saw me inside the perimeter they would haul me away. I needed good sight lines to the explosion site and a place where no one would notice me.

I looked around. Half a dozen pickup trucks, probably belonging to the construction workers, were parked on a residential street half a block away and well within sight of the disaster scene. Perfect. I climbed into the bed of a mud-spattered Ford Ranger. As I crawled under a blue tarp, I banged my knee on something hard and lumpy. Great. A big ol' bruise there to match the scrape I had from falling.

The heat from the explosion was so intense it warmed my cheeks and dried my eyes, even from that distance. Smoke obscured much of the scene, but it looked like the lead car on the light rail was destroyed. One side had been blown away and the top was missing, with the blue and yellow paint peeled back and melted-away ads on the sides of the cars

I doubted any of the passengers could survive. Still, I wanted to run right up to the train and pull people away, to cradle the children and tell them it would be all right. My arms ached at the thought that there was nothing I could do to save anyone. It broke my heart, but I dug back into last year's newsroom seminar on how to cover disasters. Let the first responders do their job and you do yours, we reporters were told. My job was to stay out of their way and report the disaster as accurately as possible. I needed to get the description of the scene, which was easy to see in the full moonlight and the glare of the fire, to the newsroom.

Barely catching my breath, I whipped out my iPhone and hit the speed dial for the newsroom Bat Phone, a dedicated line the editors monitor twenty-four/seven. Circuits must have been overloaded because I kept getting a busy signal. Same with the newspaper-issued piece-of-crap phone. I sent an email to content@Citizen.com, a general address monitored by many editors but emails can be slow. I thought about Twitter, but tweets can be read by anyone. I needed to word them deftly so they didn't tip off the TV stations, but I didn't have the time to choose my words carefully.

That left texting.

"I'm here. Talk to Fred," I texted directly to my editor, knowing Fred would tell her I had taken off toward the train.

By now the hundred feet between me and the burning train was swarming with cops and firefighters. Sirens wailed. A helicopter *whoop, whoop, whooped* overhead. But I didn't see any other media. It looked like I had managed to get inside the perimeter the cops had set up around the burning train.

"Ours alone, I think." I texted it with both my iPhone and the paper's piece-of-crap phone, just in case one got through better than the other.

On a breaking story like this we don't take the time to write full paragraphs. It's better to shoot just one sentence back to the newsroom as soon as you have a detail. An editor will pull it all together, hopefully taking out all the typos. In these days of the internet, every minute is deadline.

I counted twenty trucks from all the firehouses, each with their sirens blaring as they approached. Oddly, it was scariest when the siren stopped near my hiding place. The sound told me what my eyes and nose knew: I was very close to the horrendous scene. Cops, firefighters and first responders scurried everywhere like fire ants.

The catastrophe's foul odor hung in the air. Acrid. Electrical. Like a hair dryer that's been overheated times a thousand. Then the overpowering stench of burning metal. Fire engines wailed as thick black smoke, orange flames and yellow flames shot to the sky.

I heard a *Pop. Pop. Pop.* The sound may have been the big windows on the train exploding, but I didn't know for sure. The deafening rush of fire almost overcame the screams from inside. Almost.

Sirens from a dozen ambulances added their own discordant notes to the cacophony. Fire hoses squirted water at the train as people inside pounded the stuck doors, desperate to get out. Grim-faced first responders were doing their best to help, but it wasn't going well.

I kept texting.

Count 20 trucks from all firehouses. Cops everywhere.

First car on train fully engulfed. Smells like hair burning.

Popping noise. Don't know what. Electrical something?

Ads on train for Citizen and Metro Transit bubbled, melted on sides of cars.

I hoped someone in the newsroom, our newsroom, was getting all this.

Cops set up command center.

Hear rush of fire.

Windows pop out on train.

More sirens. See 6 ambulances.

Doors stuck on car. People pounding to get out.

Count two choppers above.

Fire hoses squirting at train.

In what seemed like seconds, cops set up a command center about thirty yards away from my hiding place. It wasn't long before a cop turned in my direction. Trying to hide, I ducked under the tarp in the truck bed, finding myself nose-to-nose with a giant rusty wrench. When I poked my head up seconds later I was caught in the steady gaze of Minneapolis Sergeant Victoria Olson. She gave me a slight nod, then said something to one of the other cops. I could see the vapor from her breath in the cold air as it mixed with the heat of the fire.

Someone was going to roust me, and soon, I figured, so I had to send back as much detail as possible because, as far as I could tell, I was the only representative from the public on the scene.

I texted as fast as I could.

Smoke clearing some. 2nd car scorched. First car totaled.

Grass around train burned for about 30 feet.

Looks like cops evacuating nearby houses.

Rescuers pulling people from 2nd car. 5 or 6 kids, I think. 25-30 adults.

People lying in dirt. Couple look dazed. One with broken arm? Heads bleeding. People limping.

Rescuers began pulling people from the cars. Some were lying in the burned grass that surrounded the train. *Were those people alive?* I felt a magnetism that made me want to run to the victims, but I tamped it down. I would just be in the way of people who were trained to handle emergencies.

Finally I got the reply that said my texts were getting through. "Keep it comin. Slick & Dick @ press conference."

I couldn't tell who sent it but it didn't matter. Someone in the newsroom was receiving.

Thank God.

* * *

Another explosion. I ducked under the tarp again, this time to protect myself. Good thing, too, because shards of glass, chunks of metal and clumps of dirt rained down on me. Unfortunately, I moved so fast that I banged into a pile of hammers.

As I rubbed my forehead, someone snapped the tarp away. "What exactly are you doing, miss?" said a white guy with a close-cropped haircut. His FBI badge hanging around his neck glistened in the light from the fire.

"I'm covering the explosion, sir," I said.

He unceremoniously hauled me from the bed of the truck that had briefly been my fortress. I hadn't done anything illegal, but that didn't mean he couldn't detain me.

"Who are you?" he asked.

I dug in the pocket of my filthy jeans to pull out my newspaper ID. He stared at it.

"Skeeter Hughes, Staff Reporter, Minneapolis Citizen," he read aloud, then handed it back to me.

"Has anyone claimed responsibility?" I asked.

No reply.

"Any idea what caused the blast?"

"Come with me please, Ms. Hughes."

"How many dead? How many injured?" I asked.

No reply.

"Why is the FBI here? Is this an act of terrorism?"

Silence.

"Did the train malfunction somehow? Faulty engine? Hit a car on the tracks?"

Nothing.

Ignoring all the questions I fired at him, the agent silently escorted me to a car, then told the driver to take me to their emergency holding pen for the press. It turned out to be a corrugated metal shed with a concrete floor, which had been commandeered for the purpose. There I cooled my muddy heels.

The otherwise barren room brimmed with twenty or thirty journos—digital, print, TV and radio, even a couple neighborhood bloggers—shuffling about in the cold dampness. They were waiting for a police official to give them official information that, officially, would likely be barebones. One TV reporter was dealing with a runny nose, which would be a problem for her live shot. Others, drinking what smelled like stale coffee, looked like they were afraid to go to the bathroom for fear of missing something official. A TV cameraman sat on the concrete floor next to his equipment. Apparently he had done disasters in the past because he came prepared. He was reading a current New Yorker.

In the movies, these scenes are depicted as mayhem, with arrogant newsies shooting impertinent questions at public servants who are just trying to do their jobs and make it home for dinner. That's not how I've seen it. I've covered press conferences like this and hated them, not because of the discomfort, but because the "official" word really means the highly varnished truth.

Among those milling around were Slick Svenstad and Dick Richards, my newspaper's two reporters, who are happiest when nestled at the official teat. They're known as Slick and Dick, split from the same zygote before anyone knew what a zygote was. But no one can figure out why Slick is short and stocky and Dick is tall and thin.

"Big story, huh?" Slick said. "Where you been?"

"A lot closer to the disaster than here," I said.

"Aren't you a friend of the mayor?" Dick asked. "I hear the cops are waiting for Her Honor to show up so she can talk at the press conference. Can you get her to shake a leg? Tick tock."

Rachel! Where was she? I had been so busy texting reports back to the newsroom that I hadn't checked my email, the method Rachel usually used to connect, because, she said, she had too many important words to fit in a hundred forty characters.

I pulled out both my phones and thumbed through the emails

until I found the most recent one from Rachel.

"I decided to take the train because cabs are too expensive," she wrote. "Besides, how would it look with the mayor getting out of a cab in front of her house? I had a great time tonight. You guys are the best. Love ya."

Rachel. Oh my God, Rachel.

Rachel was on that train. Was she in the first car where I saw no survivors? Or the second that had some survivors? I don't think I saw her taken from the wreckage. I read through her email again but there was no telling.

I could hear my heart pounding in my temples, and my legs went slack. No. No. No. Not Rachel. I couldn't imagine life without Rachel. She was a bridesmaid in my wedding and I in hers. She was the one who told me purple eye shadow looked horrible on me. When her husband walked out on her I took her to chick flicks. I held her while she sobbed.

The combination of beer on an empty stomach and the thought that I had lost my best friend roiled in my gut. I stepped outside to a trashcan half full of sand for the icy sidewalks. I grabbed the rusty sides of the sand barrel and barfed. And then I cried.

When I was done I stepped away and wiped my mouth with a dirty tissue I had stuffed in the pocket of my jeans. The adrenaline of the last few hours had seeped from my body. I took a deep drag of the cold March air. I took another and another, trying to calm myself. I leaned my head back to stare at the heavens. The clouds were painted that gray that's too warm to snow and too cold to rain. Odd thoughts popped into my head. I wished it would snow again, or melt away all together, anything to get rid of the March crust.

When my focus returned, I texted the newsroom.

Mayor was on train. Not sure which car.

The bosses would call Slick and Dick, who would find out officially if the mayor had died in the bombing. They would beat me out of the story of the decade, but I didn't care. I knew I couldn't make myself write a word. I was frozen by all the messages that overloaded my brain, like a computer that hadn't had its memory updated.

Rachel was my best friend. Was my best friend dead?

I knew a lot of other men, women and children were dead. The light rail had blown up. How could I write a detached report?

I stumbled away from the throng of press and walked a few blocks. Along the way I called Rachel's cell about a dozen times but only got "Hi. This is Rachel. You know what to do." How could the woman who sounded so chipper be dead?

Whether Rachel were alive or dead, I just couldn't leave the scene so I headed back. I knew I wouldn't be much good, that Slick and Dick would take it from here. But I stayed until after deadline at eleven o'clock, just because that's what I do.

Finally, I went home, slipped into my nightshirt that says WILL WRITE FOR FOOD, then tiptoed into my daughters' bedrooms to inhale the sweet scent of their sleeping breath. I pulled up the covers on Suzy, who always kicks them off, and brushed Rebecca's hair away from her face. I took some solace that they were safe in their beds on this horrific night.

Michael, my husband, snored in our bed. I didn't want to wake him because he hadn't been sleeping well and he would be getting up in a couple of hours with the girls. Plus, dealing with him drains all my energy when my life is going well. There was no telling what might happen if I woke him tonight.

I called Rachel's phone a couple more times, then crawled into bed, putting my phone under my pillow so I would be sure to hear it in case she called back. But sleep wasn't an option, so I got up and began checking the websites for our paper, the St. Paul paper, CNN and the New York Times. They all carried reports of the explosion but nothing about Rachel.

I must have dozed off, because I startled and found my cheek resting on the keyboard. I stumbled back to bed when I remembered an old prescription for Ambien. I dug through the drawer in my bedside table, found the bottle, took the remaining two pills, then burrowed beneath the covers.

When I awoke several hours later, I dug my iPhone from under my pillow in hopes there would be a message from Rachel. Then I went to my newspaper's website. There it was, in a headline I couldn't deny: "Mayor, 63 others killed in train explosion."

CHAPTER THREE

When I finally got up the next morning, I made my way downstairs and found the house empty and the newspaper on the kitchen table. Apparently, Michael had gotten Suzy and Rebecca off to school and left. "What a shame," Michael had written on a Post-it note stuck to the headline.

So this is what it feels like to lose your best friend. Although my tears were spent, my eyes felt like they were full of sand. Vomiting had left me dehydrated. Even though I knew plain water would help and caffeine would only worsen the effect, I made a cup of coffee and sat down to read the coverage. It said investigators were still looking for the cause of an explosion that blew up a two-car light rail train as it pulled away from the Cedar-Riverside platform heading south from downtown Minneapolis toward the Mall of America. The train driver and sixty-three people were killed, including Rachel Rand James, the mayor of Minneapolis. Another two dozen were seriously injured and taken to area hospitals where they were treated for wounds ranging from serious to very serious. Six were treated and released.

The paper suggested that readers check its website for updates on the conditions of the injured. Our city hall reporter also wrote a profile of Rachel. I noted that it left out a few facts, but gave him a pass. Usually newspapers write obituaries of famous people and file them to be pulled out, freshened up a bit, and printed when the person dies. There was none for Rachel. She was too young for anyone to have done that kind of reporting in advance.

The photo of Rachel was from her campaign literature. I stared at the picture through my tears. Her hair was big and brown and lush, her eyes deep and muddy as a puppy's. Her mouth was set in a smile exuding confidence that seemed to say, "Vote for me and I will take care of this city as it's never been taken care of before."

Slick and Dick had joint bylines on all the lead pieces of the explosion coverage. I had to admit they did a good job. No, they did a great job. They gave context to the tragedy that the television stations, even the national big guns, couldn't. They produced transit engineers who gave critical detail about the likely location of the bomb, the structural damage it had caused, and the effect on the surrounding area.

I made another pot of coffee and read all the coverage a third time, then came to a decision: I wanted to report the follow-up on this story, not just because I'm ambitious, which, truth be told, I am. But there's more to it than ambition. A million questions burned through my brain. Was this about Rachel? Was she in some kind of trouble I knew nothing about? Would someone kill a whole trainful of people to get to the mayor? Who would kill all those men, women and children? What could possibly motivate someone to do that? Was this an act of terrorism? If so, why? And why Minneapolis? Why the light rail train? Why not the Mall of America? Why not Chicago or Los Angeles or some other bigger city? Or was this an accident? A bomb that went off too late after the train pulled away from the stop in front of City Hall. Who would do something like that? I had to find out, not just for me, but for all the people whose lives had been changed forever. I vowed I would find out: Who bombed the train?

I sent my boss an email that I was taking a sick day, which I assumed she'd already figured out, and then crawled back into bed. I woke hours later to the sound of the girls chattering with Michael. It was sweet music to my ears as I stumbled out of bed and to the kitchen.

"You look like hell." That was Rebecca, our fourteen-year-old fashion critic.

"What? You don't like my night shirt?" I asked. I didn't mind one bit that she was being sarcastic and snotty. I was used to it. Just seeing my girls gave me a lift that I really needed. "C'mere, you guys. Give me a hug."

We three wrapped our arms around each other and squeezed, while Michael looked on, expressionless. "I like bunchy hugs." That was Suzy, our eleven-year-old.

"Is Rachel really dead?" asked Suzy.

"Yes, she is," Rebecca told her.

They both started to cry and I hugged them again, only tighter. Although they had six uncles, my brothers, they had no aunt, only Rachel, who loved them dearly.

"Remember the time she took us to play laser tag?" Rebecca said.

"Of course," I said. "Last year."

It was an early spring evening when Rachel pulled up at our house in her Ford Explorer. She'd divorced a while before and had been mourning that it was unlikely she would ever have children. I reminded her she was Auntie Rachel to mine.

"Look what I've got," she shouted. She'd walked in our living room without knocking.

"Who wants to play laser tag?"

Rebecca heard her first and came running.

"So cool, Auntie Rachel," she shouted. "Let me see."

"Rachel, what were you thinking?" I said as she pulled the weapons from four huge Toys R Us bags. There were two toy Glocks and two AK47s and four vests.

"I was thinking that if your girls are going to compete in a man's world they should learn to play boys' games," she said.

"I was hoping that by the time they're women it won't be a man's world anymore," I said.

"Don't be naïve." She gave me that superior look I had come to know so well.

By this time, both girls had unwrapped the goods and donned the vests. Rebecca pretended to shoot the AK47 while Suzy was pointing the Glock at her.

"We are a peaceful family," I said. "We don't do guns."

"Oh, Mom, come on," Rebecca said. "Just once. This is so fun."

"You can't play laser tag in the city," I said. "Someone'll think you've got a real gun and call the cops. Next thing you know I'll be posting bail for you."

Rachel had already thought of that. "My cousin has a place on six acres in the western suburbs," she said. "I already called her. They're going out of town tonight. She said we could use her place."

"To play laser tag!" Rebecca shouted.

"To play laser tag!" Suzy mimicked her. "What's laser tag?"

"See what I mean?" Rachel said. "These girls've got some learning to do."

I looked at Rachel, in her black turtleneck shirt and black cargo pants. Suzy had on a pink flowered shirt and jeans, and Rebecca was in jeans with fluffy slippers and a ribbed navy knit shirt.

"Think of it this way," Rachel said. "It's a moist spring night. The air smells so good and we'll all get plenty of running. Think of it as exercise."

"We?" I asked.

"That's why I got four," she said. "It's time you got a little exercise yourself."

Michael came up from his office in the basement at just that moment, his glasses about to slide off his nose, a business magazine tucked under his arm.

"Who's getting exercise?" he asked. When he saw the guns, he put both hands in the air and said with a smile, "Don't shoot."

Rachel explained, ending her idea with "Skeeter's skeptical."

"Reluctant," I said. "I'm reluctant."

"I think Rachel's right," he said. "Go. All of you. Go."

Rebecca and Suzy squealed like girls.

"All right," I said. ."But if either one of them grows up to be a Marine, I'm going to hold you, Rachel, personally responsible."

Within half an hour we were all dressed in black, speeding along in Rachel's truck toward the wide-open fields of the second ring suburbs of the Twin Cities. Along the way, Rebecca explained laser tag to Suzy.

"You mean we shoot at each other but nobody dies," Suzy said. "This is gonna be fun."

It was fun. We ran through the fields like huntresses. Each kill was followed by a resurrection and a chance to shoot or die again.

After a couple of hours we were covered in mud, exhausted and hungry. On the way home, we stopped at a Dairy Queen that had just opened for the season. I bought four Blizzards, knowing full well each had more calories than all of us had expended combined.

"Auntie Rachel," Rebecca had said after we returned home, "you are the best auntie I've ever had."

"Yeah, the best," Suzy had said.

"We'll never get to play laser tag with her again," Suzy said.

"No, honey, you won't," I said. "But I'll still play with you."

"It won't be the same," Rebecca said.

CHAPTER FOUR

Newsrooms can have the feel of a frat house. Hence the ongoing debate about who has the biggest list of sources.

"Mine's bigger," Dick has been known to say about his phone list, among other things.

"Yeah, but half of those names collect their mail in the cemetery," Slick has replied.

"Well, three-quarters of yours are senile," Dick has fired back.

But not immediately after the bombing. Our newsroom was eerily quiet when I went in the next day. Although everyone was still working to give readers the latest information on what had happened, the mood was somber as follow-up stories passed among reporters and editors.

Hardly anyone was talking, except Slick and Dick, who are better wired into the cops than most cops are themselves. They refuse to let anyone get a better cop story. It's rumored that Slick sleeps with a police scanner by his pillow. Dick has been known to kick loose an electrical plug to stop power to a television camera from a station that stole his scoop. There's also a story about one of them standing next to the microphone for one of the radio stations, whispering "fuck, fuck, fuck, fuck, fuck" to make the audio impossible to air, but I don't believe that one.

Their work on the explosion was the kind of reporting that would probably get a Pulitzer for breaking news coverage. Just like the careers that were built on the reportage from the fall of the 35W bridge in 2007, this one had the potential to land a reporter a much more prestigious job with a national, or even international, news outfit. Unfortunately for them, Slick and Dick are in the winter of their careers, and the time for them to jump to new professional heights has passed.

My career, on the other hand, was just beginning to pick up steam. Like most journalists, my first beat had been covering one of the suburbs. A series of stories about a girl gone missing earned me a promotion into the main newsroom in downtown Minneapolis. I was assigned a new beat, missing persons, and in the first month managed to actually figure out what happened to a woman who had disappeared. Until yesterday I was searching for three more people. But that project was now on hiatus, at least in my mind.

"It was one of those Somali gals who planted the bomb," Dick said as I slid into the chair in my cubicle, which is across from theirs. "But your politically correct editor cut it out."

"Why do you think it was a Somali woman?" Long ago I had learned that it was better to just let Slick and Dick talk rather than argue with them. It certainly was more entertaining.

He reminded me of recent reports that terrorists had been turning to Muslim women as suicide bombers because they can easily hide bombs under their loose clothing.

"The guys in the cop shop say those long dresses are just the ticket for shoplifting," Dick said with a sly wink. "And you know most of those East Africans are tall and thin. Whenever I see one that looks fat, I know she's picked up a thing or two at Macy's."

"That's one of the more novel spins on the abaya that I've heard," I said. "So you think they all shoplift and blow up trains? I cannot believe you guys."

"Hey, he was exaggerating," said Slick, who got his newsroom name because he's always cleaning up after Dick, even though they agree on almost everything. "Of course, there was the Somali guy who was convicted in our fair city not too long ago for recruiting Somali high school boys to be terrorists."

"Just because the train blew up in the heart of Minneapolis's Somali community doesn't mean the bomber was Somali. Or Swedish, Irish or German." I could feel my blood pressure rising. "In fact, there's no evidence that there was a bomb. It could have been something wrong with the train itself."

"They killed your best friend," Slick said. "Aren't you mad

as hell?"

And there it was, I thought. Rachel would savor the deliciousness of my dilemma. Me, the raging liberal who believes in open immigration. Who believes we should educate all kids in the United States, whether they were born here or not. What if one of those immigrants whose tuition I'm paying blew up my best friend and sixty-three other innocent men, women and children? What if Dick is right?

"Or maybe someone wanted to kill Her Honor the Mayor," Dick said. "Maybe she was involved in some kind of bad deal. Maybe there was a problem between her and one of the zillion developers in town. Or a crooked city council member. Ever think of that?"

Actually, I had thought of that possibility, but discarded it immediately.

"I doubt it," I told Dick. "I can't imagine anyone killing so many innocent people in order to get Rachel."

CHAPTER FIVE

Fortunately, at that moment my new editor, Leona McGee, strode past my desk.

"Hey, Leona." I said.

My former editor, Thom, who was the rock I needed in my last story, had been recently terminated. Not because he had done anything wrong, but because he had done so much right during the fat years when owning a newspaper was a license to print money. His downfall was that management rewarded him with raises and promotions that removed him from the Newspaper Guild. When the lean times came, he was being paid too much for the newspaper to sustain. I looked upon his story as a cautionary tale. If you're going to climb in this sad-sack industry you've got to move to different, larger, newspapers every few years with a salary jump each time so management thinks you're a hot hire. That's what my new editor had done when she took Thom's job.

"What d'you need, Skeeter?" she asked.

"Can we go in one of the small conference rooms to talk?"

"No, I'm on my way to a meeting. Talk here."

I didn't want to make my pitch in front of Slick and Dick.

"Can we have lunch?"

"I'll get back to you after lunch," Leona said.

Not a good sign. Thom would have sat right down in the chair next to my desk to listen, because, he told me in a weak moment, he liked to hear my ideas. He appreciated the work I'd done in the past and knew what I could do in the future. Also, I often had dark chocolates sitting on my desk in a dried-up glue-pot, a relic from the 1970s when my mom was a reporter.

"I want on the follow-up team for the bombing," I said.

"Why?"

Not what I had expected.

Thom would've said 'sure' and that would've been the end of it. I couldn't tell her I wanted in because it was a career-making story, or because I was sure Slick and Dick would pin it on the Somalis, even if there were no evidence. I certainly couldn't tell her I wanted to rout out Rachel's killer because she was my friend. None of those reasons would have convinced her that I was the best choice for the story.

But I had another reason that would appeal to her as a news editor.

"Because I have friends in the Somali community who will talk to me, and nobody else," I said.

"Oh yeah? How? Who?"

"A few years ago, before you were here, I did a story on Somali women."

"Why does your connection with the Somali community mean you're best qualified to follow on this story?" she asked.

Hmmm. Good question, I thought, then chose my response carefully.

"Because the train blew up within walking distance of Riverside Plaza, the heart of the Somali community," I said. "It's ground zero."

"Are you saying someone in the Somali community blew up the train?"

"No, but Slick and Dick are."

That brought a rise to her right eyebrow.

"Look," I said. "I'm guessing Slick and Dick aren't alone. I overheard a couple of women walking behind me on the street this morning. One of them said she was sure the cops would arrest 'some Somali' soon in the bombing. The other said, 'I never trust men with orange henna in their beards."

"You point is ....?" she asked.

"My point is that maybe the bomber is Somali. Or maybe not. But at least I have a place to start asking questions."

"Slick and Dick are tight with the cops," she said.

"And how close did that get them to the burning train?" I asked.

The same eyebrow ticked up again.

Leona hadn't been at the paper or even in town when I reported the story on the Somali women—which was very well done, if I do say so myself. She had no idea of how hard I had worked. She didn't know that story took months of hanging out at Cedar-Riverside, the neighborhood where the train blew up. She was clueless that it had what we call "a very long on-ramp," meaning it took a very long time to get access to sources, probably the longest I had ever encountered. She didn't know that most, maybe all, Somalis have cell phones rather than landlines, and cell phone numbers are impossible to find, unless you know someone. And I knew plenty. Even at that, the phone numbers change all the time. Tracking down who you need to talk to can be tough. But she didn't know that either.

"You haven't had much time on the missing-persons beat." She played with a whisker on her chin that definitely needed shaving—or better yet, plucking.

True, I had only been covering missing persons for a month, and I did enjoy the beat. I'd had a good story or two. But that was before someone blew up the light rail. Who knew the story of the decade in this town would come so soon after I took the new beat?

"I think you should stick with missing persons for a while before trying something like this." She walked away.

What? She was going to rely on those two old windbags when I had better contacts than anyone in the room? Not likely. Maybe she just needed enlightening. Yeah, that's it. She hadn't seen the fine work I did before she arrived. Easy to fix. I called what we used to refer to as the library and asked an intern to pull a paper copy of the Somali women piece and send it to Leona. Then I wrote her a note—on paper, not an email—explaining everything I had done to gather those sources. While she was in the meeting, I sashayed to her desk and paper-clipped my note to the envelope, which I rested on her keyboard.

I spent the rest of the hour surfing the 'net, making it look like I was doing something beyond steaming. After my blood pressure went down and I managed to unclench my jaw, I ate a quick lunch—a bag of popcorn and a salad from home—then headed for the glass tube that is the skyway to my favorite dessert: a cappuccino. Coffee has always been my friend. It gets my muscles moving, my heart beating, and my brain engaged. Smoking used to be equally useful, but smokers are pariahs these days, probably for good reason. Actually, there's no doubt about it. But I can't say I don't sneak a quick one from time to time.

"The usual?" the barista asked me.

"Yep."

As she dropped the nozzle into the metal cup of skim milk, I felt a presence behind me, like someone was watching the back of my head. I turned to see she-who-was-not-Thom, Leona.

I can't lie. She's fat. Probably 350 pounds on a five-foot-six body of indeterminate age. She usually wears a navy blazer over black slacks in the newsroom. I imagine her at-home outfit would be a sweatshirt and jeans—if she ever went home. Her long black curly hair is usually held back in a ponytail. Paper clips keep errant strands from her eyes. Deodorant and a smile would go a long way for her. Newspaper people tend to have faces best used on radio and voices meant for print. Leona was no exception.

She's also smart. Very smart. Undergrad at New York University, master's in journalism from Columbia. She came to the *Minneapolis Citizen* from one of our sister papers a couple months ago. Scuttlebutt from there was that her family has serious New York money, which she disdains.

"Skeeter," she said with a tiny nod.

"Leona," I replied. As I turned around to the task at hand, paying for my cappuccino, I wondered if she'd had time to ready my carefully crafted note. On the first of the month I put twenty-five dollars on my plastic coffee card. It's my own little savings plan. My goal is to have a little bit of money left on the card at the end of the month. Unfortunately, I usually had a little month left over at the end of the money.

As I dug through my purse looking for the card, I gave myself a little talking-to. Okay. Leona is not my favorite editor, or even person. But I seriously want to work on the follow-up to the train bombing. To do that I need Leona's blessing. Every job has times that require sucking up. This is one of them.

"How's your day going?" I asked as she paid for her coffee, lots of cream, plenty of sugar.

"Good," she said. "I wanted to talk to you."

"About ....?"

"Dick told me you and the mayor were friends."

"True."

"He and Slick think you should not be working this story because you're mourning the death of your friend and that will cloud your objectivity," she said.

"That's nuts," I snapped back. "Damn those two. Yes, Rachel and I were friends—good friends, in fact. But that is not an obstacle to reporting the story objectively. "In fact, it's what drives me to find the bomber."

We walked together toward the newsroom, each of us carrying our coffee. I haven't worked with Leona long enough to know her body language, but she seemed to be thinking before she finally spoke.

"I read your note. You make a compelling case," she said. "These are incredibly difficult times. Newspapers are circling the drain. Nobody knows how to make us viable again. I think it's time we went back to the days when reporters wrote what they felt."

Get to the point, please, Leona. This was definitely sounding better. Should I tell her of my personal vow to find Rachel's killer?

"Go on," I said.

"I recommended to the big guy that we assign you to find out who bombed the train," she said. "He's okay with it."

"Good idea, Leona," I said.

"Thought you'd agree." She took a sip of her coffee.

"But be aware. I'm taking a chance on you because you are driven. You and I need to be Velcroed at the hip on this. I don't want any surprises that are going to get me in trouble up the chain of command. You tell me every move you plan to make. Understand?"

"Got it."

"Slick and Dick want the story, but they don't have your passion," she said. "On the other hand, someone has to look into whether the mayor was the real target. I've decided to assign them that angle of the story."

I was not pleased with her decision, but I understood it.

"Do you want us to work together?" I hoped she'd say no.

"Keep your work separate from theirs," she said. "There's a conflict of interest if you're investigating your deceased good friend. I'll be directing their reporting just as I'll be directing yours."

I hadn't scored as I had hoped, but I could live with the situation. As I watched her walk away I said to myself, "She has lovely hair. Maybe she's not so bad, even if she isn't Thom."

CHAPTER SIX

Being careful, of course, to not spill my cappuccino, I practically ran back to my desk. I dug through my drawers for the notebooks I'd kept from that story I had written a few years ago about Somali women. It's a standard of journalism that what we put in the newspaper is public for anyone to see, and what we put in our notes is not. Notes can contain hunches that prove untrue, or confidential information we won't share. If notes are thrown out long before a lawsuit commences, they cannot be subpoenaed. End of story. The other reason for throwing stuff out is we don't have enough file space to hold on to everything.

But the story I had written about Somali women was different. I kept all my notes. I'd had an inkling that one day I would want to review the information I had collected because I was so moved by the stories I had heard. Fortun, Hakeema, Shukri each had a different take on what it's like to leave a hot, arid homeland to come to cold, wet Minnesota, to leave a murderous government for a land where freedoms like speech and religion are guaranteed. I wanted my own record, so I wouldn't forget what their lives meant.

Journalists' gold, in the form of phone numbers, was buried among my notes. I called about a dozen. At least ten were no longer in service, but a couple went through to voice mail. I left messages.

Then I called Sgt. Victoria Olson, a source from stories past whom I thought had blown the whistle on me to the FBI at the train blast. I didn't know if it was karma or luck, but Sgt. Olson seemed to pop up often on my stories. I put LM, for left message, next to her name on the log of phone calls I keep.

My next call was to a neighbor who had worked at the FBI

years ago and might be able to point me in the right direction. She was retired but sometimes, over a glass of wine, would reminisce about her days in the bureau. She, too, got LM next to her name.

The final call was to a cousin who had been fired by Metro Transit last year. He was a bitter, unreliable drunk who had deserved to get the boot, but who still knew all the transit gossip. It would only take a few beers to get him talking. I got through to his wife, who said she would have him call me. He got a question mark after his name, because I wasn't sure his wife would pass the message along.

CHAPTER SEVEN

While waiting for them to return my calls, I reread some parts I had written for the series.

Fortun was one of two wives of a powerful man in her village. They had both married the man when they were fourteen years old and thought of themselves as sisters. When the other wife, Amin, became pregnant, Fortun took her to the hospital to deliver her baby.

Barefoot, they made their way through the sea of men, women and children, dressed in dusty rags that had once been swirls of oranges, reds and blues.

The girls cut back and forth among huts thrown together with plastic sheeting and prickly branches. The loamy smell of burning trash, camels and cattle hung in the air. Flies buzzed around three hunks of meat hung in a butcher's stall. A couple dozen electrical lines crisscrossed overhead, intersecting at a stoplight that no longer worked because there was no electricity.

After walking for what seemed like hours, they finally saw the hospital with its dirty white walls and windows without screens.

Fortun looked around. Young mothers rocked children in their laps. Lucky babies lay in paint-chipped metal beds squirming, crying. Less lucky babies lay still, silent, staring.

Fortun had been pregnant three times, but each time the baby had died. She knew her husband was displeased, especially about the boy. As Fortun was waiting for Amin's baby to be born, she noticed a note scribbled on a torn piece of paper stuck to the wall on a rusty nail. It said a new mom was looking to give away her twin baby boys. Did anyone want them?

Fortun searched the medical center, nearby shops, even the huts on the edge of town looking for the babies, until she found them. They looked healthy and their mother seemed desperate to find them a better home. Fortun took them home and named them Mohamed and Abdi.

It was a happy year for Fortun. She and Amin took care of the twins and Amin's baby as if all three were their own. Fortun fed the boys and kept them clean. Amin cooked, cleaned house, and fetched water. When Amin didn't want to be with their husband, Fortun took her place. It was a cooperative arrangement that worked well for everyone.

But Fortun and Amin's husband was not happy about the mouths Fortun had brought into their home. She paid them too much attention. Worse, they were not his sons.

"I divorce you. I divorce you. I divorce you," he told Fortun one day. Under Islam a husband need only say those nine words to his wife to end their marriage.

Years before, Fortun's mother had been granted political asylum in the United States. Fortun pleaded with her to bring Fortun to her home. It took years, but finally the paperwork arrived.

Fortun was a divorced young mother of twin teens on her way to Minnesota.

The series won several awards. Just as important, it impressed Rachel, who wrote me a note on paper marked with the mayoral seal. She must have liked the stories a lot because she mailed the note, instead of texting or emailing. I had tucked it away in the file. "Way to go, kiddo. The part about Fortun and her boys really defines what the Somali experience and all immigrant experiences are about. You rock!" she'd written by hand with a flourish. I read her note over twice. God, I missed her already, and she hadn't been gone very long.

I needed to stretch my legs and get more coffee, so I made my morning trek to my favorite coffee spot on the skyway. When I came back, there was a message on my desk phone from Fortun.

CHAPTER EIGHT

I called her back right away. "It's great to hear from you. I bet the train explosion was scary. How are you?"

She said she was "fine" but her voice didn't sound "fine." It sounded more like she was terrified.

"Can I talk with you about the train bombing?" I asked.

"I don't think so," she said.

"Why not?"

"I don't have time." She spoke so softly I could barely hear her.

I found that hard to believe. After I had finally established rapport with her when I was writing the series, she always made time for me.

"Are you working more hours?" I asked. "At Target?"

A brief pause, then she said, "Yes… Yes, I am."

"What about Hakim or Shukri? Do you think they would have time to talk with me?"

"What do you want to know?"

"Look, Fortun, we've known each other a while. You know you can trust me."

"You want to know what happened to the train," she said.

"Yes, I do," I replied. "Do you know?"

"No."

"What about Hakim or Shukri? Do they know?"

"I can't say," she replied. "I have to go now."

"Wait. Just one minute, Fortun. Can I call you later to see if we can chat?"

"Okay. Bye."

I heaved a sigh of frustration and took another swig of coffee.

"Problems?" Slick was passing by, his newspaper tucked under his arm. He did this every day at about this time after finishing his morning ablution. "Somebody won't talk to you?"

"Yeah," I said.

"You know, I once knew a top-notch reporter at the *Miami Herald* who had a plan when something like this happened. If a source refused to talk, he would politely say thank you and hang up. He'd wait ten minutes, then call back and ask to talk again. Half the time the answer was yes. If the answer was no, he never called back again." Slick sat down in front of his computer, opened his paper and began to read.

Hmmm, I thought. Not a bad idea. I waited ten minutes then called back again.

"Hi, Fortun," I said. "I'm thinking you're upset about something and it would be good if we talked."

"Not on the phone," she said.

"Can we talk in your apartment?" I asked.

"Okay."

"When?"

"Now."

CHAPTER NINE

Fortun lives in the Cedar-Riverside neighborhood, also known as Little Mogadishu. The intersection teems with women in multicolored hijabs and men wearing embroidered kufis atop their henna-dyed heads. Many of the shops cater to the Somali population. A money transfer company, a halal grocery store, and several small shops, selling everything from battered pots and pans to bolts of fabric, line the street. Expedition Coffee is a beehive of activity from early in the morning to late at night for the Somalis, who stop in to trade information about everything, especially news from home. Fortun and I would never meet there, however, because only Somali men are welcome.

If I had the time and were interested in my health, I'd have walked. But I didn't and I wasn't so I drove two miles to Riverside Plaza, also known a few years ago as "Crack Towers," on the edge of the University of Minnesota west bank campus. When I was a journalism student at the U, most of the residents were Hmong immigrants, who were new to written language. Now most are Somali immigrants. I've always wanted to write about the intriguing residential towers with red, blue and yellow panels built into their sides in no discernible pattern. It was designed by a fancy architect in the 1970s as a grand experiment in urban life. The tallest tower shoots up thirty-two floors, offering a panoramic view of the Mississippi River and downtown Minneapolis. The idea was that it would house a mix of college students, professors, immigrants, and people who would walk to a potpourri of jobs downtown. But as time went on the dream faded. A developer who recently bought it is remodeling. These days the locals call it the Somali Hilton.

I punched the elevator button and waited several minutes for it to rattle its way to the ground floor, then stepped in and hit twenty-two. With an inch gap between the doors, which had not closed tight, the elevator slowly rose. The sight of the concrete on the inside of the shaft made me a little nervous. I'm kind of an elevator-phobe. I much prefer to ride in a car that doesn't show me the shaft, even if I know intellectually that it's there.

When the doors finally opened all the way, I took a quick right down the long narrow hall of chipped tile and cinderblock walls painted off-white enamel. Women in flowing abayas of many colors floated past, chattering in Somali and Oromo. Occasionally, a man in a white cotton shirt and brown trousers, his beard tinted orange with henna, passed by, but the women ignored him. No one seemed to pay much attention to me, even though I looked nothing like them.

I knocked on Fortun's door.

"Hi." She pulled the scarf from her head as soon as she realized it was me, not a man. Her hair was a rich chestnut brown and reached her shoulders. When I saw Muslim women on the street before I knew Fortun, I often wondered what they wore under the beautiful flowing fabric. Now I know. When they're home they wear slacks, sometimes jeans, and a blouse, shirt or sweater like Western women.

"Come in."

Thick rugs in deep reds, purples and browns covered the tile floor and hung on the cinder block walls, sound-proofing her two-bedroom home. A small TV was tuned to a noisy game show. A kitten wrapped itself through the legs of a table stacked with pamphlets about how to become a naturalized American. Heavy drapes blocked the light from her window. I sniffed the faint scent of jasmine, which made me feel more comfortable in her already comfortable home.

"Good to see you again," I said as she directed me to a thick, upholstered chair.

She gave me that shy smile I remembered from the last time we talked. Her skin was smooth as chocolate milk. Her eyes pierced through me. Once again I thought she looked young. Even though we're about the same age, she has adult sons while my girls aren't even in high school yet.

Two Somali women I had never met were in Fortun's kitchen. Soon, one handed me a cup of tea with orange fingertips from the Somali-chic henna dye, while the other set a plate of figs covered in sliced bananas on the table between us.

"These are my friends," Fortun said. Each told me her name but I couldn't always decipher their words so I ripped a piece of paper from my notebook, dug another pen from my purse, and asked them to write their names and phone numbers down. Then they returned to the kitchen.

Her eyes looked strained and there was a bend in her back that hadn't been there the last time I saw her. We had first met a few years ago when I was a volunteer assistant in an English class for recent immigrants. Somalia has not had a written language for long, so it's particularly difficult for their students to learn written English. Fortun was at the head of the class, because she's smart and she studied at home, which the other students did not.

"How are sales going?" I asked.

"Good." Fortun supplements her income as a check-out clerk at Target by selling Amway products. Until the local bank shut down transfers to Somalia, she sent $200 to friends and relatives in Somalia every week. "I have a new hand cream. Want to try it?"

"Sure. How are your boys?" I rubbed the creamy stuff into my chapped hands.

She told me Mohamed and Abdi, angry that their biological mother had abandoned them, had returned to Somalia last summer. It was a difficult search but they finally found her. Their birth mom told them that they were numbers ten and eleven of her children, their father had been killed in the war, and she had no choice but to leave them in someone else's hands. Fortun said the boys returned to Minneapolis, still angry.

"I told them to forgive their mother," Fortun said. "She did the best she could."

"Where are they now?" I asked.

"Mohamed is back in school," she said.

"And Abdi?"

Her eyes clouded over like the sky just before a March snowstorm as she told me about him.

For the past couple of years, Abdi studied computer science at Minneapolis Technical College during the day and drove a cab at night. He studied while he sat in the taxi queue at the airport waiting for his turn to pick up a fare. Some nights he made a few dollars, other nights he got a lot of school work done. Fortun saw him for an hour or two most mornings when he stopped home to change clothes. About three months ago, she had to leave for work before he came home. The pattern continued and they began to miss each other most days.

"Was there any sign he had been home?" I asked.

She nodded. "He'd leave dirty clothes or dishes for me to wash."

Her eyes clouded with tears and she wiped them with her sleeve. "He disappeared a few weeks ago. I left messages on his cell phone, but he never called back. Finally, a week ago, I got a message on my phone from Abdi."

Fortun's friends returned from the kitchen, and sat solemnly around her. One held her hand, the other wrapped an arm around her shoulder. There were lines on her beautiful face that I hadn't seen before. Clouds had gathered outside. From my perch near her window on the twenty-second floor, I felt like I could reach out and grab a handful of the biggest, the blackest, the one with lightning sparking through it. The smell of rice bubbling in a pot in the kitchen filled the tiny apartment.

"He said, in Somali, 'I love you. You will never see me again.'"

By this point in her story Fortun was sobbing. "I love my son, but what can I do? Only cry."

I offered her a tissue from the bottom of my purse and put my arm around her as her body heaved in sorrow. After she settled down a bit I encouraged her to drink some of the tea.

"Where do you think he could be?" I asked.

"I don't know," she said.

"Maybe he's gone back to Mogadishu? Can someone in Mogadishu help you look for him?"

"I tried," she said, shaking her head.

"Maybe his friends here? Or Mohamed?"

She shook her head again.

"Can you help me?" The tears pooled in her pleading brown eyes.

"I'd be happy to ask around if it would make you feel better," I said. "But you have more friends in the Somali community than I do."

"I need you to ask your friends who aren't Somali." She just hung her head.

"Why?" I asked.

She shook her head and heaved a huge sigh. "First you must promise me you will tell no one what I say next."

"Okay," I said.

"I think he blew up the train," she whispered.

"What?"

"I think Abdi blew up the train," she said a little louder. The expressions on the faces of the other women in the room confirmed for me that they knew what she said, and probably agreed with her.

"What makes you think he blew up the train?" I asked.

"Because of this," she said, showing me her cell phone.

The text message said, "I'll never see you again. I love you. Always remember me."

"I don't understand," I said. "This doesn't say he blew up the train."

"The message came an hour before the explosion," she said. "I haven't heard from him since. What else could it mean?"

"It could mean he went back to Somalia, or that he's gone on a trip to somewhere else," I said. "What does Mohamed think?"

"Mohamed tells me what he thinks I want to hear," she said. "He says Abdi went back to Mogadishu, that he doesn't want me to worry."

"Did Abdi send a picture with the text?" I asked.

"No."

"Did he tell anyone about his plans?"

"Mohamed and Abdi are men now," Fortun said. "They only talk to men. If Abdi told anyone about a plan, I would not have heard about it."

I knew she was right. Somali men talk to Somali women only when they must. But sometimes Somali men will talk to non-Somali women. Like me.

A picture of Abdi would help my search for him. I looked around the room but there were no pictures of her sons, or anyone else for that matter. Conservative Muslims don't keep pictures, I recalled. The thought of Fortun trying to remember her son without a picture almost brought me to tears.

"I'll see what I can do to find out what happened," I told Fortun.

CHAPTER TEN

I needed some fresh air, even if it was filled with a March mix of rain and snow, so I headed for one of my many favorite coffee shops, Mapp's Coffee and Tea on Riverside Avenue, a couple of blocks from Fortun's home. I'd like to think it was owned by somebody with a sense of humor named Mapp because the walls are covered with maps. Outside, the wind blew yellow caution tape from the bombing in and around the buildings, a mailbox, and a tipped-over trash receptacle. The Blue Line Light Rail had been suspended and replaced with buses while the city tried to clean up. Traffic was a mess.

Anyway, I was sitting on my favorite broken-spring couch watching the crowd, a mix of university students and professors, Somalis, and someone dressed in business casual undergoing a job interview when my cell phone rang, or rather twilled. Do any phones ring anymore?

"You the lady wrote the light rail bombing stories?" the caller asked.

"That was my colleagues," I said.

"But you're the one asking around about the bombing?"

"That would be me." I wondered how he knew my name. Maybe my drunken cousin told him, or told someone he knows.

"Skeeter. Skeeter Hughes?" he asked. "Where'd you get a handle like Skeeter?"

"When I was a kid my older brothers thought I was as pesky as a mosquito. A skeeter. The name stuck. What can I do for you, sir?"

"I know who blew up the light rail," he said.

My first reaction to a caller like this is skepticism. The newspaper puts my phone number at the end of every article, which usually just brings out the nut cases. Sometimes it's someone who doesn't have enough to do and wants to waste a reporter's time for entertainment. But sometimes the caller is legit. I always listen, then decide whether to follow up.

"And who might you be?"

"Name's Angel."

"Angel, huh. Angel who?"

"Angel deAngelus."

"So, who blew up the train, Angel?"

"Guy I know."

"And who would that be?"

"Ya gotta hear this face-to-face," he said.

He asked me to meet him at Grumpy's on Washington Avenue, which continued to exist happily as a dive on the east side of Minneapolis, even after the new football stadium went up nearby and the neighborhood became gentrified. It was only a few blocks from Mapp's.

"Now?" I asked.

"Sure," he said. "Now."

"How will I know who you are?" I asked.

"I'll know who you are," he said.

That felt creepy, but I hadn't figured out what to do about Fortun's problem yet, so I thought, why not? Go talk to the guy.

I looked around the near-empty bar and spotted a guy nursing a beer at one of the high tables in the back room. He wasn't hard to spot. About sixty years old. An aging hippie from the tip of his white braided ponytail to the flip-flops on his feet. He looked like the kind of guy who would acknowledge the depth of winter by wearing jeans instead of shorts with his Tommy Bahama shirt under his black leather jacket.

"Hi," I said, sliding into the chair opposite him as I passed my card to him. "I'm Skeeter. I believe you called me."

"What makes you think I called you?" he asked.

I looked around to the other side of the room. A couple of bikers were shooting pool. If Minnesota hadn't banned cigarettes in bars, the place would have been thick with month-old smoke.

"Because there's nobody else here but those guys, you and me, and I'm betting neither of those bikers called," I said. "Business is a bit slow."

He laughed deeply enough to stir the rust in his lungs. "Ya got me," he said with a wink and a tip of his beer.

"What's your real name?" I asked. "It's not Angel deAngelus."

"I'd just as soon not say," he replied. "It's simpler if you don't know."

I hate anonymous sources. People who aren't willing to attach their names to whatever they have to say are either cowards or liars—often both.

"This makes me very uncomfortable," I said.

"When you hear what I got to say, you'll understand," he said. "You check out what I tell you. You'll see I'm right and this is important."

"All right, Mr. Ponytail, what have you got to share?"

"I know who bombed the train," he said. "And it wasn't Somali terrorists like everybody's been saying."

"Who was it?"

"A computer guy I worked with years ago," he said.

"His name is ...?"

"Steve Bridgewater."

"Steve Bridgewater?" I said. "Isn't the condo across the street called the Bridgewater?"

"Steve Bridgewater," Ponytail replied. "Weird coincidence, huh?"

"Why do you think Steve Bridgewater blew up the train?"

"Because he was trying to kill me."

That set off my skeptic's scanner, but I let him go on. I was here. I might as well get the rest of it. A guy dressed in black chains and a black t-shirt, with biceps big as apples brought us glasses of water, then disappeared.

"Why do you think he was trying to kill you?" I asked. "And how does trying to kill you correlate with blowing up the train?"

Mr. Ponytail took a big swig of beer, then set his glass on the chipped Formica tabletop and belched, before launching into his story.

He and Bridgewater were part of a dying breed of geeks who understood how to read and write COBOL, a computer language written for banking and other business uses in the nineteen sixties.

"A lady named Grace Murray Hopper wrote COBOL," Ponytail said. "She was a Navy commander. They called her 'Amazing Grace.' Bridgewater and I and a few other guys worked for her in the Navy. "

The computer code worked well, he said, but no one got around to writing a manual that explained how it worked. As time went on, new computer language was written to replace COBOL. When Amazing Grace died in 1992, Mr. Ponytail, Bridgewater and the other guys were called the Legacies in computer circles because they were the last to understand COBOL. The banks hired Mr. Ponytail and Bridgewater in the mid-1990s to revamp their computers.

"While he was there, my buddy Bridgewater did a little, shall we say, creative computing that netted him a million dollars."

"How do you know that?" I asked.

"Because I saw him doing it during lunch one day," Ponytail said.

CHAPTER ELEVEN

"How did he do it?"

"The plan was so simple," Ponytail said. "He wrote his own side code. He'd tag bank accounts that people never reconciled. They usually had a balance of a couple grand, immediately available. It took a while, but over time he identified about a million of those. Then he set them aside in an encrypted file. Meanwhile, he set up his own account, which embedded a code. When he wrote a check for a certain amount, say $25.25, it initiated a program to go through the million accounts in his file, debiting random amounts that averaged about a dollar each. In minutes, his account grew by a million dollars. The genius of his plan, Ponytail said, was that the checking account holders didn't miss a few pennies. And a million dollars was piddling compared to the billions the bank had under management.

"Either the bank never noticed the money was missing, or Bridgewater had done such a good job that they never traced it back to him. Or, the bank figured out someone had taken the money but was too embarrassed to make a fuss about it. Whatever the reason, Bridgewater never heard anything more about it."

He chuckled again and shook his head. I wondered if his response was admiration for Bridgewater or disdain for the bank. Probably both, I figured.

A couple of years later, when the banks didn't need their help any more, Mr. Ponytail and Bridgewater were let go.

"When we were laid off—actually fired—Bridgewater thought of his stash as severance pay," Mr. Ponytail said.

"Then came the Y2K scare," Ponytail said. "Remember that? Everyone, especially the bankers, were afraid that all the computers would crash at midnight of the year 2000. Minneapolis has the largest debit-processing center in the country, so the folks here were especially nervous. If they couldn't debit accounts, the whole banking industry would crash. So they hired Bridgewater and me to save their asses."

I was just starting to follow him when our server, a woman with more nose rings than I ever thought possible, stopped by our table. "Can I get you anything?"

"Coffee," I said. "And a basket of your fabulous tater tots."

"Another beer," he said, then returned to his story.

"I remember sitting in a coffee shop with him. Not Starbucks or Caribou, or even Dunn Bros. It was an independent. Something with the name Java in it. One of the Legacies ran it because he couldn't take the corporate world anymore. I remember exactly what Bridgewater said:

"'Those sons of bitches. They hired me to write their computer code, then fired me when they didn't need me anymore. Now they're making nice because they know I can save them from meltdown when their systems click over to the twenty-first century.'"

"Why did he go back to work for the bank if he hated them so much?" I asked.

"He said, and I quote 'I'm broke. Damn, it's amazing how fast it goes.'"

"Anyway, I went back to work at the bank with him and we fixed their Y2K problem. Ran like a dream right through the flip to the new year," Mr. Ponytail said. "But during the down times while we were working on that, I know Bridgewater was doing more of his 'creative computing.'"

"I don't get it," I said. "How does that mean he bombed the train trying to kill you?"

"Hold on, lady. I'm getting to that." He took another gulp of beer. Belched. "January fifteenth they fired us."

"Did you rob the bank too?" I asked Ponytail.

"No." He drained his beer.

"Why not?"

"Here I was, saving the whole banking industry for a mere hundred dollars an hour. It was unfair, but I've always thought of myself as an honest man. I just couldn't steal like that and live with myself."

"I still don't understand how that means Bridgewater bombed the train," I said.

"Hold on. You reporters sure are impatient," he said. "I didn't see Bridgewater for years after that. He was always an arrogant asshole and a braggart. I avoided him. About six months ago I ran into a buddy, the guy who owned the java place. He said Bridgewater had come into a large chunk of change. Said he met some woman and was moving to Antigua."

Our server came with his beer and my coffee. "Go on," I said, as I poured in the half-and-half and stirred.

"Bridgewater was smart. He waited years before he finally activated his plan a few months ago. I'm guessing that on a Friday an hour before the bank shut down for the weekend, he used his magic debit account again. Maybe he bought himself a pair of twenty-dollar sunglasses, whatever, to write a check that would trigger his plan. Even though all the workers had left the bank by the time it went through, the computers were still doing their jobs. "

"Why on a Friday afternoon?" I asked.

"If the program is tripped on a Friday afternoon, it takes a few pennies here, a few dollars there from debit accounts in the encrypted file Bridgewater set aside and moves them into his account. The bank doesn't reconcile those accounts over the weekend, so it's Monday before there's even a chance the bank will notice the money is gone. By then it's fattened his account. I hear Antigua is the place of choice these days."

"So go on about how all this is related to the train bomb," I said.

"A few weeks ago, an investigator for the bank called me," Mr. Ponytail said. "He wanted to know what I knew about Bridgewater. The bank is on to him."

"What did you tell him?" I asked.

"Nothing, at first," Ponytail said, looking around Grumpy's. "Damn. I wish an honest man could still light up a smoke in this place."

"Nothing?" I asked. "Why nothing?"

"Because I just listened at first. I hate the bank. I don't trust the government, either."

I recalled that I had heard similar sentiments from other people over the years. There were days when I could agree with him.

"Then he offered me a twenty-percent fee if I could help him trap Bridgewater. There's plenty I can do with two million dollars."

Suddenly I found myself listening more closely.

"What did you do?" I asked.

"Told him I'd see what I could do for twenty-five percent," he said with a chuckle. "Nobody should get away with stealing ten million dollars so he can run off to Antigua with some chick."

Mr. Ponytail said he started doing some online sleuthing and was just getting somewhere when Bridgewater figured out his old buddy was on to him.

"Guess he found out I was working for the bank again, because he came back to town," Ponytail said. "He started following me."

He got up. "Gotta hit the head. Back in a minute."

As soon as he left, I looked around to see if anyone was watching, then I rifled through the pockets of his tattered black leather jacket, which he had left on the back of his chair. Men take quick potty breaks, so I knew I wouldn't have much time. I snapped a quick picture of his driver's license, Discover card, and Social Security card with my iPhone, returned them to his wallet, and his wallet to the same jacket pocket. I was checking my email on my phone as he returned.

"Why would he come back to town after he had made a clean getaway?" I asked.

"Because he wanted to kill me." Ponytail looked deeply into his beer, gave it a swish and chugged the rest.

His movement felt theatrical. Too theatrical. More times than I care to count I've gone on a wild goose chase courtesy of a guy who wanted to see his name in the newspaper. Still, what if his tale were true? Not only would I have the answer to who bombed the train but a story about a bank robbery, too. I needed to press him more.

"Why did you call me and why are you telling me all this?" I asked.

"Because, as I told you, he blew up the light rail trying to kill me," he said. "Are you listening to me, lady?"

"Why do you think he was trying to kill you?"

"The day the train blew up, I got on in front of the Government Center. I looked over my shoulder and who is getting into the car ahead of me but my old buddy Steve Bridgewater. I was creeped out, so when the train made its next stop, at the Vikings stadium, I got off. But I don't think he saw me."

"How did he know you were going to take that train at that time?" I asked.

"Because I work at the coffee shop in the Government Center," he said. "He knew I always take the train home after my shift."

"So that's how you knew who I was," I said. "I've bought coffee from you."

"Yep." He continued, "The way I figure it, Bridgewater left a bomb on the train then got off at the next stop, Cedar-Riverside. Before it got to the Franklin Avenue stop—KABOOM! It went off."

That was quite a tale. I wasn't at all sure I should believe him. But stranger things have happened. Who would have thought that Richard Nixon would be brought down because one of the Watergate burglars taped the lock on the office door horizontally instead of vertically? Was my heart beating faster because I started channeling Woodward and Bernstein? Or was it the coffee?

"Why should I believe you?" I asked him.

"Because there's no other explanation for blowing up a train in Minneapolis instead of Chicago, New York or Los Angeles," he said.

"Come again?" I asked.

"Haven't you been listening?" he said. "I told you, Minneapolis has the largest debit processing center in the country. Nowhere else could anyone pull off a heist like Bridgewater did. It would be worth blowing up a train for ten million dollars, especially if it got blamed on a bunch of Somalis."

I could almost hear Rachel whispering in my ear, "How are you going to verify this one, Miss-hotshot-reporter-pants?"

For starters, I'm going to run Sherman Heraty's name and social security number through every data base I can find.

CHAPTER TWELVE

I got in my car and drove back to the newsroom. I could almost feel my thighs thicken with every block I drove instead of walking. I'll get back to exercising and lose some weight after I'm done with this story, I told myself. Then I heard Rachel say, "Yeah, sure."

Rachel and I had met within the first month both of us worked for the newspaper. I remember sitting beside her in the back of a conference room while the orientation leader filled us in on all the do's and don'ts of the newspaper. How to fill in a time card for overtime pay, why joining the Guild was not necessarily in our best interest, that the publisher of the newspaper had actually signed a statement that said sexual harassment was verboten.

"Did you fail your piss test or did you cheat?" she asked me as we left the room together. The newspaper required a urine test of all new employees, just to make sure no one was on drugs, at least for the first few days on the job.

"I cheated." That was a lie. I haven't touched drugs since I was pregnant with Rebecca.

"Me, too. We'll be friends."

And we were.

As reporters, Rachel and I were seated next to each other in the hinterlands of the two-block-long newsroom, the ghetto for newbies. Rachel thought the feng shui was bad because the configuration of the desks put her back to the editor's office, so she brought in a small mirror that allowed her to view the rear as well as the front of the newsroom. Rachel was the only person I knew who could be practical and mystical at the same time.

She was a big woman. I don't mean fat, but truly large-boned, standing about five feet eight inches, plus another two inches for the heels on her boots. Her hair was a deep brown and always curly. In Minnesota, where the air is so dry, most of us have our straight-as-pins coiffure moments. Not Rachel. She usually wore it pulled back in a chignon. One day she came to work with her hair balled up under a bowl-shaped contraption with a metal design that made it look like the dome on a Catholic basilica. By early deadline she had yanked the thing out.

"I decided it would be better if I used it to steam broccoli," she said.

Discussions about men consumed most of our talk, especially after she met Tad James, the blond Brit who would become her husband. I couldn't have chosen a mate who stood in greater contrast to her. She was loud, opinionated and profane, with a deep laugh that resonated through the newsroom. He was, well, reserved, meaning if you could see his teeth you knew he was ecstatic about something. She was an ethnic Jew, not a religious Jew. He was a conservative Presbyterian. She said they were complementary. I had my doubts from the very beginning.

Politics, combined with typical newsroom poor planning and serendipity, had brought them together. She was eating lunch at her desk two days before the 1998 governor's election when an editor strolled through the newsroom looking for somebody to cover the election night returns at the campaign site of wrestler-turned-candidate Jesse Ventura. No one, except Ventura, thought the World Wrestling Federation pro would win the governor's seat.

"You," the editor said to her as she took a bite of the bagel she was having for lunch. "I need you to go to Canterbury Park tomorrow night."

"Why?" she mumbled.

"Because that's where the Ventura campaign will be. He'll concede by 8:15 and you'll be done by 8:30. File something short and sweet."

Rachel's political persuasion leaned Republican, Ventura was an Independent, and Tad was a Democrat. Tad visited the Ventura campaign headquarters that night because he had an inkling the professional wrestler was going to win and he wanted to witness one of the quirkier nights in politics. Turned out Tad was right. Ventura's victory party ran until two a.m. Tad and Rachel were the last to leave.

For the next two months, Rachel talked about nothing other than Tad. Tad this, Tad that. "How can I be involved with a Presbyterian ?" she'd ask me in a hoarse whisper. I listened and listened. The following March, they were married at city hall, with Michael and me standing up for them. They honeymooned in Duluth because neither of them had much vacation time.

But the marriage was not meant to be for very long. A couple years later, Tad left her, saying she was too much for him—too loud, too bossy.

She took a brief sabbatical from the paper. When she returned, she was a different woman. Our discussions revolved more around politics, less about gossip. She had gone into journalism because she wanted to make the world better. After Tad, she saw journalism as a dead-end for people who stood around watching as other people actually did things. She left the paper that summer to run for city council in Minneapolis's thirteenth ward, where she had bought a small condo. Even though the thirteenth consistently turned out the most liberal voters in the state, she won handily. A year later, when the mayor was convicted of taking a bribe, she ran for his seat and won again.

Our friendship changed when she left the paper. We were still friends, but we were no longer buddies. She had commitments just about every moment of every day, which left fewer moments for us to share. We were both passionate about our work, but hers was different from mine. And of course, I had kids, she didn't. I think we made the mistake many women do as we age and our other interests are more, well, interesting. We let our girlfriends go away, thinking that when things settle down, we'll find time to cry and laugh together again. We were just beginning to rekindle our friendship the night she died.

Did this wonderful woman die because Steve Bridgewater got greedy? Or did she die because Abdi, Fortun's son, had been sucked into a vortex of terrorism? Was her death the result of an international incident, or was it something altogether different? I was back at my desk in the newsroom when, in my head, I vowed to Rachel that I would find out.

CHAPTER THIRTEEN

Leona came by on her daily check-in with her reporters.

"Whatcha got for me today, Skeeter?" she asked. "Tell me you've got a story, because it's time to feed the beast. Our dwindling readership is demanding great stories every day. Where have you been?"

I told her about Fortun and Mr. Ponytail. "I don't know what to believe."

"So where's the story?" she asked, again.

Sheesh. Editors. Always with the what-have-you-done-for-me-in-the-last-fifteen-minutes demands.

"I got nothing for you for today," I said. "Sorry."

"It's okay. Slick and Dick have enough cop stories to fill the page," she said. I picked up on the subtle hint.

"I need to check out Mr. Ponytail." I told her about the photo opportunity of his driver's license.

"Good work," she said. "Run him through our usual databases."

"Will do," I said.

Because there were so many funerals related to the explosion, the editors had set up a rotation of journos to cover them. Maybe I drew the Mass for a mother and daughter in an Irish Catholic family because that's how I was raised.

I hate covering funerals. By definition they are sad events, no matter how hard people try to call them celebrations of life. A funeral means somebody is dead. When the dead are whole families, or even parts of a family, I find it impossible to divorce myself from the service enough to create some kind of objectivity in my reporting. If there's a class in journalism school about covering funerals, I'd sure like to hear about it.

Only in Minneapolis would a Catholic Church be named St. Olaf, I thought as I arrived early for the funeral service, took a seat in the far back pew, and looked around. It's a fairly simple sanctuary, compared with others I've seen, with straight, clean lines and not a lot of ornamentation. Kind of like Scandinavian furniture.

Peggy O'Connor and her ten-year-old daughter Kelly were on the Blue Line light rail headed for a little shopping at the Mall of America when they were caught up in the tragedy. Mrs. O'Connor had been born and raised in south Minneapolis. Kelly was a fourth grader at Clara Barton Open School.

When young people die, their funerals are usually packed with mourners, and this was no exception. Timothy O'Connor and son Kevin were the last to enter, after about a hundred fourth graders. I watched them walk slowly down the aisle, each slow footfall creating a cadence of sorrow before they took a seat in the front row in full view of two caskets.

When Father Curt Swenson took to the lectern to speak about the mother and daughter, the sounds of sniffles and wiggling were background to keening.

"We don't know why God lets things like this happen," Father Swenson said. "It's not our place to ask. When tragedy befalls us and we all know there is nothing we can do to avert it, we have no choice but to accept it."

"Peggy and Kelly O'Connor were good Catholics who died too soon," he said. "But look around. I see neighbors, relatives, friends, and perhaps friends of friends. Mrs. O'Connor's entire bowling league and all of Kelly's classmates have filled the church to send this mother and daughter on to heaven where they will be together for all eternity."

When I looked at the assemblage of mourners, I wondered if the bomber responsible for their deaths might be tucked away in the crowd. I didn't see anyone who looked like a bomber—but then, I had no idea what a bomber looked like. The service ended with the children's choir singing "On Eagles' Wings." I wondered if all the other funerals were as gripping.

It was all I could do to walk back to the newsroom and write the report for the next day's paper. As I was finishing writing the piece, I looked up to see my friend Fred, who was just coming in to start his shift. Copy editors usually start work late in the afternoon and go until about 11 o'clock.

We hadn't had much time to talk since the explosion, and I was very glad to see him. I even gave him a hug in the newsroom, something that is reserved only for significant occasions.

"Looks like there's a little overtime in my future," he said. "I see you and I are scheduled to cover a Somali funeral tomorrow."

"That could be a problem," I said.

"Why?"

"Because under Muslim tradition women aren't allowed at burials for Muslim men," I said.

"I'll talk to Leona," he said.

So Fred ended up covering six Muslim funerals, alone.

"They were very quiet compared with the others," he said later. "No weeping, no wailing, which surprised me. The imam read from the Quar'an and the men responded. That went on for a while, then they picked up shovels and filled in the holes. No casket, no headstone. That's Muslim tradition."

"Muslim practice does not allow weeping or wailing at funerals. That's why it was quiet," I said. "Were they all wrapped in shrouds or were some still in their clothes?" I asked.

"The ones I saw were all shrouded," Fred said. "Why?"

"Because the Quar'an says that martyrs are not washed and shrouded. They're buried in the same clothes in which they were found."

"Meaning?"

"Meaning that as far as this Muslim community knows, none of those buried were martyrs who had blown up the train," I said.

CHAPTER FOURTEEN

Rachel's funeral. The words sounded so foreign to me. I had never thought I'd say that phrase. Rachel and I had discussed everything, but never our funerals.

The newspaper covered every funeral from the bombing. Sometimes the report was a short five or six inches, sometimes longer—however many words were needed to capture the essence of the person.

Rachel's funeral was the last, and the most dramatic, set on the stage at the Guthrie Theater. Rachel would have loved having her service at the Guthrie Theater, a big Ikea blue box with an appendage that cantilevers over the Mississippi River. "All the best weddings and funerals are at the Guthrie," she would have said. It was the perfect place for her final performance, where the stage thrusts into the audience. Everyone who attended could see not only the service but everyone else who was there—an important advantage for politicians.

I sat in the tenth center row with our good friend Fred on one side of me, Michael on the other, and our daughters, Rebecca and Suzy, sitting next to him. I held hands with both Michael and Fred, who had been with me and Rachel the night she died. When tears ran down my face I didn't care. I didn't want to let go of either hand for a tissue.

The governor, Minnesota's congressional delegation, both senators, and the full city council sat in the first nine rows. As I looked at their backs dressed in various shades of gray and black, I couldn't help but think that Rachel would have said something like "Good, God, couldn't at least one of them have worn fuchsia?"

Then I started to chuckle to myself. Michael fired a stop-that-right-now look at me, which made me start to cough, and then I dissolved into sobs. Again.

I pulled myself back together as the president of the city council, with whom Rachel had battled fiercely, stepped on the podium and walked to the lectern, which was bordered by sprays of gladiolas, lilies, and roses, all white. Rachel would have said it was the first time the Guthrie smelled like a funeral home.

"Rachel Rand James was a trailblazer in many ways," the city council president said. "The second woman to hold the office of mayor of Minneapolis, she accomplished a great deal for the city, even though her term was cut short. She beefed up the police and fire departments, held property taxes steady, encouraged development within the city, and was the first in the nation to oversee city-wide Wi-Fi connections, bringing low-cost internet access to every neighborhood in the city.

"Although the light rail was up and running before she took office, Mayor James continually encouraged city residents to use the train at every turn, with her once-a-month free tickets. She knew that the more riders on the train, the more small business and large residential developments along the line would prosper."

"Mayor James was a woman of her word," the council president said.

A woman of her word. No kidding, I thought. Moreover, her words packed a punch. I thought back to the day she closed on a condominium after her marriage was over. She had spent a lot of time looking for that place. Sometimes I went along.

It was for sale at a bargain price because the sellers were going through a divorce. They were still fighting when they sat down to sign the documents to close the deal, with the man verbally abusing the woman when Rachel called a halt to the proceedings.

"Stop that," Rachel said to the soon-to-be ex-husband. "I'm in a very good mood this morning and I won't have your bickering. It will destroy the karma. We are going to take a one-hour break, and the two of you are going to leave and sort out your differences. If you are not respectful to each other when you return, there will be no closing."

The closing resumed an hour later. Rachel was smiling and the couple was at least civil to each other. That was Rachel, I thought, ever the negotiator, the problem-solver.

The council president's words cut into my reminiscing. "I remember the day we considered her first budget. Now we all know the budget isn't very sexy to the public, but it drives everything else. When I examined Mayor James' proposed budget. I thought it asked too much of taxpayers and not enough of residents who wanted city services. She promised me that if I voted for her plan, her next budget would be more to my liking. I did, and it was."

Rachel would have scoffed at his words and said something like, "That SOB. After all I've done for this city, he can only talk about his precious budget. The bastard was gunning for my job before I was dead. I bet he put his campaign committee together the moment he learned I was toast on the train."

When my mind returned to the present, Rachel's brother, Sam, stood at the lectern. He was a male version of Rachel. Dark hair, dark eyes, a nose that some called Grecian, but Rachel called "too big, with a bump for added height."

"Most of you called her 'Mayor' but I called her Rach. She was my sister. The only person besides me who really knew what it was like growing up with our parents." He paused to fight back tears.

"She was the one who told me when it was time to get off the school bus all through first grade, long after I had figured it out for myself. She told me what to get Mom for Mother's day, and reminded me of upcoming family birthdays. After our parents died when I was in college, she called me up on the phone three times a week to make sure I was okay. She was my rock, my talisman, my big sister."

His voice was cracking at this point and I could see tears rolling down his cheeks. Just like they were on mine. He stopped, took a deep breath, and looked up at the lighting.

"But boy, could she be a pain in the ass." This drew a chuckle along with some nodding heads. "She was so bossy. In fact, she was sure she was never wrong, even when we both knew she was. She grabbed the limelight at every opportunity. She was theatrical.

That's why I think it's not appropriate for us to end this service with a moment of silence. Instead, I think we should offer applause for a life well-lived."

The clapping started like a trickle then grew into a stream and then a river and finally an ocean, with everyone standing. There wasn't a dry eye in the house. Tears streamed down my cheeks, my nose ran, and I didn't care. Rachel's memorial ended with a video of her life, with the final piece being Barbra Streisand singing "Don't Rain on My Parade" from *Funny Girl.* I could almost hear Rachel whispering in my ear, "Did they have to pay for permission to use that? Good God, the taxpayers put on a fine farewell."

CHAPTER FIFTEEN

After the service, family, friends, and even a few of Rachel's political enemies mingled among teacakes and coffee on little round tables in the hallway outside the stage. The crowd would have energized her. She wouldn't have referred to them as mourners, because Rachel never mourned. She just moved on. She would have shaken hands with and hugged every politician in the room, and there were plenty. Both U.S. senators, representatives of Congress, the governor, and mayors from just about every city in the state.

"Skeeter, it's downright multicultural in here," she would have said.

Indeed, it was. A gaggle of Muslim women awash in blues, reds, purples and greens, who had voted heavily for Rachel in her last election, fussed around the food table. A leader in the African-American community was deep in conversation with the police chief, who was standing just behind the president of the University of Minnesota. Presidents of all the banks headquartered in the Twin Cities stood in a knot by one of the floor-to-ceiling windows looking upstream, talking quietly, intently. My reporter's antenna began to buzz a bit.

"Probably fixing interest rates," Rachel would have said with a chuckle and a wink.

Some people were dressed in their best, others looked like they were about to clean out the garage. Men in dark suits and white shirts mingled with men in jeans and hooded sweatshirts. Women in casual slacks and sweaters hovered around the refreshment table with women in tailored pantsuits. Rachel would have liked that, I decided.

"For my funeral, the rule is 'come as you are,'" Rachel would have said. "And for God's sake, eat up. I'm not taking any of this food with me."

I was helping myself to my second cookie and more coffee when I literally bumped into Rachel's older brother, Sam.

"I hear you were out drinking with Rachel just before the... explosion," Sam said.

"I don't know if I'd call it 'drinking' but, yeah, Rachel, Fred, a pitcher of beer, and I were at the Loon," I said.

"When did you see Rachel before that?"

That was an odd question, I thought, but people say unexpected things in the fog of funerals, so I thought back.

"I don't know. Maybe a month. Why?"

"I hadn't talked to her in six weeks," he said ruefully. "She seemed a little odd."

"Like how?"

"I don't know. Distracted I guess."

"She was mayor. She had lots of distractions."

"Yeah. Say, we've been going through her stuff in her apartment, cleaning it out, you know?"

"Must be a tough job," I said.

"Yeah, it is. Anyway, she'd just got a new Mac desktop computer. I've already got one and don't need another. D'you want it?"

Our family Mac was six years old, and the girls had been complaining that it had none of the new software that can make Apple stuff so cool.

"Sure, I'll take it," I said.

"She's got—had—some other crap we don't know what to do with," he said. "Clothes, boxes of chotskies she'd picked up somewhere along the way. Want any of it?"

I knew what he meant by crap. Rachel kept all kinds of it. Coffee mugs from Gooseberry Falls, an 1880s brick from a city street that was repaved, not to mention table napkins from the weddings of friends. Plus, six months ago I had loaned her my favorite scarf. I wanted it back, dammit.

I returned to my thought that I had felt Rachel slip away over the last couple of years. Maybe some of her stuff would help me get back in touch with her.

"I'll take whatever you want to give me," I said.

"I'll drop it off in a couple of days," he said, then faded back among the mourners and politicians.

"Ready?" It was Michael, nodding his head toward the door. The girls stood next to him wearing their coats.

"I'm really going to miss her," said Suzy who wrapped her arms around my waist.

"Me, too." I stroked her hair then gave her a kiss. Rebecca took my hand, something she hadn't done in at least a couple of years.

"No, I'm not ready," I said. "But I guess it's time to go home."

I didn't want to leave. I didn't want to leave Rachel. I didn't want to go back to normal life. Every day going forward would be a day further away from our friendship.

And then I heard Rachel's voice. Not imagined or dreamed but, I swear, really heard Rachel say, "I need you to find out who bombed the train."

Damn straight I will. "Let's go home, guys," I said to my family.

CHAPTER SIXTEEN

I had promised Fortun that I would do my best to find Abdi. I could understand why she would not know where he was, but I figured his brother, Mohamed, might have an inkling. Fortun said he was taking classes in computer programming at Metropolitan State University on the edge of downtown Minneapolis. I called his cell phone and made arrangements to meet him in Loring Park.

Male and female ducks swam aimlessly in pairs in Loring Park's largest pond. Even though it was March, the early birds had apparently begun courting. I love this time of year, despite the snow still stuck to the edges where earth meets water.

Mohamed was sitting on a bench in the park when I arrived.

"I'm Skeeter Hughes. You must be Mohamed," I said, extending my right hand to shake his. He stood and moved his right hand across his chest to his left breast, leaving mine flapping in the breeze. Damn, I thought. I keep forgetting that Muslim men, even the younger ones, don't touch women, even older women. I was embarrassed by my error, so I pretended to use that hand to dig in my purse for my notebook.

"Thanks for agreeing to meet me. Can we walk a bit?" I asked.

"Sure," he said, and we started to walk along the path.

Like his mother, and most Somalis, Mohamed had a long face on a tall thin body. He wore a black leather jacket, dress pants, and a white shirt. As I looked at him, it dawned on me that I had never seen a Somali man in jeans.

"Your mother is worried about Abdi," I said.

"I know. She worries too much." His accent was pure Minnesotan.

"She thinks he may have bombed the light rail train," I said.

"She told me." Moisture from his breath created clouds of smoke in the damp chilly air.

"Did he?"

"I don't think so."

"Why?" I asked.

"Because he loves America," he said.

He kicked a stone into the lake. I got the feeling he was holding something back.

"Is there an 'and' that goes after that or a 'but'?"

"Abdi is a good Muslim. He's against violence," he said.

"What would be a typical day for Abdi?" I asked.

"Why?"

"I'm just trying to understand him. In school? Driving a cab? Working at a parking ramp?"

"He worked at the money exchange," Mohamed said.

"The one on Cedar Avenue?"

"Yes."

"What did he do there?"

"Something with money," Mohamed said. "I don't know what."

"Have you heard from him?"

"No."

"No text, no email, no phone call?"

"No."

"Does that surprise you?" I asked.

"Yes. We have separate lives, but we talked."

"When did you talk to him last?"

"A couple days before the train blew up. Look, I've got to go. I drive my taxi tonight."

I thanked him for his time and gave him my card. "Please call me if you think there's anything else you'd like to tell me."

"What are you going to say in your article?" he asked.

"I don't know yet," I said. "But you should know that I'm also trying to help your mom."

He nodded and headed down the path near where a pair of ducks was swimming. As he walked toward them they began to swim away. Apparently they wanted to be alone.

CHAPTER SEVENTEEN

Real life. Back to real life. Here I was back in the newsroom the day after Rachel's funeral, seeking normality in the backwash of tragedy. Newsrooms for daily morning papers have a comforting rhythm about them. Morning starts about nine-ish with reporters and editors stretching, yawning, reading the paper, chatting each other up. Slick and Dick have been known to wander among the desks of their buddies telling off-color jokes. It's usually about noon when the tempo picks up. Newsrooms can vary in size but seldom in temperament.

My first reporting job was in Rochester, Minnesota, a company town that houses IBM and the Mayo Clinic. You can't be a reporter there without making friends—or enemies—in the medical or computer fields. I mostly made friends, carefully, always playing fair, never misquoting anybody, always careful to give context to what I was saying. That was very important in the land of the WFMC, or World Famous Mayo Clinic, as it is sometimes referred to with more than a hint of sarcasm. At the time I did it because it was the right thing to do. But it turns out there was another benefit, which I realized when I saw someone from Rochester on my caller ID.

"Skeeter? This is Bob. Remember me, Bob?"

"Of course I remember you, BOB," I said. His name wasn't Bob, or even Robert, but that had been his self-chosen code name when he fed me some critical information a few years ago. "How's it goin'?"

"Good," he said. "I heard something today that might interest you. I've been reading about the light rail blow-up. Hell, everybody's been reading about the bombing. Damn shame. All those people dead."

"Yes, it is," I said. "What are people thinking in Rochester?"

"Well, they're thinking it was another terrorist attack," he said. "You guys have got tons of Somalis in Minneapolis. Big city, you know. Must have been one of them, is what people are saying."

"Nobody knows that for sure, Bob," I said.

"Anyway, I was talking with a friend about this and he told me something I haven't seen in the newspaper yet," Bob said.

"What's that?"

"The driver of the train lived."

I could feel my blood pressure shoot up, hear my heart pounding in my ears. The old adrenaline switch always flips to "on" when I hear about an exciting story.

"What? How does your friend know that?"

"Ambulance drivers know more than you think," Bob said.

"Where is he?"

"She. You want to know where she is," Bob said.

"Okay, she. Where is she?"

"I don't know," he said. "You're the reporter. You figure it out."

"What's her name?"

"Don't know."

"I sure would like to talk with your friend who told you," I said. "Can you arrange that?"

"Sorry. No can do. My buddy's a wreck about this. Only told me over too many beers, you know what I mean?"

"Does he know you're talking to me?"

"Yeah."

"And he's okay with that?"

"Yeah," Bob said. "He thinks the cops are too slow finding the bomber. Thinks if the newspapers knew the driver lived it might goose the cops a bit. Hey, I gotta go. My break's over."

"Thanks," I said. "I owe you."

"I'll collect sometime." His chuckle turned into the harsh cough of a heavy smoker.

I hoped Bob was healthier than he sounded.

Well now, I thought, isn't this fun? But how to get to the driver? Wait a minute. I could swear our story said everyone in the first train car died. That would include the driver. I did a quick search to find the story Slick and Dick had written. Yep, it identified the driver as Harriet Lansing, age fifty-three. I checked funeral information. It said there was a private cremation. My face must have looked puzzled because my new favorite editor, Leona, slid into the chair next to my desk, one hand digging into an extra-butter bag of microwaved popcorn.

"Why the face?" she asked. "Something up? Remember our deal. You get to work on this, I get to hear every detail before you make a move. We are Velcroed."

I picked up the cup from my desk and swirled the coffee a bit before I spoke.

"The train driver lived." I took a sip, giving me time to observe her reaction. I just love when I get to drop a huge story on an editor. The wide eyes. The sly smile. The response is always muted. They never jump up and shout. Well, almost never. Leona was no different. But she added a dimension I hadn't seen before. She began to tap her left foot.

"How did you come upon that information?" she asked.

I explained about my days in Rochester and my friend, Bob.

"Do you believe him?" she asked. "A guy in Rochester knows a guy in Minneapolis who knows the driver lived, and nobody else has reported that? Our story said the driver died along with everyone else."

"Sure did. I guess Slick and Dick were wrong."

"About what? We're never wrong," said Slick, whose head had popped over the supposedly soundproof cubicle wall at the mention of his name.

"Skeeter says the driver of the train lived," Leona said, her eyebrows slightly arched.

Slick sat down again and began tapping his keyboard. Seconds later, the press release from Metro Transit appeared on my computer screen. It listed everyone who'd died. Harriet Lansing's name was at the top.

Slick, Slick, Slick, I thought. When will you learn to be skeptical of anything "official"?

"Looks like they lied," Leona said.

"I'm shocked, SHOCKED," I said.

"Anybody else know about this?" Leona asked. By "anybody else" she meant our many TV, print and yes, blog, competitors.

"Not that I know of."

"It won't be long. Find the driver, find out what she knows. Keep me in the loop," she said.

When she got back to her desk, she shot me a text message: *Remember to keep Slick and Dick out of this.*

CHAPTER EIGHTEEN

Find the driver. Easy for her to say, I thought. I know assignment editors have tough jobs. They're pressured from every corner. Top editors lean on them to get the story for last night's website. They also want the story to be true and accurate, so they lean on the assignment editor, who leans on the reporter. Besides that, assignment editors have to deal with reporters who can be mercurial, obstinate and obnoxious all at the same time. I feel Leona's pain. But sheesh. I want everything she wants, but I've got an added burden. I need to produce it. She just needs to tell me to find the driver.

I learned long ago that whining about editors is useless, so I set to work finding the driver. This is where my calls registry comes in handy. I flipped back several pages to find the list of people I had called right after the bombing. I put through another call to Sergeant Olson. No answer. I left a message and put a check next to her LM. My neighbor who used to work at the FBI hadn't returned my call either. I called again, and while I was leaving a message I remembered that she had told me she was going to Mexico for a couple of weeks in March. Good idea, I thought, as I looked out the window across the newsroom at a gray, cold day.

That left my alcoholic cousin who had been fired by the Metro Transit last year. He answered on the third ring.

"So, Geoff, how are you?" I asked after I had identified myself.

"The last time you asked about my health was at Millie's wedding," he said. "Remember that?"

Actually, I did remember even though it was a couple years ago. I asked because I smelled alcohol when he gave me a hug that lasted a bit too long.

"Okay, here's the deal," I said. "You know I'm a reporter for the *Citizen,* right?"

"You still working there?" he said. "I thought they folded."

"Nope, we're still putting out a paper every day," I said. "You should pick up a copy and read it."

"I don't trust you newspaper people. You all lie. Never get your facts straight. Everything is that liberal elite bias."

"Sometimes," I said. "Anyway, I'm doing a story about the light rail bombing. I heard the driver lived. Have you heard anything about that?"

"No shit?" he said. "She lived? When I saw the news on TV I figured she was toast."

"Did you know her?"

"Harriet? Harriet ...what the hell's her last name? Landing? Blanding? Sanding? Something like that."

"It's Harriet Lansing," I said. "The MTC says she died but I heard she lived. What do you think?"

"I think...I know the MTC lies, all the time about everything," he said. "No way she could have lived through that. But if anyone could, it would have been Harriet. Tough old broad."

"Well, it was nice talking to you, Geoff. Be well."

"Yeah, see you at the next family wedding," he said.

I made another dozen fruitless calls before the morning's coffee got to me and I had to go to the bathroom. Maybe I was going about this search the wrong way, I thought. Many people were hurt in the explosion and went to emergency rooms all over the Twin Cities. Minneapolis and St. Paul have three level-one trauma centers, which seems like a lot for a community of about two million people. Anyway, Hennepin County Medical Center is very close to the site of the train wreck and has the best burn unit. I decided to start there.

Given that Metro Transit had put out a press release that said the driver was dead, I found it unlikely that hospital officials would invite me to her room and offer me a cup of coffee while we chatted. There had to be another way.

Before I had kids, I volunteered once a week reading books

to children in the pediatric waiting room. Earning a volunteering spot there is not easy. I had to go through a background check and a tuberculosis test and sign a passel of pledges, including one that said I would not divulge anything to the press. Although that was a few years ago, I assume that the rules are the same today. Just finding out if the driver was there was going to be tough. The hospital is just a few blocks from the newsroom, and it was a nice day, and I was hungry for lunch, so I decided to take a walk to HCMC.

Actually, the food in the hospital cafeteria is neither bad nor expensive. In an unusual fit of healthiness, I ladled myself a cup of vegetable soup and placed a breadstick on my tray.

"What, no fries and coffee, Skeeter?" asked the checkout lady.

I looked up to see Shukri, who had been working the same job during my volunteer days. We had often chatted about food as I went through her line. One day as I was leaving I saw her waiting for a bus outside the hospital. It was cold and snowy and she looked miserable. I offered her a ride to her next job as a cashier at a parking lot. She flashed me a big smile as she got out of my warm car and walked toward the uninsulated glass booth where she would spend the next eight hours while I went to my warm home and family. I've often thought about the luck of birth that led to the difference between her life and mine.

Since then, she had changed from a flowing hijab to a headscarf with a long-sleeved blouse and a long black skirt. But the smile and the twinkle in her eye were the same.

"I'm trying to be good," I said, grabbing a cellophane-wrapped cupcake from the end rack.

"How's that working out for you?" she asked.

I laughed, then leaned in a little closer to her. "You still overhear a lot as people go through your line?"

"People think my hijab blocks my ears," she said. "Or that I'm invisible. Not sure which."

"Hear anything about the driver of the light rail train that blew up?"

She looked to her right. The cashier who worked next to her apparently wasn't on duty yet. She looked to her left where a man was intent upon figuring out where the soup spoons were hidden.

Then she looked behind me. There was no one else in line.

"All I know is they moved her to Michigan," Shukri whispered.

I did my best not to jump up and down and shout "Score!"

"How do you know that?" I asked.

"I overhear a lot," she said with a sly smile. "Americans think a Somali bombed the train. They all say we did it. But they're wrong. We are peaceful people who left war in Somalia. We only want to live in peace."

I paid for the soup, the breadstick, and the cupcake and offered Shukri a genuine smile. "Thanks," I said. We both knew I was thanking her for more than the change.

I hustled back to the newsroom where I ate my lunch at my desk while I did a quick Google search that revealed that the University of Michigan has a well-respected burn unit. I placed the call and asked to speak with Harriet Lansing.

"She can't take any phone calls," was the reply.

"Can you at least tell me her condition?" I asked.

"It's 'serious,'" she said.

I thanked her and hung up.

"Found driver," said the subject line of the email I sent Leona explaining where she was. "Any money in the travel budget?"

"I'll check," Leona wrote back instantly. "Did you find out anything more about the bank robber? Or the missing Somali kid?"

"Ah, no. I've been looking for the driver."

"Yeah, well, don't forget about the other two angles," she said.

Feed the beast—it's never sated.

CHAPTER NINETEEN

The travel budget was tight, but Leona got me airfare, which was going to be pricey given that I would be leaving the next morning.

"I need a seat on the 11:55 a.m. flight to Detroit," I told the person who books the flights for the newspaper.

I could hear the clicks as he ran his fingers over the keyboard of his computer as though he were playing a sonata.

"That flight is full," he said.

"What about the next flight?" I asked.

More with the magic fingers. "We have five flights to Detroit today. They're all booked until the last, leaving at 11:45 p.m. and arriving at DTW at 2:23 a.m."

Crap. "Then put me on that one, please," I said. "Can you put me on standby for the earlier flights?"

"Sure can," he said pleasantly.

I was up way too early the next morning, headed for MSP in hopes I would get a standby seat earlier in the day. I found a place in a waiting area next to an electrical outlet where I plugged in my laptop and spent the day working. As it turned out, there were no empty seats on any of the earlier flights so I ended up leaving just before midnight. It was a long, tiring day. Ahh, the glamour of journalism.

When my plane arrived in Detroit, afraid that I would fall asleep at the wheel if I rented a car, I opted for a forty-five-minute taxi ride to Ann Arbor. I arrived about four a.m. at the quaint—and cheap—bed-and-breakfast I had booked. The next morning, four hours later, I was up at eight and took the opportunity to slowly eat the sumptuous breakfast of bacon and eggs, homemade banana bread, fresh strawberries, freshly squeezed orange juice, and coffee. At the rate the paper was reimbursing me, that meal needed to last me most of the day. The woman who owned the B&B told me a city bus stopped on the corner every ten minutes and went right by University of Michigan Trauma Burn Center.

"That's where they took the underwear bomber when he tried to blow up that airplane on Christmas," she said. "It's the best place in the country for burns. That terrorist didn't deserve it."

Fortunately, I had downloaded a map of the University of Michigan Medical Center, which sprawls across many acres, before I left Minneapolis. Despite its excellent reputation, the trauma burn center was hard to find. I walked around long enough for my boots to hurt. But eventually I found the right door, the right receptionist, and the wrong answer to my request for a visit with Harriet Lansing. I wasn't family and I refused to lie about it.

Instead, I wrote her a note on the back of my business card asking for an interview. Figuring she'd never call, and with a whole day to kill, I headed for Aunt Agatha's Bookstore in downtown Ann Arbor. A bit of browsing through my favorite mysteries is good for the soul, I figured. I was about to pay for Harlan Coben's latest when my cell phone rang.

"This Skeeter Hughes?"

"Yes."

"I'm Harriet Lansing. You left me your card?"

"Of course, Harriet. How are you?"

"A little fuzzy from the drugs and bored out of my mind," she said. "What d'you want?"

"I'd like to talk with you about the explosion on the train."

"Well, supper's gonna be here in about half an hour. They make you eat so damn early the sun hasn't even thought about going down yet. But if you want to come over here after that, I could talk to you, even though I'm not supposed to. The cops have me stashed away here. Know where I'm at?"

I assured her I did and I'd be happy to visit in about an hour.

"Thank God," she said. "Somebody to talk to."

I brought my book and headed back to the burn center. Figured I'd read while I waited for an hour to pass.

I didn't quite know what to expect when I walked into Harriet's room. I'd heard horrific stories about people with severe burns so I prepared to see the worst. As it turned out, I was surprised.

Harriet was sitting in a chair near the window in her private room. Although the Metro Transit press release said she was fifty-three, she looked to me to be in her late fifties, early sixties. Her voice was deep and raspy, like someone who had smoked for decades. Her brown teeth that matched her brown eyes supported my assumption. She was severely overweight, which was not surprising for someone with a sit-down job. Gray hair was beginning to sprout on her shaved head around patches of ointment. A port was taped to her right arm, to give her fluids, I surmised. Her hands were bandaged but she seemed to have use of her fingers. Despite her wounds, her eyes were bright and she managed a smile.

"So you're Skeeter," she said. "Wasn't that the name of the girl in *The Help?* I loved that movie, but I've seen it too many times already. They don't have much of a selection."

"I was considered a bigger pest than a mosquito long before *The Help* came out," I said.

"So the pest grew up to be a reporter," Harriet laughed. "Don't that beat all? What can I do for you, Skeeter?"

"I'd like to ask you a few questions," I said while pulling out my phone to use the recording app. "Do you mind if I record our conversation?"

"Put that thing away. No you can't record this. I hate the sound of my own voice on recording."

Not a good sign. Did she nix the recorder because she was nervous, or because she was about to lie?

"I like to use the recorder to make sure that I get the story straight," I said.

"If you're gonna record this, you and I are through right now," she said.

What was I supposed to do? Sure wasn't going to walk away from this interview. I took out my long skinny reporter's notebook and a pen. "This okay?"

"Sure," she said.

I started doodling in my notebook as soon as she began to speak because I wanted her to get comfortable seeing me take notes. Sometimes it's unnerving to a source if the reporter appears to be writing down only part of the interview.

"Tell me about the day the train blew up."

"You get right to the point, doncha?" she said.

She took a sip of water from a white Styrofoam cup on the table next to her and settled herself into her high-back, green fake-leather chair, as if to say she had a tale to tell and she wanted to be comfortable when she told it.

She started out by saying she hadn't planned to work that evening, but another driver had called in sick, so she'd agreed to take his shift. "I can't quite say how, but I had a funny feeling that I shouldn't do it. I even told one of the other drivers that I had the heebie-jeebies before I went into work. But I needed the money."

It started like every other shift, people getting on, people getting off, she said. Young, old, black, white, Hmong, Vietnamese, Somali. Folks headed to the Mall of America to shop, or to work in one of the hotels. Some were dragging suitcases, marking themselves as travelers headed for the Minneapolis St. Paul International Airport. "Lots listening to God-knows-what through those earphones." She took another sip.

"It was the beginning of my shift," she said. "They like to put on extra drivers during high-peak traffic. Not that we really drive, you know. The train stays on the track—or it's supposed to. But drivers start and stop the train. That's critical. I remember one time a mom was getting on the train with her baby in one of those fancy strollers."

She stopped at this point and started to pick at a corner of the tape that was holding her port in place. Her voice got a little quieter, softer when she continued.

"Anyway, the mom was pushing the baby ahead of her while she turned back to yell something to somebody on the street. Something about pizza, I think. Anyway, the baby stroller, with the baby in it, is on the train and mom is still on the platform. The doors start to close like they do after that computer voice tells everyone the train is about to leave. Mom's not paying attention, but I am. I can see what's happening because I'm watching her in the mirror. So I slam on the switch that stops the doors from closing right on that baby. That baby woulda been killed if I hadn't been watching."

Harriet's comment about the doors closing reminded me that one of my colleagues was gathering information for a story about safety on the train. As she talked I wrote a reminder in my notebook to share the anecdote with the reporter.

"That would have been tragic," I said, returning to her. "You're a conscientious driver. Tell me about the day the train blew up."

"The train's pulling out of the Cedar-Riverside station headed for Lake Street when I hear a huge boom, then a giant whoosh. Right away the door behind me felt hot. Before I could even turn around I felt the heat. Felt like sticking your head in an oven heated to four hundred degrees, know what I mean? Then the smell of burning rubber. I'll never forget that smell. "

She took another sip of water, then looked down in her lap. When she brought up her head again, tears were streaming down her pale pink cheeks. She snatched a tissue, wiped her nose, then scrunched the tissue in her hand. "I heard people scream. Babies calling for their mamas."

I let her sit a moment before my next question. Sometimes reporters are like therapists. Just letting the interviewee vent can be helpful—for her and me. In those situations, I make it a point to just nod as the person talks.

"How did you get out?" I asked.

"A door separates the driver from the passengers. The bomb went off in the second car of the train—remember I was in the first car—then bounced like a ball from one car to the other. The glass door between the passengers and me held off the fire, so I had just enough time to kick out the front window. Those windows are low to the ground so it was easy to jump down. I ran to the sides of train to try to help people get out of there. I tried to pull open the doors and the windows, but the fire was too hot."

She raised her bandaged hands to show me, then went on.

"Metal and glass from the train were everywhere. I remember hearing it crunch as I tried to get to people. Funny how you remember some things, ya know? There was blood everywhere…and body parts. Every time I close my eyes now I see this one little boy lying near his mother, his arms reaching toward her. I'm not going to tell you how they died, but you can imagine it was horrible. I didn't want anybody else to see what I saw, so I pulled her headscarf over her face then covered them both with her long robe."

With tears in her eyes, she gazed through her hospital room window. I doubt that she saw the fluffy white clouds against the blue sky outside. I was fighting back tears myself when she pursed her lips and turned toward me and took a big breath, signaling that I should continue with my questions.

"Why are you in Michigan instead of Minneapolis?" I asked.

"It was my bosses. The first thing they said was 'Don't talk to anybody until the lawyer gets to you.' But the cops wanted me quiet, too. Besides, this is supposed to be the best place in the country for burns, so I'm not complaining—at least not about that. They're paying for it. But I don't want to be trapped here forever, ya know?"

"So why are you talking to me?" I asked.

"Because I'm pissed that they sent me here. It feels like I'm in prison for something I didn't do."

I suspected there was another reason she was willing to talk with me. I had a friend who was a bus driver. He said the drivers at the end of their shifts get together to share stories about their riders, one more outrageous than the other. I'd bet an espresso that Harriet would get top honors with this one. She wanted to practice on me first.

"But I don't get it," I said. "Why did the cops say you had died?"

"Because I saw the bomber."

CHAPTER TWENTY

"You saw the bomber?" I was flabbergasted.

"Yep."

"Who was he?"

"I said I saw the bomber. Didn't say I knew the bomber."

"Okay. What did the bomber look like?"

"It was getting dark. I didn't see much."

"What did you see?"

"I saw someone in a University of Minnesota hoodie," she said.

"Man? Woman? Kid?" I asked.

"Don't know. Anyone can wear a hoodie."

"You're sure it was University of Minnesota?"

"Yeah. Maroon and gold. My neighbor boy has one just like it. He's thirty years old now, but I swear he wore that filthy thing every day he went to college. Still wears it when he mows his mother's lawn."

"That's gotta narrow it down to about a hundred thousand possibilities," I said.

"No need to get sarcastic with me," she said, with a half-smile. The tears in her eyes had dried. Clearly she was enjoying this interview now.

"Sorry. What did he or she wear on the bottom half?"

"Black pants."

"Jeans?"

"Couldn't tell."

"Do you think the person was male or female?"

"Male, maybe, but I couldn't tell for sure. Maybe female."

I wrote “gender?” in my notebook. Before I could get my next question out, a nurse came in Harriet’s room to take her vitals. I stuffed my notebook under my thigh so she wouldn’t see it. But Harriet saw me and gave a quick wink. Neither one of us needed someone on the hospital staff to question what I was doing there. After the nurse left the room, I pulled my notebook out again. Harriet had a huge smile on her face but she said nothing about my subterfuge. Clearly, she was enjoying the intrigue of the moment.

“Let’s assume it was a man,” I said. “Tall? Short? Fat? Thin?”

“You sound just like the cops,” she said. “Kinda tall.”

“How did you happen to see him or her?”

“I always check the mirrors before the train leaves the station,” she said. “Wanta make sure everyone is safely on the platform or inside the train, like that mom and baby in the stroller I just told you about.”

“So you saw a person in a hoodie. How did you know he was the bomber?”

“Because I saw him, or her, get on the train with a back pack as I was starting my shift,” she said.

“And?”

“And he didn’t have the back pack when he got off.”

“Are you sure?”

“Yes, I’m sure. I told you I eyeball most of the riders when I start my shift. I learned that when I was driving the city bus before the light rail. I like to study people, ya know. Makes the time go by faster.”

“Didn’t that make you suspicious?”

“Yeah, but my job was to drive the train, not check out something left behind. People leave stuff all the time.”

“What color was the back pack?”

“Black.”

“How do you know it had a bomb in it?”

“I don’t, for sure,” she said. “But it was mighty full and heavy. I could tell by the way he was carrying it.”

“Maybe it was just his stuff. A computer, gym shoes, a racquet, maybe.”

“That’s what the cops said, but he was acting kinda hinky,”

she said.

"What do you mean—kinda hinky?"

"It's hard to describe," she said. "But after you've been driving a while you get to pick up feelings from people. If they're too nervous, that's a sign. Or if they're too still, that's another sign. I don't know how else to say it."

Actually, I knew what she meant. I rely on my intuition in my work. I watch for body language, word choice, or demeanor. I can almost always pick out a liar. In this case the needle on my internal Lie-O-Meter was telling me that Harriet spoke the truth—at least as she knew it.

"Which was he, too nervous or too still?"

"Too nervous," she said. "He was just a kid."

"How do you know he was a kid?" I asked.

"I guess I don't know that. But he was tall and skinny like a teenager."

"Or a Somali man?"

"Or a Somali woman," she said. "You sayin' the Somalis did it? Wouldn't surprise me."

Actually, I knew of two people, Fortun's son Abdi and Steve Bridgewater, who might have bombed the train, but I let it go. First rule of interviewing: don't argue with a source on a roll.

"Was there anyone else on the platform with him?" I said.

"Couple of Somali girls, guy who looked like a businessman, a Somali guy in one of those cotton zip-up jackets they always wear. I looked in my mirror, saw them begin to walk away, and started the train. I was halfway to the Franklin Avenue stop when I heard the boom."

"So, if that was the bomber, how did he set off the bomb if he was standing on the platform?"

"Lots of ways," she said. "Simplest is it could have been on a timer. Or he could have done it with a cell phone, or even a clicker like you use on garage doors."

"Is that what the cops said?"

"No, it's what I said. I've been reading up on it. And it wasn't just cops. Couple of FBI agents have been here, too. They are so cute, especially that Agent O'Reilly."

"The FBI interviewed you?"

"Yeah, couple times," she said.

"What did they ask you?"

"Same questions as you," she said. "They wanted to know about my family, lord knows why. I told 'em I got none." She sighed and rubbed her eyes.

"Look, Skeeter, you're a nice lady, but I'm getting tired. I've told you all I know. I think you had better go now. It's been nice talking with you."

I certainly wasn't going to press my luck with Harriet, so I rose to say good-bye. As I tucked my notebook in my bag, I spotted the Harlan Coben book I had bought earlier. I was only twenty pages into it but I could tell it was going to be one of his best.

"Do you like to read mysteries?" I asked Harriet.

"Love 'em," she said.

"Here's a new one for you," I said as I handed her the book. "It's Harlan Coben."

"He's the best," she said. "I went to one of his signings at Once Upon A Crime bookstore in Minneapolis. D'ya know he's about six-foot eight?"

"Was that last year?" I asked. "I was at the same signing."

"It was last year," she said. "How about that? We were in the same place at the same time and didn't even know it."

On my way out, I stole a look at the whiteboard posted across from her bed. It listed Harriet's name, the name of the nursing assistant on shift, and Harriet's direct phone number, which I wrote down on my hand. I didn't want to trust it to memory. Later, when I had time, I would put Harriet's name and hospital phone number in my iPhone. Another rule of good reporting—always have a way to get back to your source so you can check information.

As I left, the nurse who had taken Harriet's vital signs was heading into her room with some pills in a white paper cup. We almost bumped into each other. As she stepped back I felt her eyes taking my measure. I gave a quick finger wave goodbye as Harriet said, "Bye, Skeeter."

Damn. I wish Harriet hadn't said my name. If someone asks me for it, I usually tell the truth, but I didn't want my name broadcast, especially because it's unusual. Then I realized that the chances of a Michigan nurse recognizing the name of a Minnesota newspaper reporter were pretty slim.

I stopped in again at Aunt Agatha's and bought another copy of the Harlan Coben book, which I would put on my expense report. As I took the bus back to the B&B, I thought about everything Harriet had said. The business about the boom followed by a fireball fit. Slick and Dick had reported about the people standing on the platform and how they had gotten away unscathed. I couldn't quite remember their descriptions so I would have to check their story when I got back to my laptop. I didn't remember reading anything about a black backpack, either. I wondered how I could check that.

To catch my 7:30 a.m. flight I had to be up by 5 a.m. to eat the huge breakfast and make it to the airport on time. As the flight lifted off, I thought about how much this story would raise my value in the editors' eyes. Hell, even being able to report that she was still alive and secreted away was probably Pulitzer material. The details were added value. I should have remembered that I get into trouble when my hubris takes my focus off the story.

I had called Leona from the bus to the B&B. This story was burning a hole in my brain and I wanted it in print soonest. Was that a smile I could almost hear in her voice? "We'll talk it through when you get back."

"You don't want it now?" I asked. "I could dictate something."

"Does anyone else know about the driver?" she asked.

"I don't think so, but you never know."

What was going on? I wondered. Wasn't she just talking about feeding the beast? Was the beast suddenly on a diet and I hadn't gotten the email?

"As long as there's no immediate competition on this story I think we should slow down," she said.

"Fine," I said. "See you tomorrow."

Even though she told me to wait, I wrote the piece on my laptop during the trip home. I was too antsy to just look out the window at the farmland. The story said the light rail driver had lived and she claimed to have seen the bomber. At Harriet's request, I declined to say where I had found her. She didn't want a horde of reporters descending upon her, and neither did I. As the other passengers disembarked, I attached the story to an email to Leona and hit send.

CHAPTER TWENTY-ONE

My story went through three editors the next day before Leona got back to me. "We have a lot of questions, Skeeter. Why isn't she more badly burned? Aren't family or friends looking for her? Are you sure Harriet is telling the truth? You'd better get somebody to corroborate what she said."

"Look, Leona," I said. "She is badly burned but I didn't dwell on it in the story because I didn't think readers wanted to read the gruesome parts. If you want, I can add some painful detail."

"No need," Leona said. "That was just something the new guy asked. He was trying to impress the big boys. He thinks gory details draw more readers. He's probably right, but that's not how we want to do it."

I pointed out to Leona that because no reporter is supposed to know Harriet's there, I couldn't exactly ask the hospital for her clinical condition. My story says she's badly burned and likely to be in the hospital for several weeks. I think that's enough.

"Agreed," Leona said. "What about her family?"

I told her that Harriet had no family and her few friends, all bus drivers, found it believable that she had died in the wreck.

"What about corroboration on possible suspects?" Leona asked.

I knew she was going to hit hard on that point. I'd spent a lot of time on the train thinking about how I could get more sources when Harriet was the only one to survive the bombing. She said she saw the bomber. Anyone who might have seen what she saw, or gotten an even better look, was probably dead. Maybe even the bomber was dead.

"What about the cops, or the FBI? Can they give you any way

to check what she said?"

I had played with that idea, too. I had already called the FBI and got the usual neither-confirm-nor-deny nonsense. Just for entertainment, I had called the public relations person for Metro Transit, five times. I knew the spokesperson would not want to speak. No one had called me back, so I took that as a "no comment." That left the Minneapolis police.

"I've put in some calls to my friend on the force but she hasn't called back yet," I said. "She might be willing to confirm what Harriet said."

"Would that be Sergeant. Victoria Olson, who, I've heard, has saved your ass a few times already?"

"That's the one."

"Find her. As much as I love this story, we can't go with it until there's at least some corroboration," Leona said.

I went back to my desk and called Olson yet again, leaving both my cell and desk number, even though I knew she had both in her own phone.

Sergeant Victoria Olson and I have some serious history. I've gotten into a few scrapes along the way in my career—nothing that I really want to talk about. Suffice it to say, Sgt. Olson always showed up just in the nick of time.

She's a big woman. I don't mean fat. I mean she has a large frame. I once watched her walk out of a convenience store with one of those measures on the door frame so terrified clerks can get a better idea of the height of the guy sticking a gun in their faces. Looked to me like her hat brushed the six-foot mark.

Cops go way back in her family. Father, brothers, uncles. But she's the first woman to be a cop. I know all this because my father was a firefighter, and those guys all know each other's business. She must have learned at a very young age the required cop stance: arms akimbo, feet shoulder-distance apart. She stands sturdy and steady as an oak tree, her face as impassive as bark. She's about a half-generation older than I, but I consider her a friend...some days. I guess you could say I have a grudging respect for her, and I sense she feels the same way about me.

Even though she shows up when I need her, she's lacking in

the returning-phone-calls skill set. It had been at least an hour since my last fresh coffee and I still hadn't heard from her, so I headed for the Starbucks on the skyway. I returned to a call at my desk from Olson.

"Skeeter, you called." It was a statement not a question. "This is Sergeant Victoria Olson returning your call. I'm off today but you can call me on my cell phone. You have the number."

Yes, I did have the phone number, which she had given me at a time when I needed her help. I never discard a phone number. My phone has probably got a zillion gigs of email addresses and phone numbers in it. Likewise with the newspaper's piece-of-crap phone, but I don't trust it to remember every name I put in it.

"Hello, Skeeter," she answered when I called her back. "I haven't heard from you since the Blue Line was hit."

"That's what I want to talk about." I explained that I had a, pardon the expression, "explosive" story, and I wanted to check some facts with her.

"I always like to see facts," she said. "I'm home today. You may come by."

Wow, I thought. To her home? First time that's happened. She gave me an address in South Minneapolis, which I committed to the memory that is my iPhone, then headed for the paper's employee parking lot. My hot Honda Civic del Sol was waiting for me.

I bought it a few years ago after turning in the minivan. Decided I was ready for something snazzy, like a two-seater red convertible. Unfortunately, it was firebombed while I was covering a story that involved Sgt. Olson. I scoured the internet for a month before I found the make and model for sale. I flew into Midway Airport outside Chicago, met the seller in a parking ramp, gave her a certified check, and drove that baby home.

I parked on the street, careful to align the car with the curb in a spot far enough away from a fire hydrant. Didn't want a parking ticket I couldn't list on my expense account. I sat behind the steering wheel a moment to take a good look at her house.

It was a typical Minneapolis bungalow: white stucco with brown trim, probably three small bedrooms with kitchen, dining area and living room. Screened front porch. I guessed there was a

TV and treadmill in the basement. Because this was early spring, little sprigs of green grass were starting to poke through the white snow. Last night was probably the last time this season we would get an inch or two. Or at least that's what I hoped. The snow that remained had been shoveled neatly to the side. Her next-door neighbor's walk had the exact same shovel marks, which led me to guess that Sgt. Olson had done that walk as well.

I made my way to her front porch and was just about to ring the bell when she came to the door. Her short graying hair was mussed and she wore a weathered black sweatshirt and jeans. In bold white letters on her shirt was Fight Back. Join the National Rifle Association.

"Come in," she said, holding the screen door open. "Leave your boots on the porch. Would you like a cup of tea?"

"Uh, yeah," I said, hopping from socked foot to socked foot on her cold wooden porch.

I had expected stuffed fish and cheetah and a set of antlers or two on the walls, but I was wrong. Nary an antler in sight. Instead, the walls were painted a soft tasteful gray-green. As I followed her across the living room, I noted the floor of finely polished dark oak, the well-cared-for woodwork, and, in the dining area, a built-in buffet with a mirror back. Then I stepped into the kitchen, which was painted a sunny yellow.

The NRA sweatshirt didn't surprise me. The homey kitchen did.

"When was this built? Around 1920?" I asked. Journalism 101: establish rapport with the interviewee right off. She and I had a newsroom/cop shop relationship so far. Time to change the tactic to something more personal.

"It was 1924," she said. "Cream? Sugar? Lemon?"

"Lemon," I said. "How long have you been here?"

"About fifteen years," she said. "Bought it from my aunt's estate. She lived here alone most of her life."

"I like what you've done with it," I said.

She gave me tea in a dark blue Minneapolis Police Department mug. Now that's more like it, I thought. She motioned for me to sit down at her kitchen table.

"Shoot," she said.

"I found the woman who drove the Blue Line when it was bombed." I sat back to watch her reaction.

"No shit?" She was genuinely surprised. "How? Where?"

I told her the story, leaving out the part about my hospital cashier friend, finishing up with, "We need corroboration, and I was hoping you could help."

"The FBI took it over because it's a possible national threat," she said. "Minneapolis police got cut out of the investigation right at the start, so anything I told you would be speculation, because I don't know the facts."

"Do you think the driver has the story straight?" I asked.

"If the driver lived, the feebies would stash her away somewhere," she said.

"But what about her seeing the bomber?"

"Could be," Olson said. "Or she may have seen someone who wasn't the bomber."

"You know, those FBI guys pride themselves on how many attacks they stop," she said. "They're most proud of the attacks they prevent from happening, so you never hear about them. And trust me, there are plenty. I bet they're kicking themselves right now. There are two FBI offices in the Twin Cities full of people who do nothing all day but monitor chatter on the internet and phones. You'd think one of them would have caught a whiff about this bomb and done something to stop it."

"But that implies that the bombing was done by terrorists," I said. "What if it was just plain old bad guys?"

"Yeah, what if?" she said. "But why would a plain old bad guy blow up the train?"

"I don't know," I said. "I'm just trying to explore all the possibilities. Do we know for sure it was blown up, and not just something wrong with that particular car on the train?"

"A fire that big wouldn't happen just because there was something wrong with the train."

"Does anyone know exactly what caused it?"

"If they do, I haven't heard," she said. "More tea?"

"I'm good," I said. "Remember when you sicced that FBI guy

on me at the scene?"

"You were very close to getting hurt and I wanted you out of there. Why?"

"He looked familiar but I just can't place his face," I said. "Of course, there was a lot going on and I had a lot of distractions."

"Yeah?" she said.

"Yeah. What's his name?"

"Whose name?"

"The FBI guy. Come on, Sergeant. Help a girl out here."

"There's nothing more I can do for you," she said.

I stirred my tea slowly. She looked at me with one bushy eyebrow raised, a half smile on her face. She loved the game of cat and mouse we were playing. I found it frustrating. I could tell she loved that I was frustrated.

"Just tell me this," I said. "Is the train driver's version true?"

"It's probably what she thinks is true," Olson said.

It was not what I wanted to hear, but I let that comment hang in the air for a while as we both gazed through her kitchen window to the snow outside. Snow angels, one bigger than the other, were imprinted in the snow.

"Who made the snow angels?" I asked.

"My nieces came by," she said. "You know, I liked her."

"Her?" I asked.

"Rachel…the mayor. Mayor Rachel Rand James."

"Did you know her personally?" I asked.

"Sure," she said. "I was her driver her first year she was in office."

Why didn't I know that? I asked myself. She should have been the first person I contacted on this story. Was I slipping? Then I thought a little harder. During Rachel's first year in office, I was covering some godforsaken suburb. There's no way I should have known that.

"You know Rachel and I were friends?" I asked. "We were having drinks just before she got on the train."

"I'd heard. I thought that was the reason you were so quick to the scene," she said.

The air in her kitchen changed from formal to almost familial, like a shift of plate tectonics. Her face softened a bit and her voice quieted. Was that a tear welling up in her eye? I wondered.

"No, I didn't even know she was on the train when it blew up," I said. "I just got there fast because, well, that's what I do."

"I was surprised she took the light rail." Olson leaned back in her chair and ran her index finger around the rim of her coffee cup. "When I was her driver, I would have taken her home. Why didn't the cop who drives her now take her?"

"Who's her driver?"

"The detail changes every couple of years. I don't know who was driving this time," she said.

I wrote *Find Driver* in my notebook.

"I only knew Rachel as a friend," I said. "What was she like as a boss?"

"Demanding," she said. "But what mayor isn't? As far as I know, she was the first mayor to request a Prius. Usually they want a Crown Vic."

"I bet you heard plenty of interesting conversations while you drove her around."

"Yeah, she was always on her phone or brought somebody along so they could talk while she was on her way to somewhere."

"Any stick in your mind?" I asked.

"That would be a violation of my confidentiality agreement," she said.

Usually when an interviewee says that they have a look that says, *I'm dying to tell you this. Please push me into it. Please.* But not Sergeant Olson. Her face remained passive, her eyes unblinking. But that wouldn't mean I couldn't give it a try.

"As much as it pains me to say it, the mayor is dead. How could you violate any agreement between you?"

"You know, Skeeter, that's why I've always liked you. You always ask that extra question. Even when we both know you aren't going to get an answer."

I tried to give her a smile. "And…?"

"And, I'm still not going to tell you anything." Olson sipped her tea, then put the cup down. "You and the mayor were friends. Good friends?"

"Very good friends in the beginning. Lately, though, we were drifting apart."

"Why?"

"I suppose we both got busy with other parts of our lives."

"And you feel guilty about that, now that she's dead." It wasn't a question. It was another statement.

As I thought about it, she was right. I did feel guilty. I had let my family and my work get in the way of our friendship. It was something I would never be able to make up to her. But jeez, I thought, some days I barely have time for the girls. And then there's Michael, who sucks the energy right out of me. If Rachel were still alive, we could grab a quick happy hour and I could tell her how overwhelmed I feel. How sometimes I don't have brain power left to put together a grocery list, let alone my marriage, which was already held together with bubblegum and Legos.

"So it's more than chasing a story," she said. "Your guilt is driving you to find the bomber? Right?"

"I hadn't thought of that, but you may be right," I said. "What? Now you're a shrink?"

"Reporters aren't the only ones who get pretty good at reading people," she said.

With that she stood, clearly indicating this discussion was over. She walked me to my boots, which I slipped on, then fumbled for my coat from the nearby coat tree.

"One thing," I said, at the door. "This story is mine alone. I'd appreciate it if you didn't mention this to anyone, especially another reporter."

"And I would appreciate it if no one knew we had this conversation," she said, just before she closed the door.

Walking down her perfectly shoveled walk to my car, I thought about asking Rachel about the sergeant's comments. Then I remembered—Rachel was dead. I missed her so much. Not just because she was my favorite sounding board, although that was true, but because she was so good at putting all the pieces together.

I could just hear Rachel now. Maybe she was talking to me from the grave. *Look at the big picture, Skeeter. Why is Victoria telling you all this? Because she wants to be your friend? I don't think so. But frankly, my dear, you've got a bigger problem. Victoria didn't even come close to corroborating the engineer's story, which you've already told Leona about. Basically, you've got squat. So what are you going to do about that, Ms. Hotshot reporter? And don't lay that guilt crap on me. It does no good. Just find the bomber.*

CHAPTER TWENTY-TWO

"So, do you want it, or not?" It was Rachel's brother, Sam, on my cell phone.

"Want what?"

"Rachel's Mac, remember?" he said. "We talked about it at the funeral?"

Actually, I didn't remember. Totally forgot, in fact, that Sam had offered me Rachel's desktop computer. I did, however, recall talking with him that day. Bumping in to him was one of the interludes I remembered clearly. I guess I was just too foggy to remember what we had talked about.

"Oh, yeah," I said. "The Mac. She just got it. I remember now. Becky and Suzy are complaining about our five-year-old desktop. The operating system is way behind. Sure, I'd love it."

"It's still sitting on her desk in her condo. Wanna stop by for it tonight? I'm trying to get all her stuff out of there so we can put the place up for sale. It's taking longer than I thought."

"Let me make some phone calls and I'll get back to you," I said.

I called Leona and told her Olson hadn't been much help in corroborating Harriet's story about possibly seeing the bomber. She said she could hold off the other editors one more day and that I could go home, since it was late in the afternoon.

"I don't think you've been home much," she said.

"No kidding," I replied.

The switch to daylight savings time was a couple of days away, so it was dark when I walked up our front steps, opened the creaky storm door, and pushed my way into our vestibule. There must have been a dozen pairs of shoes and boots and balled-up socks scattered about the oak floor. Do these things reproduce? I wondered. Are we raising centipedes? I kicked off my boots just to add them to the pile.

"Now, no foolin' around, Mr. Left and Ms. Right," I said to my boots.

"What?" Michael was in the kitchen, stirring spaghetti sauce, filling a pot of water to boil and setting the table for three.

"Nothing," I said. "Just that I love the smell of garlic bread."

"You're home early," he said. "I'll set another place."

I opened the fridge, took out a head of lettuce, washed it, and began breaking off chunks for salad. Then dug around for a tomato, sliced it and threw it in the big salad bowl along with the lettuce.

"We out of Italian dressing?" I asked.

"Till I can shop tomorrow," he replied without looking at me.

I mixed some vinegar and oil together and tossed the salad. "Let's eat."

Dinner was quiet. The girls talked about school and the start of soccer season. Michael and I listened and ate. I wondered if something was amiss with him. A couple of weeks ago, we had argued, then reconciled over a box of dark chocolate, but he seemed especially quiet on this night. He can get that way when he's working an article in his head, I told myself. I'm not going to worry about it, not right now, at least. I had plenty on my mind, too.

It wasn't until after nine o'clock, when the girls had settled in for the evening and Michael was working on a freelance piece, that I finally got away and headed for Rachel's—or what had been Rachel's place. She had lived in a townhouse on the light rail line in the Longfellow area, a middle-class professional neighborhood south and east of downtown Minneapolis. I'd been to Rachel's home many times and admired her decorating. The interior design on her townhouse was classic Rachel. Big bold letters above the fireplace spelled out YES. A four-foot-by four-foot sketch of Marilyn Monroe looked down from the top of the stairs to the second level. The kitchen was lime green and shocking pink. I rang the doorbell.

"Come in." Sam came to the door with two glasses of white wine in hand.

Hmmm, I thought. Why had I never noticed how attractive Sam is?

"How are you?" I gave him a hug and took a glass. "I'm glad you called."

Sam was two years older and two inches taller than Rachel. Aside from that, they could have been twins. Same dark brown curly hair matched his big brown eyes. He wore horn-rimmed glasses, which make him look professorial, even though he's a lawyer.

"Big job ahead of you, huh?" I asked.

He plopped down in Rachel's comfy black leather chair. The fire in the hearth behind him crackled. It smelled mighty fine on this damp March night.

"Like her life, her stuff is complex. But it's better for me to do this than our parents."

"Find anything interesting in Rachel's affairs?" I asked.

"I haven't found any 'affairs,' if that's what you mean," he said. "Although with Rachel, who knew?"

"I meant financial affairs, not romantic," I said.

"I know what you meant," he said with a smile.

Sam went on to say Rachel's finances were intricate. She held significant amounts of stock in high-tech, construction and transportation companies.

"Wasn't that a conflict of interest for Her Honor the Mayor?" I asked.

"Don't think so, but I haven't been through everything yet," he said. "Tell me about you. How are you doing with all this?"

The wine, the hour, and his interest all made my body melt. All of a sudden I could feel the muscles in my arms and legs relax. My jaw unclenched. For the first time in a long time, I was relieved of the pressures that were my life. It was as though I was talking with Rachel, who made me feel safe being me. I began to pour out my feelings, my frustrations with Michael, my sorrow at the loss of Rachel.

Sam leaned back in the chair, his ankle crossed at his knee. He listened. Just listened. His eyes said that he understood.

"Rachel was my go-to on all matters," I said. "She told me when I was right, when I was nuts."

He nodded and took another sip of wine. "Are you hungry?"

"As always."

"Let's see what we can find in Rachel's pink-and-green kitchen," he said. "Jesus, I don't know how she ever managed to cook anything in there."

"We both know what she made best was reservations," I said.

He laughed and nodded again.

I opened the cupboard doors while he dug through her freezer.

"Got it. Byerly's frozen chicken noodle soup," he said.

"Here's a not-too-old box of saltines," I said.

We defrosted the soup in the microwave, heated it up, and sat down to a midnight feast.

"Rachel said you were divorced last year," I said. "I'm sorry."

"It's okay. Jeannie and I had three good years," he said. "That's not bad out of seven."

I laughed. "That's what Rachel said about her marriage."

"She got the line from me," he replied.

We both laughed and it felt so good. I couldn't remember the last time I laughed like that.

"Got any advice on what I should do about Michael, Mr. Experienced-Divorce-Attorney?" I asked.

"I only give advice when it's time to file the papers," he said. "Before that, you need a marriage counselor. I can recommend one, although all she did was get Jeannie and me to fight louder."

Our bellies were full of chicken soup and it was late—much later than I had intended to stay. I looked into his eyes across Rachel's kitchen table. "I need to get the Mac."

"I'll carry it out for you," he said.

We climbed the stairs to the bedroom Rachel had turned into her office. Bookshelves full of mysteries, thrillers, and romantic suspense covered one full wall. All hardcover, most of them signed. I pulled one from the shelf, a first edition of John Sanford's *Rules of Prey,* the opening book in the series. If Rachel had bought it when it first came out in 1989, she would have been about twelve years old. I doubted that, so she must have gotten it from a collector, then had the author sign it. "To Rachel, one tough lady – Camp" was inscribed on the title page.

"Rachel knew everybody," I said as I closed the book and returned it to the shelf.

"That she did," Sam said as he wrapped the cord around the base. "I'll take this part if you want to carry the keyboard and track pad."

We put it all in the trunk of my car. He returned my hug with a stronger one that felt like Rachel's arms wrapped around me.

I could feel the smile on my face as I drove home.

CHAPTER TWENTY-THREE

The next morning, I tossed all the bits of information around in my head while I drove to the newsroom—after stopping for coffee, of course. Harriet, the driver, had lived through the train wreck, and the FBI had stolen her away, telling the public she had died. Why? I couldn't think of another time when the FBI had lied about a case. Lots of times they'll say "no comment," but lie? Seldom. And what of Victoria Olson, inviting me to her home, no less. But she hadn't corroborated what Harriet had said.

I pulled my car into the underground garage and headed for the elevator to ride up with two other reporters who were using the time to complain about their jobs.

"This is one part I hate about newspapering," one of them said. "Everybody wants a great story and nobody is willing to wait for it. The office folk think reporting is just a matter of asking people questions. They have no idea of how much digging it takes to get stuff that is both good and accurate."

"Ironic, isn't it, that most editors started out as reporters," said the second. "It's like they had the reporter part of their brains lobotomized the day they parked their butts in an editor's chair. Instant news online makes the problem worse."

They got off on a different floor and I continued on.

Leona, who as an editor was a target of their whining, was just leaving the morning meeting as the elevator doors opened and I stepped out.

"I told the gang you've hooked a good one," she said. "Made

everybody happy. You're going to keep us happy, right?"

"What I got from Olson wasn't exactly corroboration." I told her the gist of the interview.

"What about the FBI?" Leona said. "Anything from them?"

I just rolled my eyes.

"Call them anyway, so we can at least get their 'no comment' in," she said. "You sure this is still ours alone?"

"I haven't bumped into any other newsies," I said. "Doesn't mean they aren't out there."

"I've got Dex monitoring all the tweets and Facebook pages of the other guys, just in case someone is stupid enough to let the whole world know what they're chasing."

Wow. Didn't know anyone did that. Must be some new trick the tech guys taught the editors. The big guns really are hot for this story. How do you spell Pulitzer? Then I came back to reality.

"Look, all I've got is that the woman who drove the train lived," I said. "I have no way to prove that what she said is true."

"Do you believe her?" Leona asked.

"Yeah. Yeah, I do."

"Then find a way to show it's true," Leona said over her shoulder as she walked away. "Or I'll put someone else on it. Meanwhile, give me a budget line."

I sat down in my cubicle, made as homey as I could by a small lamp my mother was giving away and pictures of the girls and Michael, and began to tap out the budget line.

DRIVER LIVED – Despite news releases to the contrary, the driver of the bombed light rail is alive and in not-too-bad shape in the burn unit at the University of Michigan hospital in Ann Arbor. Says feebies parked her there to keep her quiet. She doesn't want her name used to avoid calls from a million media. (Sounds like a good idea to me.) Ours alone, so far. Looking for about 50 inches plus art. Suggest Sunday. Hughes

I hit the send button and watched across the newsroom as Leona read the budget line, typed something and sent back to me.

What about her theory on bomber? That's what readers/we really want.

I typed my reply. *Still mushy. Do you want me to write it now or wait until I know something?*

Her reply came back immediately. *Know something. Fast. Deadline's coming up and we have to have it lawyered before it runs.*

If this process sounds erratic, it's because it is. Newspaper stories can morph from one idea to another faster than you can say Craig's List, which, by the way, took so much classified advertising away from newspapers that many publishers have resorted to a tin cup when the budget is short.

A day later, I was still waiting for the go-ahead from Leona when I had to make a run to the candy machine in the basement. There'd been something wrong with the building elevator for months. Management seemed uninterested or unable to fix it. I hated setting foot in it, but I hated the idea of using the stairs worse, so I decided to live dangerously and got on, alone. Sure enough, somewhere between the fourth and fifth floors, the iron box stuck. I hit the emergency button, which set off an ear-piercing scream, but no one answered. Hit it again, and again and again. Still no response. I never knew I had claustrophobia until that moment when it set in with a gut-wrenching ferocity. Because my cell phone couldn't get a signal, I picked up the one the Otis Company was so kind to provide.

"Can I help you?" asked the pleasant, confident voice on the other end.

"Hell, yes," I said. "I'm stuck between floors in the elevator. Get me out of here."

"We're sending someone over, ma'am," he said.

"Make it fast." I was beginning to sweat profusely. "And can you call my editor and tell her where I am so she won't think I skipped town in case this takes more time than I can stand?"

"I'm sorry, ma'am, but we're in Portland. I don't have that number," he said again with the voice that was beginning to grate on me.

"Portland, Oregon?"

"Yes, ma'am."

I couldn't believe it. The newspaper had outsourced the safety of its biggest asset, its employees. On second thought, it made sense. They had already outsourced subscription requests to Miami. There was talk about outsourcing copy editing of agate, that teeny tiny print that lists sports scores, to India. Why not the mere running of the elevator, which in its past had lifted huge bags of grain in this one-hundred-year-old building?

I wanted to reach through the phone and grab Mr. Otis by the neck and tell him that another minute in the iron cage was unacceptable. But, as we all know, I couldn't.

I hung up on Mr. Otis and started deep breathing exercises. Inhale, slowly exhale. Over and over again. It didn't help. Dammit, haven't I learned anything? I had gotten stuck in this same elevator a couple years ago. Déjà vu all over again.

I had to find a way to distract myself until I could get out—as if that was ever going to help. I'd never really looked carefully at the inside of the elevator before. "Capacity 1,000 pounds" was engraved on a little plaque that was almost worn from a century of people passing it by, never noticing its importance. A thousand pounds. So, ten people who each weighed one hundred pounds could fit in there. I've gained weight, but not enough to stop an elevator, I thought. With an average weight of one hundred fifty pounds, that would mean fewer people, but I didn't do the math. That's why I went into journalism, so I didn't have to do math. Who came up with one thousand pounds, anyway? Why was it such an exact number? Was that the weight of twenty sacks of grain plus a couple people? Did it have something to do with the strength of the cable that moved the could-be sarcophagus that held me suspended over God knows how many floors? Or was it some weird algorithm that determined the acceptable capacity? Some graduate student in a desperate search for a thesis topic had probably figured it out. I bet there's a story in that. Here I am, gathering string again. If I could have gotten internet reception in the elevator I would have Googled "elevator capacity in historic buildings." I was trying to come up with Plan B when the car started to move with a jerk. *Finally.*

After what seemed like hours, my would-have-been tomb reached the first floor. When the doors opened, I hesitated to put a foot out. Didn't we have a story a while back about a woman who was getting into an elevator when it started to move and she was severed between floors? But I decided I couldn't think about that, so I ran out as fast as I could and didn't stop until I reached the guard, a kid who was so young he thought a guy named Bush was a president for a long time, not that were two Bush presidents. Thank God, I thought, at least they haven't outsourced the guard.

"I was the woman trapped in the elevator," I said to him breathlessly.

"Did you get out?" he asked, staring at me.

"You are the guy who protects the people who protect the First Amendment," I said.

"Yes, I am," he said, standing a little straighter.

"No wonder the First Amendment is under constant attack."

It was more than I could stand so I just turned on my heel and headed for Starbucks. One grande vanilla latte with three shots of espresso later, my hands stopped shaking.

CHAPTER TWENTY-FOUR

Even though the newsroom is set in the oak-paneled space that was once the pit of the Grain Exchange, the journalists have made it their own, with paper, paper everywhere. Print-type people just never seem to get the email that says we're now in a paperless society. Manila folders are stacked everywhere, sometimes topped by a paper cup filled with three-day old coffee. About half the cubicles are empty because reporters are either out chasing news or taking the day off because of a forced furlough. As I passed, I heard one reporter talking on the phone: "Let me get this straight. You're angry that the post office didn't deliver the live puppy you mailed to Louisiana because it was a birthday present for your son?"

Tucked way back in the corner was the intern in charge of watching Twitter messages from other media folk.

"So, do I call you Dex or Dexter?" I asked.

"Dex," he said. "Rhymes with text, but without the 'T'."

"Is that the first T or the second T?" I asked.

"No matter."

Dex had brown hair that brushed the back of his neck from under his Twins baseball cap. He wore a purple Vikings T-shirt over jeans and flip-flops, in March. "Your job is to monitor Twitter messages all day long? How do you stay awake?"

"I prefer to think of it as competitive intelligence."

This kid clearly had a future in journalism. His left eyebrow appeared to be permanently arched in skepticism, yet he gave off the aura of an earnest early-twenty-something.

"It's actually pretty interesting. You'd be surprised how much gossip floats around. For example, the wife of a certain TV news personality tweeted about the great housing market in Los Angeles. I passed that on to our gossip columnist, who reported said anchor was job-hunting. Next day the station announced that hubby had jumped ship."

That was certainly scoop-worthy, I thought. News you can use. But I beat back my sarcasm and didn't tell Dex that. There's already enough spoken sarcasm in the room. Didn't want to put a ding in his proud "competitive intelligence."

"Leona told me to keep an eye out for other reporters talking about the Blue Line bombing, but that doesn't tell me much," Dex said. "What exactly should I be looking for?"

"Obviously you'll not breathe a word of this to anyone," I said.

"Skeeter, I'm wounded. How could you even suggest I might spill?"

"Just emphasizing here," I said.

I told him that the driver of the light rail had survived the explosion, that she was in a hospital at the University of Michigan, and that we were sitting on the story while I tried to confirm her less-than-descriptive description of the bomber. Maybe a teen. Maybe a man. Maybe a woman.

"If anybody tweets about anything that hints they may be on to this story, let me know right away," I said.

"Got it," he said.

I headed back to my desk, hoping he wouldn't find anything that would blow up my story. Love having kids in the newsroom.

CHAPTER TWENTY-FIVE

To figure out my next move, I flipped through my notes again, looking at all of Harriet's quotes.

"Couple of FBI agents have been here too," she'd said. "They're so cute, especially that Agent O'Reilly."

Where was my head when Harriet was talking? I must have been focusing on something else she'd said because it didn't hit me right away. Or when I asked Sergeant Olson for the agent's name. Suddenly, I realized I knew Agent O'Reilly. Tim O'Reilly. We had gone to high school together. He was a couple of years ahead of me. And he was cute back in high school. Very conservative. Very uptight. President of the math club and captain of the wrestling team, if I remember correctly. All the A+ girls were hot for him. Last I heard, he had joined the FBI and was living in one of the far western suburbs, but I couldn't remember which one. I put a call through to an old friend, Barb, or Barbie as I always called her, to do a little reconnaissance on him.

"Law offices," the receptionist answered. Barbie's now an assistant U.S. attorney. I wondered if she had a Barbie-sized briefcase.

"Barbara Levine, please."

"Who shall I say is calling?"

"Tell her it's Ken's proctologist," I said.

Barbie picked up right away. "It's got to be Skeeter. No one else spends as much time with assholes."

"Right you are," I said.

We swapped some bits of gossip about our former classmates and reminisced a bit about high school.

"Remember when we had the joint birthday party?" she asked. "You and I have another birthday coming up."

"You mean tomorrow?" I asked.

"That would be it. Has Michael got anything special planned for you? I heard he left the paper and he's freelancing these days. True?"

"He was laid off last month," I said. "So, yes, he's freelancing."

"How's that going?" she asked.

"The good part is he's around for the girls when I'm working. But freelancing is a tough business."

"Causing you two a little stress?" she asked.

Stress? Between me and Michael? Yeah. But our issues went back long before he was laid off. He pretty much disappeared to God knows where in January, then walked out on me. He returned and we're still living in the same house, but our marriage is tentative on good days.

"Yes, there's some tension," I said. "But that's not why I called. Remember Tim O'Reilly?"

"No forgetting that one," Barbie said.

She said he was living in Land o'Lakes, a high-priced suburb named by developers who wanted home buyers to think they were investing in a community as smooth and rich as butter. He'd done tours in Iraq, Afghanistan, and Somalia, and was back in Minneapolis working counterintelligence.

"Did you know the FBI has not one, but two offices in the Twin Cities, where dozens of people spend their entire shifts in a room without windows, monitoring internet chatter?" she asked. "Sounds deadly boring to me."

"What are they looking for?"

Barb said she didn't know exactly, but one thing she knew for sure. "They're only successful if they stop an attack. Heads are rolling because the train was bombed."

"Do you think that would include Tim O'Reilly's gorgeous head?"

"Could be," she said. "But you can check him out for yourself. My daughter's playing soccer against his daughter's team tonight.

He usually goes to the games."

"They're playing in March?" I asked.

"Just a scrimmage."

I asked for directions to the field, offered my thanks, and hung up, wondering about the best way to approach Agent O'Reilly. This wasn't going to be easy. Dealing with the feds, even former classmates, is always tough in the simplest of stories. This was no simple story.

The setting sun was in my eyes as I wheeled my way on Highway 62 to Land o'Lakes at about six-thirty. Minneapolis' forebears had the good sense to lay out streets and avenues in roughly parallel lines, then name them in mostly alphabetical order and by number. Not so in the 'burbs, where I feel perpetually lost. Thanks to my iPhone navigation system, not the newspaper's piece-of-crap phone, I found the soccer fields in short order. Then I had to figure out at which of the dozen verdant suburban acres the O'Reilly girl might be playing.

I texted Barb: *colors for your team?*

The answer came back in seconds: *blue & white.*

Girls in blue and white were warming up on one end of field six, while at the other end, green and white was predominant. This must be the place, I thought as I drove up and down the rows of SUVs, Lexus wagons, and Audis before pulling into a spot at the end.

I strolled over to the sideline space roped off to keep parents from getting too close to the coaches or players. It wasn't hard to find Tim O'Reilly. He was the dad with ramrod straight posture, a just-clipped haircut, and no beer belly. The only one with a physique.

"Hi, Tim," I said casually. "Remember me, Skeeter?"

"How could I forget you? I see your byline in the paper all the time."

How could I have forgotten his deeply blue eyes? This was one guy from high school who had definitely improved with age.

He looked back at the game. "Good job, Sarah," he yelled, clapping his hands. He turned to me. "What are you doing out here? Do you have a daughter who plays?"

"Actually, both my girls play soccer, but not tonight. I'm here to see you."

"Why?" he asked without taking his eyes off the field.

"I'm working on a story on the light rail bombing. You're FBI."

"Your information is out of date," he said, turning to look at me. "I was FBI."

"Was? Since when?"

"Since the train was bombed."

"You were fired because the train blew? Why?"

"FBI uses 'terminated,' but yes. I was in charge of monitoring internet chatter. The bosses weren't happy that we missed that one. I had to take the fall."

He turned his gaze back to the field, just as his daughter charged down the field with the ball. "Go, go, go Sarah! Score. Go gold!" he shouted.

"I don't want to distract you from the game," I said. "Can I talk with you about the bombing some other time?"

Sarah ran and scored.

"Way to go, Sport." Tim looked as happy as an FBI agent can look.

"I don't know," he said.

I thought back to our days in Rochester, right out of college, when I was a news reporter and he was a cop who was going to law school at night. I had to massage his ego a bit to get him to talk to me back then, too.

"Remember when I wrote that profile about you?" I said. "I talked my editor into letting me do it by saying I'd known you in high school. Class president, straight A's, captain of something …."

"The wrestling team," he said.

"That's right. The wrestling team."

"And debate," he added.

"I seem to recall that you graduated from law school right after that, then quickly got a job with the FBI."

"Four months."

"Four months?"

"Yeah, four months later, I went to work for the FBI, after I passed the bar," he said.

"I think I have half the story about the bombing. I understand that it would be especially risky for you, but I don't want readers to see only part of the truth. I need to give them context. You could help me with that."

"Do you drink coffee late at night?" he asked.

"Do I drink coffee?" I rolled my eyes. "Yes, I drink coffee, all day and late into the night. It's never kept me awake."

"I'm driving a bunch of Sarah's friends to Dairy Queen after the game, then home," he said. "It's going to be about nine thirty before I'm free. There's a Dunn Bros on Shady Oak Road just south of Excelsior Boulevard. It's in an old house with a big white front porch. Do you know it?"

"I used to cover Land o'Lakes. Sure I know it."

"They close at ten," he said. "If I have time after I drop off the girls, I'll swing by there on my way home and we can have a quick chat, maybe."

"Maybe?" I said.

"Sometimes the girls hang out longer," he said. "Now that I've got more free time, I like to be with Sarah as much as I can."

CHAPTER TWENTY-SIX

I arrived at the Dunn Bros inside the Smith Douglas More house about nine o'clock, ordered a double-shot latte from the barista inside, then grabbed a chair on the front porch of the refurbished Nineteenth Century farmhouse. I wasn't convinced that Agent O'Reilly would show up, but I wanted to be there early in case he did. I sipped, and stirred, then sipped again. I was checking the time on my phone at nine twenty-eight when he came up behind me. He must have come in a back door. He may have been fired but he still used the old FBI tricks.

"I almost didn't come, you know," he said as he set a ceramic mug on the table and took the chair opposite me.

"Why did you come?" I asked.

"Because we were just about to crack this case when I was 'terminated.'" He rolled his shoulders, then twisted his neck as if it were sore. "I wanted to see this one through."

"I can understand that."

"Understand this," he said in a hoarse whisper. "Our conversation never happened. You haven't talked to me since high school. Anything I tell you came from someone else. Got it?"

"Got it."

"What do you need to know?" he asked.

"The engineer of the train lived. She's in the burn unit at the University of Michigan, where you visited her."

"How did you find that out?" he asked.

I love anyone who asks me that question, especially an FBI guy. It demonstrates that I do my homework and this wasn't just a fishing expedition. I always answer the same way.

"Doesn't matter. I just thought we could start with something we both know to be true. Harriet, the driver, said that someone left a backpack on the train. She thinks it had a bomb in it that he detonated with a cell phone or garage door opener or some other technology."

"That's what she thinks." He ran his finger around the rim of his coffee cup, then took a gulp and set the cup down. "Doesn't mean that's what happened."

"Is she wrong?"

"Not necessarily, but I will tell you that the analysis of the scene turned up a backpack full of weights," he said.

"Weights?"

"Yeah, weights, like one-pound, five-pound, ten-pound weights that someone would use to exercise," he said. "In fact, they're exactly what I use in my basement for my workout."

"Could weights be part of a bomb?"

"If they were intended to be used that way, they weren't effective because they were still in the backpack," he said.

"Were there any identifying marks on the backpack? I suppose it's too much to ask that the owner had written his name on it."

"Yes, it is too much to ask. The bureau was running that down, last I heard." He shifted in his chair, a movement I'd seen before in anxious interviewees.

"You said you wanted to see this case through and that's why you're speaking with me," I said. "But I sense there's another reason. Am I right?"

"I'm not worried about getting another job," he said. "But the department has been riding roughshod over the Somali community, and I don't like that."

"What do you mean by 'roughshod'?"

"Sending agents to the high schools to talk to kids, pulling them out of class. Grabbing Somalis off the street and dragging them into a car to interrogate. There's no proof that Somalis are responsible for what happened to the Blue Line."

At just that moment the barista stepped out on the porch. "Closing time," she said, taking our empty cups from us.

"Is that unusual for the FBI? Why the heavy pressure?"

"Time's up," O'Reilly said. He pulled his trim self up to about six feet. In the half light, I saw gray hair emerging at his temples and crow's feet around his eyes.

"Remember, this conversation never happened," he said, then disappeared into the dark.

I sat on the porch for a while after the barista had shut off the lights inside and locked the door. I never heard O'Reilly's car start up or drive away. How did he do that? I wondered. Maybe he drives a silent Prius. But he never struck me as a Prius kind of guy.

CHAPTER TWENTY-SEVEN

The next morning, I was in line at Starbucks when the boing that alerts me to a text message on my phone grabbed my attention. "Fox TV guy looking for best bars in AA," Dex wrote. "He headed there for train driver?" I forwarded Dex's message to Leona, adding, "On my way in."

She had already assembled the editors when I arrived in the large conference room. I looked around. Ten men and women crowded around the table. Blue shirts with ties and khaki pants must be male editor fashion du jour, I thought. Even though there was a sprinkling of non-white guys, they all looked the same. Hair cut reasonably shaggy, but no ponytails. Women wore light jackets or sweaters like a doctor's white coat to indicate they were decision-makers. Most were squinty-eyed from staring at computer screens too long. Half-full coffee cups littered the room.

Yellowing front pages were thumbtacked to the wall. "Somali Pirates Tell Their Side: They Want Only Money," read one headline. And below it, "Banking Crisis Crosses Atlantic." "Home Sales Brisk in May, According to Realtors Report," said another. The air in the room was stale. It had been rebreathed too often.

Leona looked up as I sat down. "Here's Skeeter," she said. "She can fill you in."

"What do we know and how do we know it?" the editor in chief asked.

"We know for sure that the train driver lived," I said. "It's been ours alone, but Dex has picked up Twitter chatter that the Fox

News guys may be on to us."

"And ...?" the assistant managing editor asked. "Are we any closer to a suspect, or even a cause?"

I cleared my throat. "The driver thinks the bomber may have been Somali, but I haven't been able to corroborate that."

"We need my investigative guys on this," said the editor for investigative reporting.

I glanced at Leona.

"Skeeter has the best sources on this, and they trust her," she said. "We should stick with her. She recently talked with an FBI source. What came of that?"

Before I could speak, the public safety editor piped up. "My reporters have tons of FBI sources."

Leona looked at him with one bushy eyebrow raised, a look that said, *Back off.*

"I had a conversation that 'didn't happen,'" I said. "I was told that an analysis of the scene turned up a backpack filled with weights, and that the FBI has been heavy-handed in riding the Somali community. None of that is confirmed."

"But was the driver right that the bomber was Somali?" asked the sports editor.

"The driver hinted at that, but never said it specifically. My source neither confirmed nor denied," I said.

"Some source," harrumphed Slick. He and Dick had slipped into the meeting.

"Look, guys," said Leona. "We've got to be very careful with this. Whether the bomber was Somali or Swedish, it would be way too easy to blame a whole community for the act of one person. I say we go only with what we've got verified, that the driver lived."

The room broke into cacophony, with each editor trying to outshout the other. As the noise built, Leona leaned and whispered in my ear, "We should just get a ruler, have them all unzip, lay everyone's out on the table, and measure to see whose is biggest, then be done with it."

I stifled a giggle as the noise settled down.

"I'm with Leona." The ombudsman was the last to speak.

"Agreed," said the editor in chief. "We go with the driver

lived, and keep working to tighten the other facts. I want to see the copy. We label it an exclusive and release it online after our competitors are past their deadlines."

Folks began gathering up their pads and pens to leave. "Everyone sit back down," the e-in-c said, his voice raised. "I shouldn't have to tell you this, but I will anyway. We need to be very careful with this story. We cannot, will not, inflame readers with a story that pins the bombing on any ethnic group. There's enough buzz out there already about who might be responsible. When we find out the truth of what happened, we'll share it as we know it, but not before we're one hundred fifty percent sure of what we're saying. Understood, everyone?" Heads nodded around the room, then most editors and reporters left.

"Skeeter, a moment please," Leona said to me.

When the room had emptied and it was just the two of us at the large conference table, the energy dissipated, as though a balloon that had been blown up to about-to-pop had lost all its air and become a saggy blob.

"You're doing good work here," Leona said.

It's a rare day when an editor says "good work" to a reporter. Something inside me wanted to jump up, ring a bell, pound a drum, but I didn't. Would have been poor form to even smile.

"Thanks," I said.

"Don't fuck it up," Leona said.

Now that sounded more like what I was accustomed to.

I returned to my cubicle, logged on, and pulled up the writing program, which typed by *Skeeter Hughes, Staff Reporter,* along with the tag line with my phone number and email address. It would have been nice if the program wrote the story, too.

Now what? Writing a lede (I've never understood why they're not spelled lead) is the toughest part of news reporting. Long ago, when the inverted pyramid style of writing was in vogue, writing a lede was simple. Who? What? Where? When? Why? How? Information was imparted in a descending order of importance. That was then, not now. In these days of short attention spans, the goal is to hook the reader. Sometimes that means waving a shiny object. The lede that journalists like to quote the most was written by Edna

Buchanan, a Pulitzer Prize-winning cops reporter in Miami in the mid-nineteen-eighties. "Gary Robinson died hungry," she wrote for a story about a man who shot up a fried chicken joint because they ran out of the food he wanted. I decided to follow her simple start.

"The driver of the Blue Line train that was bombed two weeks ago lives," I wrote.

Okay, but could be better.

"The driver of the Blue Line train survived the bomb that killed sixty-two passengers."

Improving, but still... Time to get more coffee to get my heart beating a little faster. A cigarette would help, too, but that wasn't going to happen. A Depth Charge black coffee spiked with a shot of espresso would work. I headed over to my favorite Caribou Coffee and picked up some chocolate-covered coffee beans while I was at it.

Back at my desk, I started again. Although few reporters get writer's block, because there isn't time when a deadline looms, I have found that just typing anything is a good way to get the juices flowing. Some reporters start a story with Dear Mom, and pretend they're explaining the story to her. If mom can understand, anybody can, is the old adage. But that strikes me as ageist and sexist and reduces mom to a lightweight. I'm a mom and I certainly don't think of myself as a simpleton. So I don't use that method.

Caffeine was kicking in. I suggested a headline that said "Light Rail Driver Lives." Then I wrote, "The Blue Line driver who survived the March 1 bombing is dying to talk about it."

That ought to work for Leona and the boys, I thought. Once I have the lede figured, if it's the right lede, the rest of the story flows pretty easily.

Much later, just after midnight, I checked our website and found that the powers that be had gone with the headline I suggested and left the lede unchanged. I fell asleep with a smile on my face.

CHAPTER TWENTY-EIGHT

On the way to work the next day, I suddenly remembered I'd forgotten to pick up my scarf from Rachel's things. I called her brother Sam and left a message. "Sam, it's Skeeter," I said to his cell phone. "I was so caught up about getting the computer that I forgot about the scarf I loaned Rachel. I want it back. Call me, please."

I replayed the other night in my head. In my mind's eye I saw Sam in Rachel's kitchen. There was something so right, so comforting to be there with him, especially after the silent treatment from Michael.

I hadn't gone more than two blocks when my phone rang.

"So, the scarf?" Sam said.

"It was my favorite," I said. "Fall colors—gold, green, orange—all in a leaf pattern. I loaned it to Rachel last year. She's not going to need it anymore, and I do."

He chuckled at that. "How do your daughters like the computer?"

"If they've set it up by now, they haven't told me," I said.

"It was good to see you," he said. "When can I see you again?"

Hmmmmmmm.

"I enjoyed it, too," I said. "I've got to work late tonight. Probably till at least eight. You going to be around?"

He said he'd be at Rachel's again tonight, still sorting through her stuff.

"The scarf will turn up," he said. "Would you like to come by to get it?"

"Sure. On my way home," I said.

That evening, after I filed my last story for the week, a short police report about a hit-and-run, I headed down the snowy city streets toward Rachel's place. Funny, I still called it that, even though technically it didn't belong to her anymore. As organized as Rachel was about her professional life, she was a disaster when it came to her personal affairs. She never got around to writing a will, so the probate courts would be left to sort it all out.

I parked on the street, got out, and tried to step over a giant puddle glazed with a very thin sheet of ice. As usual I was hurrying and thinking more about seeing Sam than about what I was doing. Next thing I knew, my foot slipped from under me and I was flat on my butt in the icy water, which my jeans soaked up like a thirsty sponge. I cursed as a car almost ran over the contents of my purse, which spread on the street beside me. Not wanting to get hit in the fading light, I scrambled to gather my stuff back in my purse and then, hanging on the car door, pulled myself out of the puddle. Pain shot through my ankle the moment I put weight on it. Sam was just opening the door to Rachel's place as I limped up the step.

"What happened to you?" he asked.

I explained about the mishap.

"You could've been run over," he said. "Come in. Sit."

"You don't want me sitting on anything in here," I said. "My jeans are soaked."

"Take them off." He smiled. "I'll throw them in the dryer."

All I could think was, Michael would never have said anything like that. It would not have occurred to him.

I limped into Rachel's bedroom, where I took off my boots and jeans, then looked through her closet, chastising myself that I was too fat to fit into her pants. I found a thick terrycloth robe that smelled so much like her that I started to tear up as I wrapped it around me. When I walked out into the hall and faced Sam, I could see from the look in his eyes that he was thinking the same thing. He wrapped his arms around me and held me for a very long time. Neither of us said anything for several minutes. We didn't have to. We each knew how the other felt.

"God, I miss her," he said after we had broken our hug.

"Me, too," I said.

I felt more than sorrow. I felt a need to touch Rachel again, to hear her voice, to see her move. But I knew the closest I was going to get to her was Sam.

We began to kiss, gently at first, then voraciously. Sam started to push me to Rachel's bedroom. My heart was still beating fast in my ears. My mouth was dry. My hands were shaking.

"This is wrong," I said.

"Is it?" he asked. "Really?"

"Yes, really."

"It's something I've wanted for a while," he said.

"I'm married. I have two daughters at home."

"Well, I'm not married," he said. "And I've got no one. All I had was Rachel. And now she's gone."

"This isn't going to bring her back," I said.

"I know," he said. "But we can pretend."

"This isn't about sex," I said. "It's about Rachel."

"About Rachel?"

"You think, we both think, that if we have sex it will bring us closer to Rachel," I said. "It won't work. I can't do this. I just can't."

I pushed him away, went to the dryer, pulled out my toasty-warm jeans, and tugged them on. Then I grabbed my purse and shrugged on my jacket. The pain in my foot had miraculously disappeared.

I had my hand on the door to leave when Sam came toward me, holding the scarf that had supposedly drawn me back to her place.

"Here," he said. "Don't forget this."

"Oh, yeah. The scarf. Thanks."

I ran toward my car, stopping halfway to look back at him. Rachel's porch light backlit his head as he stood in the March drizzle watching me run to my car. I began to cry, for the loss of Rachel, for the loss of opportunity with Sam, for all the problems with my marriage.

It wasn't like Rachel hadn't warned me.

"Why do you stay married to him?" Rachel had asked once when Michael was out of town and not returning my phone calls. At the time I was working on a complicated story and relying too much on our neighbor to look after the girls. It was a time when all the pressures of my life made me feel like I was walking the ocean floor without an oxygen tank.

"He's the father of my children."

"Then don't you think he ought to be taking some responsibility in that area?" she said. "I mean, you've both got full-time jobs, but he seems to think that gives him justification for ignoring you and the girls."

"He doesn't 'ignore' the girls," I said.

"Who goes to all their soccer games, teacher conferences, and whatever else the parent job description entails?" she asked.

I remember those were her exact words "whatever else the parent job description entails." Only someone like Rachel, who never had kids, would think of those things as duties instead of joys.

"Rachel, what's really going on here?" I asked. "Why don't you like Michael?"

"He demands too much of your attention," she said. "He takes time that you should be spending with me. There. I've said it."

I was shocked. I'd never heard Rachel even hint at being needy. What's more, she had phrased it in a way that told me she had been thinking about this for a while.

"You think I have to choose between you and Michael?" I asked. "Can't I be close to both of you?"

"Of course you can," she said.

But it wasn't so. Our friendship took a hit. I didn't hear from her for a couple of months, until the day we had drinks with Fred, and she died.

CHAPTER TWENTY-NINE

I hadn't had time to follow up on Mohamed's comment that Abdi worked for the money exchange on Cedar Avenue. Today was the day. I hadn't planned on getting sucked into international monetary policy, but if that was a route to the answer, I had to go there, even though I had figured that by going into journalism I could avoid working with numbers.

Mohamed Express US was only open from ten in the morning to two in the afternoon, except on Friday, which is the day Muslims go to the mosque at noon to hear the sermon. Fortunately, today was Thursday.

Dust motes floated in the sunshine filtered by dirty windows inside the shop as a familiar voice was reporting on the latest in state politics on Minnesota Public Radio from some unseen back room. A young man, maybe thirty years old, sat at a beat-up wooden desk, circa 1969, talking on a cell phone in Somali. He raised one finger to motion that he would be with me in a minute.

"Are you Mohamed?" I asked when he came to the counter.

"Aren't we all?" he replied with a big grin.

I had to smile at that. "It sure seems to me that every man in Cedar-Riverside is named Mohamed."

He nodded. "What can I do to help you today, ma'am?"

His English was perfect, his accent Minnesota bordering on Wisconsin. If I had closed my eyes I would have thought I was talking to someone born and raised in the suburbs of Minneapolis. In fact, Mohamed probably was born and raised in the suburbs, like many of the younger Somali-Americans whose families first came to the US in the 1990s.

I told him I was a reporter and I was inquiring about Abdi Qassim.

"Why?"

"His mother hasn't seen him in a while, and she's worried about him."

"A mother's job is to worry," he said. "Fortun is like any other mother."

"You know her?"

"This is a small community."

"So, where's Abdi?"

"I don't know," Mohamed said. "Maybe Somalia, maybe North Dakota. I hear jobs taking oil from the ground are good there."

"When was the last time you saw him?" I asked.

"He worked for me for about six months," Mohamed replied. "Then, one day, he didn't come to work. I haven't seen him since."

"How long ago was that?"

"Maybe six months ago. It was the beginning of Ramadan, I remember."

"So it was well before the train was bombed?" I asked.

He glared at me. "Is that what this is about?" His voice was loud as he slapped the flat of his hand on the counter. "Do you think Abdi blew up the train? That he's a terrorist? A suicide bomber?"

"I don't know," I said. "Do you?"

"No way," he said. "Abdi is a pacifist."

"How do you know that?"

"Because Abdi is deeply religious. The Qur'an tells us peace is the way. So many people think we Muslims are the enemy. It's like a new McCarthyism. Instead of going after Communists, you're going after Muslims. You think we're all out to kill non-Muslims. Not true. We just want to live our lives, practice our religion in peace without interference.

"We're like the Pilgrims who first came to America. But our religion isn't Christianity. We follow Mohamed, not Jesus Christ. Sure, there are some among us who are extreme. They're like the Christian Ku Klux Klan. Did you ever think of that?"

His question was rhetorical, but I felt a need to respond anyway. "Yes, I have thought of that," I said. "Thought about it a lot, in fact. But it's my job to ask questions, and that's what I'm doing here today. "

From the look on his face, I could tell Mohamed wasn't accustomed to a woman talking to him the way I had. Somali women talk a lot, in part because their culture places high value on oral communication. But while Somali women rule the roost in their homes, they don't talk back to a man who is not their husband.

His cell phone rang and he answered in Somali. The conversation went on for a few minutes, which allowed the small tension between us to dissipate.

After he hung up, I asked him how the United States' ban on sending money to Somalia had hurt his business.

"A lot," he said. "Most of my money transfers go to Somalia. That's why I'm only open a few hours every day now. But worse, it's hurt Somalis. American Somalis wire about $100 million a year back home. That's a lot of money not going to people who need it."

Shutting down the wire transfers sent a message that all Somali Americans are terrorists, he said.

"We're not. My parents came here to get away from the terrorists in their homeland," he said. "You think that was easy? It wasn't. I watched my parents struggle. Because my mother wears a hijab, my father wears a taqiyah, because their skin is brown, people look at them, at me, like we are terrorists."

"What's a taqiyah?" I asked.

"Glad you asked. It's a small round cap," he said. "Look, I'm an American just like you. I was born in Eden Prairie, Minnesota. I went to Minnesota public schools. I'm studying for a PhD in urban planning at the University of Minnesota. But people think when they drive through Cedar-Riverside that they are going to get shot. Do you know that this neighborhood has less crime than any other in Minneapolis?"

Actually, I did know that. Besides, my reporter's DNA was telling me that Mohamed could be a great source.

"Can I have your cell phone number?" I asked, proffering my phone so he could type the spelling of his name and his number in my database himself. After he agreed, I asked him to take my card.

"I'll call you if I have more questions, okay?" I asked.

Mohamed's slight nod gave me the feeling that he didn't really trust me. I wondered if he would return my call in the future.

"One more question," I said. "Who bombed the train?"

He took a deep breath, placed both hands on the glass counter that separated us, and looked me straight in the eye.

"I don't know," he said. "I wish I did."

CHAPTER THIRTY

Note to self: Never sit at your computer, elbows on your desk, holding your head in your hands. Editors think you're snoozing. You're sure to get handed an assignment you don't want.

Unfortunately, that's exactly what I was doing. But I wasn't catching a much-needed nap. I was thinking about the train story. Trying to find a better way to figure out who bombed the train. Where is Abdi? Did he blow up the train? Was he the guy in the hoodie? And what about Mr. Ponytail? How was I going to figure out if he was nuts but knew the truth, or just nuts? And then there was all the stuff that my old high school buddy, former FBI agent O'Reilly, didn't tell me.

I felt a tap on my shoulder. It was the editor filling in for Leona.

"You know about light-rail trains, right?" he said.

"Uh, yeah. That's what I've been covering, the Blue Line train that was bombed."

"There's a meeting this afternoon outstate. The city council there is going to talk about extending the light rail through there. The regular reporter's sick. Cover it. I'm assigning Marshal to shoot it. Thanks." With that he walked away.

Why do editors always say 'thanks' like they assume you're going to do exactly what they ask? I wanted to shout at him, but I didn't because I knew the answer. They know you're going to do what they say because you are.

"What's the problem there, Skeeter? Did the boss-man give you a tough assignment?" Dick's head popped above the cubicle wall we share. "Something you don't really want to do?"

I glared at Dick. "Just because I'm working on this bombing

story doesn't mean I should be heading to the land that elected Michele Bachmann too many times just because there's going to be whining about expanding the light rail out there. I'm covering a bombing, not a train. That's crime, not transportation."

"What a shame." Slick had overheard the same conversation. These cubicles offer zero privacy, which is especially a problem in a room full of journalists who are nosey about everything. "Too bad Leona isn't here today to run interference for you."

Indeed, it was too bad. But there was nothing I could do about it, so I checked out a company car and hit the road. Besides, there might be something there that could help me get to the bottom of the Blue Line bombing, I told myself, trying to be cheery.

I turned on the radio, hoping Minnesota Public Radio would lighten my mood. They had a report on global warming that said the "mild" winters we've come to expect would continue. That was good news. Only one or two days with temperatures below zero in the winter was much better than when I was a kid. Back then, we called two weeks at fifteen degrees below zero too cold to swim but warm enough for sledding. On the other hand, global warming means far less water in the lakes in the summer, which can cut into swimming, water-skiing and fishing. I turned the radio off with a snap.

What was really bugging me? It was that I was headed to cover a community meeting. I'd reported on at least a million of those as a young reporter. They're long and tedious, and rarely produce a decent story. I've sat through board of education meetings where a dozen people can take an hour to debate whether to buy a new boiler for the high school. I didn't expect this to be much better.

Until, that is, I got close to the parking lot for the community center where the good citizens planned to meet. There was not an open spot to be had in the lot, nor on the street for two blocks. What's more, all three local news stations had their trucks parked in front, ready to shove those antennae into the sky for live reports. Holy smokes, I thought. Are they giving away free lefse tonight, or is this going to be a barnburner of a meeting?

I like to sit in the back of these kinds of events. It gives me a better perspective on the audience and the speakers alike. But there was no seating in the back. The best I could do was lean against the white cinderblock wall, which meant I would be standing through the whole thing. Fortunately, I'd worn my comfortable Uggs.

Even though it was a cold, damp March night, human bodies heated the community center main meeting area. There must've been three hundred people there, all talking at once. The decibels grew until the lady in the front with the perfectly coifed silver-blond updo banged her gavel.

"I'm Margaret Michaels, your city council representative," she said after the conversation simmered down. "I'll be chairing the meeting tonight. We have two microphones set up, one here"—she pointed—"and one there. I ask you to form lines at either mike and we'll alternate speakers. You are limited to one minute."

An angry roar went up in the crowd. "One minute?" someone shouted. "I could talk for an hour."

"You'll have to choose the best one-sixtieth," Ms. Michaels said with a smirk. "Please do not repeat what someone else has already said. After you have spoken, I ask you to sign your name to the sheet on the clipboard on the back table. Everyone understand?"

More murmurs.

"Good. We're here tonight to discuss plans to put a light rail line through the center of town. There's a map pinned to the wall near the bathrooms for those of you who don't already know where the light rail train is proposed to go. You can also access that information on the city website, and there are a few copies of the map on a table by the door. This is a listening session for myself and the other council members on the podium here with me tonight. We will not be commenting."

Lines formed at both microphones as she spoke. This is going to be a long one, I thought. I had to find a way to entertain myself, so I decided to assign an identifier, say an animal or kind of food, to the speakers, along with the order in which they spoke. Then if I decided to quote them, I could go to the sign-in sheet for spelling of their names. The technique has worked for me before. In addition to keeping me awake, it helps me remember who said what.

"I think this light rail thing is an abomination," said the first speaker, a woman of about fifty wearing a tattered North Face quilted jacket, jeans and boots. She had orange curly hair and a forehead that met her scalp halfway back her head, making her look like a clown. But there was no humor in her tone.

"I moved out here to get some peace and quiet and to raise my kids away from the city. This thing'll bring all kinds of people we don't know. It'll decimate our community, I tell you."

I wrote "Bozo" in my notebook next to "decimate," which originally meant to select by lot and kill every tenth man. It's been used improperly enough that the dictionary definition now says, "to cause great destruction or harm."

"Is there an environmental impact statement written about this train?" asked a forty-something man with long, professorial hair. "I understand that light rail is much better than cars for the environment in general, but what exact effect might it have on our town? This must be our foremost concern."

This one was definitely a granola bar. I called him "prof environmentalist."

Next up was a young woman. "I think it's a great idea. Listen people, trains that come in can go out. That means we can get on a train and get to the city quickly without driving. Think about, like, if you're in the city, and, you know, you've had a little wee bit too much to drink. You don't wanna drive home, but you wanna be sure that you can get home. You can, like, just jump on the train and here you are."

Her name had to be "kitten." She wore black high-heeled boots and tush-grabbing tights and looked too young to drink legally anywhere. I drew a pitcher of beer next to her name.

The microphone went to a thirty-something woman, who held it tightly in both hands. "I'd like to address an earlier comment, if I may. I'm concerned about my neighbor who said the light rail would 'bring people we don't know to our community.' What does that mean? Is she afraid someone who isn't white and Lutheran might pass through town?"

Now we're getting to the crux of the matter, I thought. All the times I've covered these meetings, I've never heard someone address the issue of 'not like us' so directly. I drew a star on my notepad and prepared to write down as much of her quotes as I could.

A nervous titter ran through the crowd.

Bozo stood and pointed to Star. "What do you mean?"

"It sounds to me like you don't like the idea of people of different races and backgrounds coming from the city to our town," said Star.

"Well, look what happened when they let the buses run from Minneapolis to the Mall of America in Bloomington for only a quarter. All the gang-bangers showed up. I stopped letting my kids go there. I don't want them gang-bangers in our town."

A man in a red knit shirt with the Lacoste alligator on his breast jumped up and shook his fist. "Look what happened to the Blue Line. One of them bombed it. Killed a bunch of innocent people. I don't want that happening in my town." I named him "Red" in my notebook.

The crowd erupted. Shouts of "Yeah, what about that?" reinforced others saying "Not here." People were on their feet, pumping their fists in the air. Someone let out a loud whistle, which scared the baby in the second row, who began to wail. Finally, but not soon enough, the baby's mom bundled her up, tripped over four people to get to the aisle, and ran from the meeting, shooting the whistler a nasty look on her way out.

"Excuse me. Excuse me," said Ms. Michaels, her voice raised above the noise of conflict. "This is a time for everyone to feel free to express their opinions to the council. Not a time for debate among citizens. The speaker with the microphone has the floor."

After the crowd settled down, the next person in line, a woman who looked enough like Star to be her sister, spoke. "Well, as you all know, I own the Java Lounge in town, and I think if the train stopped here it might be good for business. And I'll serve coffee to anyone and everyone." I wrote Star2 next to her quote in my notebook.

The next one up was a man—I couldn't tell his age—in a University of Minnesota hoodie, baggy dirty jeans, and sneakers. He jammed his fists in the front pockets of his jeans as he spoke in a voice so low that the microphone barely picked it up.

"I was in Iraq after them Muslims blew up the World Trade

Center," he said. "I'm back now, but that part of the world is still with me, ya know. Then I moved out here. Sometimes when I see them dark-skinned ladies dressed like nuns, I ask myself if one of them is going to blow up. If the train came through here, you just don't know what could happen. Think about it."

Talk in the room had settled to a low buzz as the man I named "Soldier" returned to his seat next to Bozo. Their body language made me wonder if they were mother and son.

Next up was a silver-haired man in a light yellow sweater over a denim shirt and clean, pressed slacks. In my head, he had to be an insurance broker.

"My wife and I are all for this light rail," he said. "Think about it. It will bring in all kinds of business to our charming town. With a little effort, we could become a destination. A few great restaurants, maybe a fancy playground with a Ferris wheel? How about a wave pool for the kids in the summer? Let's throw our arms around this. Embrace it, people. It's going to happen whether we like it or not, so let's make it our own."

I dubbed him "biz casual" and drew a couple waves next his quote in my notebook.

It went on, and on, and on like that for three hours. Some thought it was a great idea; others would have preferred planting soybeans on the land where the rail line might go.

After the place cleared out, I went to the clipboard to learn the names of the people I planned to quote. I wanted the piece, which would be far shorter than the meeting, to reflect the mixed sentiment of townspeople. Then I went to my car, opened my laptop computer, wrote the story, and filed it with my editor, all in about twenty minutes so I could make deadline. I expected it would go somewhere inside the B section and online under "local," because meetings like this one where citizens expressed sentiments happened so often, they didn't much qualify as news.

The gathering hadn't brought me any closer to finding the bomber, but it did give me a first-hand look at current thinking about the light rail. Or so I thought.

As I was just finishing up, a knock on my driver's side window gave me a bit of a jump. I held up one finger to indicate I was busy for a second, then rolled down my window. The man in the yellow sweater handed me his card. Yep, he was an insurance salesman. He gave me a big smile and a thumbs-up.

CHAPTER THIRTY-ONE

It had been a long week. I was so tired my hair hurt. As I rode the bus home, I thought of Michael and my daughters. Rebecca and Suzy loved Rachel. Even though they hadn't seen her in a while, their mourning for her had cast a pall over our home. To make matters worse, Michael's freelance writing business was in a slump that had sent him into his own slump. As much as I loved them all, I was not looking forward to a late dinner of reheated spaghetti. Especially tonight. It was my birthday, but apparently that had been forgotten. All day I had hoped for a phone call from Michael, maybe a handmade card at breakfast from the girls. I got nada.

We live in the lower half of a duplex in the heart of south Minneapolis, just a half a block from the bus stop. Summers when it's warm and light out until about 9:30 p.m., I often bike to and from work. It gives me a chance to clear my head and get in some much-needed exercise. But on this March night, it was dark as I trudged up the wooden steps to our porch that covered the front of the house from one side to the other. As I put my hand on the rail, I noticed the living room was dark. I thought that odd, but if the girls were in their bedrooms and Michael was in his basement office it was altogether possible that no one had thought to leave a light on in the living room for me.

When I opened the door to the screened front porch, it gave that familiar squeal that told me I was home. I'd always liked that sound, especially when the girls were little. I could hear it from anywhere while working in the kitchen or chatting with a neighbor down the block and know that one of them had opened or closed the door.

That thought had begun to warm my mind as I dug through my purse searching for my key, while holding the screened door open with my butt. Finally, I found my key, slipped it in the lock, and gave the door a push with my hip.

"SURPRISE! HAPPY BIRTHDAY!" a crowd shouted as the lights snapped on. Rebecca sprayed pink Silly String in my hair while Suzy blew a party horn in my face. Both girls were jumping up and down with excitement and Michael was leaning up against one side of the oak archway, his thumbs in the pockets of his jeans and a huge grin on his face.

Scanning our living room, I saw a dozen of my best friends. Hjelme, the spry octogenarian who rents our upper unit, had a mischievous twinkle in his eye. Andi, my college roommate, was there, and so were a couple of my favorite neighbors. Newsroom friends, moms and dads I knew through the girls' school. Even Fred, the copy editor who was the third leg in the stool that held Rachel and me together, had apparently managed to get the night off. The only one not there was Rachel.

"How did you pull this off without even dropping any hints?" I asked.

"When you're working all the time, it's not that difficult," Rebecca said.

Ouch. I decided to let that pass.

"C'mere, you two," I said, and gave both my girls a mama-bear hug.

"They planned this and pulled it off all by themselves," Michael said with a smile.

With that, Fred began singing "Happy Birthday." Everyone else joined in, but no one could match his beautiful tenor. Then the girls grabbed my hands and dragged me to the dining room where two candles, one in the shape of a three, and the other a seven, burned atop a chocolate cake.

"Make a wish," Suzy said.

I closed my eyes, wished that I would always feel as happy as I did at that very moment, and blew out the candles.

By the time the cake was reduced to crumbs on the plate, the girls had headed off to bed and the crowd had thinned to Michael, me, and Fred. As always, the conversation turned to the sorry state of journalism.

"The St. Paul paper offered another round of buyouts," Michael said. "Nobody is taking it, because everyone old enough to retire has already gone, and the mid-career folks know there is nowhere else to get a job."

"You seem to be doing okay," Fred said to Michael, who had left his job as a St. Paul business reporter. "You picking up freelance?"

"A bit. Barely what I need, but a bit," he said.

Unsaid in the conversation was that he was okay as long as I had a regular paying job, with health insurance. We didn't need to go into that particular conflict that hung between us.

"I was laying out some pages last night but there wasn't time to edit them," Fred said. "A senior editor actually told me that with the size of the staff we have now, what we put in the paper 'only has to be good enough.' I didn't go to journalism school and practice my craft for fifteen years to put out work that 'only has to be good enough.'"

I pointed out that the reporters who broke the Watergate scandal that led to President Nixon's resignation have said that said Nixon's White House had been a virtual den of thieves, far worse than the reporters knew at the time.

"If there's anything nefarious going on in the White House now, we aren't going to read about it with so few reporters around," Michael said, shaking his head.

"I'm bothered that journalism is not the watchdog it used to be," I said. "If Nixon were breaking into people's offices and pulling together hush money today, no one would know about it."

Fred and Michael swigged back more beer and shook their heads, knowing I was right.

"You know, Rachel would argue with you about that," Michael said.

"She would say that you're too dark, too skeptical…too suspicious," Fred chimed in.

"Well, Rachel would argue with me about anything," I said.

They both laughed at that, again knowing I was right.

“Time to go,” Fred said, as he picked up dirty plates, cups and bottles, then headed for the kitchen. “I’ll just pop these in the kitchen, then I’m going home.”

“I’m heading to bed,” Michael said.

Fred and I finished cleaning up, then he gave me a big hug and a kiss on the cheek. “Happy birthday, Doll.”

Doll. That’s what Rachel called me sometimes after we’d had another of our rip-roaring debates. It was her way of making up. God, I missed her.

After we had been working together for about a year, Rachel and I realized our birthdays were both on the fourteenth, exactly six months apart. Hers was in September and mine in March. I always reminded her that she was older. We made a pact that we would at least call each other, no matter where we were, to mark the day. If we could, one would take the other out to breakfast, lunch, or drinks. But we understood that sometimes life would intervene, so we gave ourselves an out. We promised each other that we would be in contact “within the octave” of our birthdays. We just didn’t say “octave” of what. It could be days, weeks or months.

After Fred left, I was still feeling jazzed after the party and not ready for bed, so I pulled out my laptop to check the news stories that would lead on tomorrow’s—rather today’s—front pages. Then I clicked on Facebook. To my surprise, there was a message waiting for me.

“Happy Birthday, Doll,” it said. “Hope you see this within the octave…hours, this time.”

It was signed, “Your older friend, Rachel.”

It was just like high-tech Rachel to set up the Facebook message to be delivered on my birthday. Showed she had thought some time ago about a return to our earlier, better relationship.

My first reaction was to scream. I read the message over and over again. Why? Why did it have to be like this? Why did she have to die at such a young age? I knew I would never have another friend like her. I would never hug Rachel. Never be able to thank her for writing me birthday greetings, and then set the date for them to arrive on my page. I cried until I couldn’t cry anymore.

CHAPTER THIRTY-TWO

Michael and the girls had gone to bed, Fred was on his way home, and Rachel, well, she was with me in spirit, courtesy of Facebook. From my favorite overstuffed chair, the one where I had read every word of Harry Potter to the girls, I surveyed our living room. It was a typical lower level of a top-bottom duplex in south Minneapolis. Like Victoria Olson's place, it was rich in hard oak floors and trimmings. Unlike Victoria's, it was seriously scratched, gouged even, from the blades of ice skates that had been slung over the girls' shoulders, from dragging the coffee table to the middle of the room for a game of Monopoly, from the sand stuck to winter boots scuffled through to the kitchen. Bits of pink and yellow silly string were everywhere. It smelled of beer and sugary frosting. The perfect home that Michael and I had always envisioned.

Except that it wasn't perfect. Far from it. Things between Michael and me hadn't been right for some time. When we were dating, even when we were first married, I used to think Michael was the smartest, wisest man I had ever met. He knew the answers to all my questions. He was a great reporter, an even better writer. He could fix any problem I had. He had always been my go-to guy. Not anymore.

I left the comfy chair and was scrolling through the online versions of tomorrow's newspapers when I heard that familiar squeak of a footstep on the loose board outside our bedroom. Michael was up.

I twirled the desk chair away from the computer screen so I could face him. "Nice party. Thanks."

"You're welcome," he said. "It was all the girls' doing."

In the half-light from the green-shaded desk lamp, he looked a bit like the man I had married—fairly tall, and still lean from all his biking. But his brown hair was receding and his eyes had new crow's feet. I admired, again, his long legs and tight butt as he headed for the kitchen, where he opened the fridge, grabbed the last beer, and stepped back to the living room. He plopped down in the comfy chair and swirled the beer in the bottle.

"Can't sleep?" I asked.

He nodded, so entranced with the beer that he didn't look at me.

"Me neither," I said. "Talk to me, Michael."

"About?"

"Anything. It's been so long since we've had a conversation."

"Hasn't been much time," he said.

The tick of the clock that had been my grandmother's was the only sound in the room. I ached to hear his voice. I had always liked the sound of his voice—deep, kind of raspy. Sexy. But it was clear I wasn't going to hear it so I told him about the Facebook birthday wishes from Rachel.

"Creepy," was his only reply.

"Rachel's death is still hard for me," I said. "Then I've got the pressure from Lovely Leona to come up with the definitive piece on the train bomber."

He said nothing. Just sucked down more beer.

"On top of that, Slick and Dick are trying to find a link between Rachel and the bombing. And while I appreciate that you've been with the kids while I'm tied up in this story, I...well, I miss them."

"That's the advantage to freelancing," he said, with a hint of sarcasm. "I'm here when they come home from school."

"I'm jealous."

He stared at me long and hard. The clock tick, tick, ticked away.

"You've got balls complaining," he said.

I hate it when he makes accusations instead of telling me directly how he feels.

"Meaning?"

"I'm the one who was downsized out of a job I loved while you're running around being Woodward -and -Bernstein. We both know this story will be a huge boost to your career. Meanwhile, I'm writing scintillating prose for Purchasing Management Magazine and driving Rebecca to soccer practice and Suzy to her violin lessons."

I hadn't thought of it that way, but he was right. Still, I was stung by the anger in his voice. Was I being selfish?

"So there it is, Michael," I said. "I want your job and you want mine."

"No. You don't want my job only," he said. "You want your job and mine."

"You don't know how good you've got it," I said. "You get to talk to Rebecca on the way to soccer. And Suzy? You can see firsthand how much she's improved at violin. I'd have to schedule a vacation day for either of those."

"Not that you'd ever take a vacation day," he replied.

"And while we're at it," I was on a roll, "the $300 you get paid for that fabulous Purchasing Management piece won't cover violin lessons for more than a couple of months."

The minute the words left my mouth I wanted to call them back. We had never fought about money before because we'd always had enough—not a lot, but enough. This was new territory for us. And I had taken the low road.

"I'm sorry," I said. "I didn't mean to say that."

"Yes, you did." Michael's expression said I had emasculated him. And in a way, I had. I instantly regretted it.

"Your friends, the Muslims—I think they have the right idea," he said.

"What?"

"They know the place of women."

"Oh my God, I can't believe you said that. Do you think that's our problem? That I don't know my 'place'? In what country, what century are you living?"

"Just sayin' that we might be better off if you took some lessons from the lady in the hijab." He rose, walked to the kitchen, dropped the empty beer bottle in the recycling bin, and headed back to the bedroom.

It was our bedroom, but not for tonight.

I shut down the computer and tried to sleep on the couch but it wasn't happening. My mind raced. Me, in a hijab? I laughed out loud. Know my place? What decade was this?

Michael was right about one thing. I did want both lives, mom and professional. But even I knew I'd have to clone myself to make that possible. Nobody's figured out how to be in two places at the same time. If anyone does find a way, though, it will be an employed mom. Or maybe a lady in a hijab.

I once asked Fortun how Somali women dealt with two or three of them sharing one husband. The culture seems so misogynistic. She didn't see it that way. To her it was a fair division of labor. Strong women formed a bond to run a household and raise kids in a way that was cooperative. All chores got done, children got the attention they needed, and some women ran small businesses, without any of the wives being overburdened. They did just fine taking care of matters with only a part-time husband, she told me. Maybe she had a point, I thought ruefully.

The next morning, early spring sun slipped through the living room blinds to wake me on the couch. My head split with a headache and my mouth felt like the Russian army had tromped through it. I dragged my achy body from the couch, stumbled into the kitchen, and made coffee. I wrote a note addressed to Rebecca, Suzy and Michael, thanking them for the fabulous surprise birthday party. I told them they were all wonderful and that I loved them more than they would ever know. I was gone to work before Michael and the girls were up.

CHAPTER THIRTY-THREE

Earlier in the week, I had asked Fortun to meet me. Saturday morning was the only time she was free. I had been trying to track down Abdi but was coming up dry. I thought if I could talk with her again, it might give me a different angle to pursue.

"I'm sorry I haven't got better news for you," I said.

"I understand," she said.

We were sitting in Mapps Coffee and Tea, on Riverside Avenue in the heart of Little Mogadishu, just around the corner from the storefront money transfer where Fortun had tried to wire her week's pay from Target, about $200, home to her sisters. Out on the street, three giggly teenage girls walked by, arm-in-arm. The bright green, yellow, and red of their hijabs stood out against the dirty snow of the street. They reminded me of the first crocuses that would pop up any day now, fresh, full of hope, packed with surprise.

Fortun saw me watching them and turned her attention in the same direction. The girls were all tall, with the long face typical of Somali-Americans. Despite wearing cloth from head to toe, there was a budding sexuality to them, a sway of their lanky bodies that looked urban, American. All three carried cell phones. The one in the red metallic hijab had hers tucked in next to her ear.

"The girls here are very different from when I was young in Somalia," Fortun said.

"How?"

Fortun dunked her herbal tea bag three times, then used her spoon to scoop it from the cup. With long, thin fingers, she wrapped the string from the bag around it to squeeze out the last of the tea, then set the bag on the paper napkin in front of her. As she went through the exercise, I noticed that her fingernails were newly hennaed.

"Our lives were so much harsher in Somalia," she said. "When we didn't go to school, we washed clothes, cooked, cleaned all day. Sometimes we had to haul water home. The girls who lived far from the city often were cut."

"Cut? You mean female circumcision?"

She nodded sadly.

"Were you?" I asked.

"No, I was lucky. The Somali girls born here don't know what their lives would be like if they had been born in Somalia."

"Female circumcision is illegal in the U.S.," I said.

"That hasn't stopped some families, the rich ones, from sending their girls to Dubai to have it done," Fortun said.

"They still do that?" I was shocked.

"Not everyone, but some," she said. "More still in Somalia. There's an old woman in my sister's village who does the cutting. The parents pay her to cut their girls. That's why I tried to send the money to my sister."

"I don't understand," I said. "How will sending money to your sister in Somalia stop the cutting?"

"My sister is going to pay the woman who does the cutting to not cut any more girls," Fortun said. "But Mohamed, my friend in the store? He wouldn't take my money. He said the Americans won't let him send any more money to Somalia. Why?"

I explained to her that the feds had shut down money-wiring services across the country because they believed that the money was going to arm terrorists in Somalia.

"You know the pirates that have taken ships full of cargo off the coast of Mogadishu?" I said. "Well, the pirates don't really want them. What are they going to do with ships full of oil? So, they ransom the ships to insurance companies for millions of dollars, which go to terrorists who use the money-wiring services to buy weapons. When the feds found out about it, they put the money-transfer places on a list of companies that Americans cannot do business with, including your friend Mohamed around the corner."

"How do you know all this?" she asked.

"I read a lot of newspapers."

"So I can't send money to my sisters because of pirates?" Fortun looked perplexed.

I took a sip of my coffee and nodded.

"That's crazy," she said. "Abdi never told me any of this when he worked with Mohamed. Abdi worked at the money transfer place last year, while he went to school. Did you know that?"

I nodded. "Your other son told me. Did he like working there?"

"I think he helped Mohamed take in money. Just a couple of days a week. I don't know more than that. He never said he didn't like it."

I questioned Fortun for another half hour, but she couldn't tell me anything more that figured into the puzzle.

"I have to go to work," she said.

"Which job today?" I asked.

"Target. The night shift. I close at eleven o'clock."

"How do you get home?"

"I take the bus. Actually two buses, now that the light rail isn't running," she said.

"What time do you get home?"

"After twelve o'clock."

"Isn't that scary?" I asked.

"Yes, but what can I do?"

CHAPTER THIRTY-FOUR

Was this whole thing about money? Did Rachel and all the other innocent folks die because ham-handed Somali pirates wanted to send a message to the big, bad Americans? Was the train bombed for dollars? It sure wouldn't be the first time that lust for lucre led to evil, I thought as I walked down Cedar Avenue. On the other hand, Minneapolis is an unlikely target for international terrorism. But it's also an unlikely home for the largest diaspora of Somalis outside of Somalia.

As I crossed the new 35West freeway bridge, I thought about the drivers who were on the old bridge when it collapsed into the Mississippi River in 2007. Thirteen people had died in that tragedy, and more than one hundred sixty were hurt. The cause was nothing so sinister as a bomb. It was a mistake made decades earlier when the bridge was built with metal that wasn't thick enough to hold the weight of cars and heavy construction trucks stalled in a line on a hot August day. The people who were injured and those who died were victims of bad luck, not terrorism. As simple as that.

Maybe, I thought, I was working on a false assumption. Had I assumed the cause of the bombing was international evil because it went off in the heart of the Somali immigrant community? Was the tragedy really homegrown?

That got me to thinking again about Mr. Ponytail as I walked farther along Washington Avenue, past Grumpy's, where he and I had met. Pulling that particular piece of string in this mystery ball was difficult because it required computer skills better than mine.

As I pushed through the revolving doors of the Grain Exchange Building where the newsroom is housed, I saw the little junk food shop that had been in the building since the days when sacks of grains were exchanged on the fourth floor. Rachel used to buy lottery tickets there.

"Hey," I said to Mike, the small Greek man who ran the place. "What's the lucky number today?"

"You gonna buy a lottery ticket?" he asked. "You've never bought one before."

The guy sounded like Rachel, always nudging me to buy a ticket.

"If you don't buy a ticket you're never going to win, Hughes," she would say. "I can't believe a raging liberal like you can be so conservative personally. Think of it as propping up the public school system you're always touting."

"For some reason, today seems like the day," I told Mike as I laid down five dollars on the counter.

"Five?" he said.

"Give me three dollars change. Don't want to spend it all in one place."

"Too bad about the mayor," he said as he handed me two tickets. "You were friends."

"How did you know?"

"I see a lot from behind this counter," he said.

"That and because Rachel bought a ticket every day, and lots of times I was with her, right?"

"How did you know?" A gold tooth shone below his mustache when he smiled.

I nodded goodbye, stuffed the tickets in my purse, and caught the next elevator to the newsroom, where I planned to track down Dex. As the rickety elevator clinked and clanged its way up four floors, I wondered why I had stopped in Mike's store today. Why did I suddenly start buying lottery tickets? Was I channeling Rachel? That's stupid, I told myself. I don't believe in channeling the dead. Still, I felt like Rachel was standing next to me as the floors dropped away. I remembered one particular conversation.

"I can't afford to buy tickets every week," I'd said. "It's about money. Michael and I are barely paying the rent. Besides, I can't believe that a right-wing conservative like you would throw your hard-earned money away on a bet as bad as a lottery ticket."

"Every time I buy a ticket and lose, a dollar goes to Minnesota education, freeing yet another dollar for the outrageously greedy teachers' union. That would be the folks who make more than we do but only work nine months out of the year."

"What are you talking about?" I asked. "Two of my brothers are teachers, and I've never seen anyone, including you, work as hard as they do."

"Are you saying I don't work hard?"

"That's not what I said, Rachel. I said my brothers are hard-working teachers."

"They're probably the exception," Rachel said. "If teachers were really working hard, we'd have better-educated kids."

"If we started spending more on education and less on defense, we'd have a better-educated populace and probably wouldn't even need an army," I said. "How about bake sales to raise money for the Department of Defense and appropriation without question for the Department of Education instead of the other way around, which is how we do it now?"

"Now you're quoting bumper stickers? Really, Skeeter? You're better than that," Rachel said. "You want our country's defense to depend on cupcakes?"

"No," I replied, "but I don't want it to rely on lottery tickets, either."

That one ended the way they all did, with Rachel and me looking at each other and then bursting into laughter. We were each other's favorite sparring partners.

As the elevator doors opened and I set out in search of Dex, I recalled what I had said in our conversation from so long ago. It's about money. *Or is it?*

CHAPTER THIRTY-FIVE

It's well-known in the news biz that if you want to get a lot of play for a story, you release it on Sunday, when the competition for spots on the front page is the weakest and editors are hungriest for something to serve up in the Monday paper or online. It's especially helpful if you don't want the initial news carefully scrutinized, because most reporters are off work on Sundays, and even if they are in the newsroom, they will find it difficult to reach sources who can opine on the event at hand. Early evening is even better because the television stations will likely lead with it for the ten o'clock news—not that what TV stations do these days could even remotely be called news.

Michael and I had spent Saturday simmering down. Given that the girls wanted to order pizza and we didn't, we decided to go to dinner at Wilde Roast, our favorite place overlooking downtown Minneapolis and the Mississippi River. It's named after Oscar Wilde, set in his late 1880s London era, with tattered leather furniture, velvet drapes, and peacock feathers. Good food, but not too expensive. You get the idea.

I had planned this dinner carefully. I wanted to tell him about Sam—that I had come close to doing something I really didn't want to do, but did want at the same time. That I had pulled back at the last minute because I wanted our marriage to last, because I wanted to work on it. I had chosen this night because it was time, this place because it was an old favorite from the days when we were truly together, a team. I wanted us to talk as two adults, no screaming, no tears, in public. I wanted to tell him that I was willing to work hard on it, but I couldn't do it alone.

Marriage takes two, I would say. Michael and Skeeter. Skeeter and Michael. Neither Skeeter nor Michael alone. I'd figured a Sunday night was a safe time, because, well, news seldom breaks on Sunday night. Ironic, on many levels.

Our server had taken our orders, poured our wine, and returned promptly with our dinners.

"I've always liked this place," Michael said.

Tinkling glass. Tinkling glass.

It was the sound I'd set for my cell phone when a text message arrived. I didn't want to hear it. "This is a cliché, right?" Michael said. "The text message just as we're about to eat?"

"It is, but I can't ignore it." I pulled my phone from my purse.

Be ready 4 big story. 8 p.m.

It came from my favorite FBI agent, Tim O'Reilly.

That the heads-up came from my buddy Tim was encouraging. It meant he was willing to go rogue, at least a little bit.

Gimme a hint? I texted back.

The reply came seconds later: No.

"I know," Michael said. "You've got to call Leona. Then you've got to go."

"I'm sorry, Michael." I genuinely was sorry. Probably sorrier than he would ever know. Michael didn't reply, and I wasn't surprised. It's his way to steam silently. His facial expression doesn't change, but the vein on the left side of his head begins to pulse rapidly, like the rattle on a snake.

"I'll drive you home before I go to the newsroom," I said. I asked our server to box up our dinners to take with us. At least Michael would get something to eat. Neither of us said anything all the way home.

We know who bombed the train. Was that the news the FBI was about to release, I wondered as I slid my magnetic pass through the door lock to get into the building. Or was it something more mundane? I hoped Reilly hadn't wrecked our Sunday dinner for word that the FBI had finally caught the Gentleman Bank Robber, as Slick and Dick called the suspect whose exploits they had been reporting.

It was a bit eerie walking alone down the freshly polished tiled floor to the newsroom. I imagined that if I stopped and listened closely, I could hear the ghosts of grain traders a hundred years ago calling out what they expected to pay for hard red winter wheat. I turned into the newsroom and glanced over to see Slick and Dick's cubicles empty. I wondered if they were out interviewing someone who would tie Rachel to the bombing. I had to hand it to them—they had kept their investigating quiet. I had heard no rumors about who they were talking to.

In fact, as I looked around the newsroom I was struck by how few of my journo friends were in residence. Leona, who had told me she was on her way, hadn't arrived yet. There was only the weekend editor and the two poor suckers who had drawn this particular day for their Sunday rotation as warm-body-on-call, and, of course my Twitter-feed-watching friend, Dex.

"So, what's up with the new girlfriend?" I asked Dex.

"You mean former girlfriend," he replied without taking his eyes off the screen or his fingers from the keyboard.

"Oh no," I said. "Tell me it ain't so."

"Sure is, and it isn't pretty. Neither of us can afford to move out. Thank God we've got a two-bedroom place."

"Is the breakup at least civil?"

"Depends on what you mean by civil," he said. "It's shocking pink Post-it Note communication. I found this one on my bedroom door last week."

YOU WRECKED THE LINER TO MY SHOWER CURTAIN. BUY ME A NEW ONE. YOU'VE GOT 36 HOURS.

"What color did you get her?" I asked.

He hung his head. "Blue. I'm such a schmuck. What really pisses me off is she can get her own shower curtain, using her employee discount. She works at Target. What do they cost? Maybe two ninety-nine?"

"Love can be cruel, Dex," I said.

I grabbed a cup of coffee that tasted like charcoal from the pot that had been sitting all day long—coffee shops near the Grain Exchange are closed on Sundays—and settled into the blue swivel chair. Fortunately, the desks in the cubicles can be raised or lowered to accommodate the current resident. Mine is just where I want it. I looked around the cubicle at my paltry collection of stuff. A coffee mug emblazoned with a years-old picture of the girls holds assorted pens and pencils. A picture of Michael just after he rode his bike a hundred miles in the MS Ride-a-thon. He sure was cute in his bike shorts back in those days. An industrial-strength magnet held a sheaf of papers to the dirty-tan fabric-over-metal wall of the cubicle. A portion of the First Amendment marched across my computer screen: "CONGRESS SHALL MAKE NO LAW...ABRIDGING THE FREEDOM OF SPEECH, OR OF THE PRESS."

"Showtime soon?"

I was so deep in thought, trying to guess what the big news was, that I startled at Leona's loud New York accent. I hate it when people sneak up on me like that.

"Hope so," I said after my heartbeat settled down.

"Take Dex with you to tweet the news as it happens," Leona said. "And be sure to get a photo we can use. Our only photog working today is at a fire."

An email message pinged on my screen. The FBI would be holding a press conference in the Minneapolis Federal Court building in fifteen minutes, it said. It was addressed to all media. The good news for me was that the federal courthouse is directly across the street from the newsroom, giving me plenty of time to be the first there.

"We're on," I said to Leona as I grabbed my purse.

As I've already mentioned, I hate news conferences because of the bogus theatricality the stagers usually employ. But this was different. I knew there would be news from this one.

"So what's new?" I asked Robert Beherens, the FBI's special agent in charge in Minnesota. We were the first two in the lobby of the federal courthouse.

"If I told you first, I'd have all the other reporters mad at me, now wouldn't I?" He wore a white shirt, black tie, and slate gray suit.

Sheesh, I thought, don't these guys ever go business casual?

"And that would be a problem because?" I asked.

But by then half a dozen TV folks, including the on-air chick in full makeup, spike heels, and coifed hair, and her cameraman in jeans, boots, and a scruffy beard, had arrived.

"Thanks for coming, ladies and gentlemen," Beherens said. "I'll read a statement that is being emailed to your respective newsrooms at this moment." He looked down at his paper.

"With help from the Somali community, the Minneapolis office of the Federal Bureau of Investigation has thwarted a plan to bomb the Mall of America," he said.

There was sudden silence from the handful of journos who had made it to the courthouse in time to catch the opening remarks.

"For more than a year, the FBI has been following a potential terrorist cell, which was uncovered with the help of a local money exchange," he said. "The potential terrorists have been tied to Somali pirates who launder ransom money through Somali banks doing business with small wire transfers in the United States. The plan to blow up the Mall of America was intended to send a message that the pirates were displeased when the federal government forbade Americans from wiring funds to Somalia."

I looked over Dex's shoulder to watch him tweet *FBI says plot to bomb Mall of America averted.* His fingers move like magic, making it more likely that our message would be up on Twitter before our competitors at the press conference.

Beherens continued, "Muhktar Hussein Mohamed, nineteen, was arrested Saturday, moments before he was about to detonate a bomb in the Mall of America rotunda. Mr. Mohamed was born in Mogadishu and immigrated to the United States with his parents when he was two years old. He became a naturalized American citizen last year. His mug shot is attached to the email sent to your editors." He looked up.

"I am prepared to take questions for the next twenty minutes."

I've got more than twenty minutes worth of questions, I thought, as I shot my hand in the air. I'd have to take my best shot first. "Bob, what stopped him from detonating the bomb?"

"As I said, we have been watching this for more than a year. When a member of the Somali community told us about the plan, we embedded an agent in the cell. I can't give you his name, but he is an American hero who has saved many lives. He saw to it that the detonator Mohamed thought was real was a dud."

Agent embedded in terrorist cell, Dex tweeted.

In the background I heard another TV crew arrive, the on-air reporter asking, "What's going on?" I had to smile when someone replied, "Good question."

"You're talking about a 'cell,'" a reporter from the St. Paul paper said. "That implies more than one person. Are there other terrorists still out there?"

"Our information tells us three other individuals who were working with Mohamed have returned to Somalia. As you know, the Somali government is severely weakened. Nonetheless, we are working with officials there to find and extradite those individuals involved in the plot."

"Their names?" asked another reporter as I waved my hand in the air again.

"Until we have made an arrest, we cannot name the individuals. Skeeter?"

"Bob, you talk about help from the local Somali community. What kind of help? From whom? Can you give us names?"

"No, I can't," he said. "We plan to protect their identities. I can tell you, though, that we are concerned about the safety of the local Somali community. I'll let the chief speak to that."

Minneapolis Police Chief Michele Nichols, who had joined Beherens at the head of the growing crowd of reporters, stepped up to the microphone. "The Somali community is an important and valued part of the fabric of Minneapolis. We have increased patrols around Muslim community centers to ensure there is no retaliation."

"That will be all," Beherens said, with an air of finality. "Thanks for coming, ladies and gentlemen."

"One more," I shouted as he walked away. "Is this related to the bombing of the train?"

Beherens stopped and turned my way. "That is still under investigation, so I can't comment."

My phone was vibrating in my pocket before I exited to cross Fourth Street to the newsroom. It was Leona. "I'll have Dex comb the web for whatever we can get on this Mohamed fellow. When you write the story, include reactions from the community, Mall of America, Bloomington cops, … and a dozen more I'll think of before you get here. We need this to be online ten minutes ago."

I composed the lede in my head as I crossed the street, against the light. By the time the elevator doors opened on the newsroom, I had the next two paragraphs mentally written. Dex, bless his heart, had already sent the B matter—background information—to my mailbox. I had the first fifteen inches written and sent to Leona in ten minutes, a personal best. She whipped through it and sent it back to my queue with two questions inserted in the text. She wanted Mohamed's age (nineteen) and where he was being held (Beherens hadn't left enough time for anyone to ask). I clicked another button, sent it to the copy editor, who wrote a headline, then performed some hocus-pocus I didn't understand, which sent it into cyberspace. Just as the FBI had hoped, the story, Feds Thwart Mall Bombing, was lead on our website. I spent the next couple of hours calling Mall of America public relations, and the go-to-guy we always quote from the Somali community, while Dex called some store owners in the mall, looking for quotes. We pasted the additional material on the end of my story, which would be stripped across the top of Monday's front page.

The trick to doing all this so quickly, I learned a while ago, is to keep my emotions out of the import of the story. I turn myself into a robot, a thinking, highly focused one, but a robot just the same. In my head, I treat it as though it were everyday stuff. News is change. It doesn't matter what the direction, just different. What was up is now down, what was left is now right. Something out of the ordinary.

I seldom read my own articles because I know what they say. But this story was different. After deadline I would care about this one.

I dumped out the stale coffee from the pot of yesteryear, made a new brew, and sat down to actually read what I had written. I found two typos. That had been my average since the powers-that-be had shaved the staff down to a mere six-pack of crazed, overworked copy editors to take care of all our errors. I marked them, then called the copy desk and asked to have them corrected at least online. Then I took a slug of coffee and delved into what was reported in my story.

It was pretty simple, really. No bomb blew up. The Mall of America folk were happy that no one was hurt and confident that shoppers would always be safe. An "alleged" bad guy was behind bars.

I was most vexed by what wasn't in my reporting. The key point missing was whether the thwarted bombing was related to the train bombing. I had to think so, but so far had no confirmation. Besides that, the story didn't say much about how the FBI had made this arrest, or even what information it had to hold Mohamed. And how lethal was this potential bomb? If it had been detonated, would it have blown out a quarter of the mall, or just incinerated a trash can? What kind of bomb was it? Are we talking C4, or a bag full of nails and broken glass? And why the Mall of America, anyway? Minneapolis—actually Bloomington, the suburb where the mall is planted—isn't New York or Los Angeles or even Chicago or DC, much more likely terrorist targets. Any self-respecting bomber knows the Upper Midwest of the United States is considered second tier, at best. Had there been other bombing attempts that were stopped but we just hadn't heard about them? Why tell us about this one? Why now?

Dex had figured out that the would-be bomber had gone to South High School, that his father ran a small halal grocery store in Cedar-Riverside, and even that he had eight siblings. It was good work on a very short deadline, but it didn't tell us who Muktar Hussein Mohamed really was. How did he get into this? Had he been falsely accused? What was he doing before his arrest? Going to school? Working at a car wash? Driving a taxi? Who were his friends? Where did he hang out? And what about the three who reportedly went back to Somalia? Who were they? Why did the FBI think they were involved? Were they local? U.S. citizens? Could one of them be Fortun's son, Abdi?

And then there were the underlying issues that would never see ink, or electrons. Why did Agent O'Reilly give me the heads up? Certainly not out of the goodness of his heart. What were the politics behind the news the feds had decided to share today? I had to think it had something to do with the bombing of the train—but what?

I wrote all this up in an email to Leona, for multiple reasons, the biggest being that I was covering my ass lest she think I was slacking on the story. Also, I wanted to set my own direction of the story before she, or worse yet, someone higher up, did. And I had promised that I would keep her aware of my every move.

Her response was swift. *You're going to have a busy day tomorrow. Copy to me by 4 p.m.*

CHAPTER THIRTY-SIX

On my way out, I stopped by Dex's cubicle. "Nice job today," I said.

"Thanks," he replied. "Any chance I can grab a ride home with you? My car's in the shop, and the buses only run on the hour this late."

Of course I was happy to give him a ride. He was a good kid and I wanted to get to know him a little better.

"How did you get into this mess with the girlfriend?" I asked as we drove east on Lake Street toward Dex's apartment.

"Ex, that's ex-girlfriend," he said. Traffic was sparse. Lights shining down from the bars and bodegas mixed with the oil to create a kaleidoscope of color on the wet street. "I don't know how we got here, but I can't wait to get out of our apartment. One more month, the lease is up. Today's angry Post-it note was a doozy."

He pulled it from the pocket of his jeans and straightened it out on the dash. I looked over to see something written in bright red capital letters.

"What's it say?" I didn't want to take my eyes off the street long enough to read it.

"It says, KEEP THE DOORS TO YOUR BEDROOM SHUT AT ALL TIMES. THERE'S ENOUGH CHOCOLATE IN THERE TO KILL BOTH MY DOGS."

"Ouch," I said. "Vicious."

"Ah, yeah," he said. "Can we turn the radio station to something else? I can't stand listening to MPR."

I smiled to myself, thinking how much he reminded me of my daughters. "Sure."

"Did you know that Target has one of the most sophisticated forensics labs in the country?" Dex asked.

"Really?"

"I tripped across a story about it. Besides working with local cops, they do stuff for the FBI, the ATF, and even Customs."

"Customs?" I asked. "What would they do for Customs?"

"Something about checking incoming cargo containers," he said. "I didn't really have time to get into it too deeply. I can send you what I found in the morning."

"Send it tonight," I said as he thanked me for the ride and left the car.

I was pretty sure Michael wouldn't be waiting up for me when I got home, and he wasn't. Everyone was in bed. I was still jazzed up from the evening's work. May as well spend some time on the computer if I wasn't going to be able to get to sleep, I figured.

Dex had already shipped the links to my computer by the time I had settled onto my couch, beer in hand, laptop fired up and ready go. I read for about an hour, amazed to learn that all this time, when I was buying toilet paper and light bulbs at Target, I was also funding a vast private surveillance operation. As a citizen, I didn't quite know how I felt about face recognition software following me as I pushed that red plastic cart up and down Target's aisles. Geez, can't a shopper get any privacy? When I finally fell asleep, I dreamed I was wearing a red shirt and khaki pants working in the checkout lane. I had to call a supervisor because I couldn't find the bar code on a backpack. When I opened the pack I saw a bomb and a dozen exercise weights.

As I drove to work the next morning, questions swirled through my head. Was Abdi a suicide bomber? Had he died in the explosion? Or had he gone back to Mogadishu? And if he had, why? In recent years, a couple dozen young Somali men had returned to their homeland to join al-Shabab. Until now, perhaps, al-Shabab had confined itself to terrorizing its own government, raising money through links to pirates. Was Abdi one of them? Had he returned to the United States as a terrorist? And if so, why Minnesota? Why not New York? Or Los Angeles? Or even Chicago? Just because fifty thousand Somali refugees live in Minnesota, the largest enclave in the country, is no reason to blow up public transportation in Minneapolis. Or is it? I didn't see a tie. Was there one?

I'm a journalist. I earn a living asking questions, finding answers. But this story went farther than that. Beyond the professional questions were the personal. Did the son of my good friend Fortun kill all those people, including my best friend, Rachel? Why? Why did they all have to die? Why did Rachel have to die? Was it just her time? I didn't buy that. Was there some point to her death? All I could do was hope that the answers to the professional questions would give me insight to the personal.

Was the LRT bomb set off with some device from a distance, like a garage door opener or a message from a cell phone? Or was the detonator a suicide bomber? Could there be DNA evidence on bomb particles that would point to anyone in particular?

Answers to these kinds of questions are usually highly classified. I didn't want to go to FBI Agent O'Reilly again until I had a good handle on what all the questions would be. I needed someone with bomb and firearms experience. Slick and Dick.

"Guys," I said after I had settled in to my cubicle. "I need to talk to you."

"Imagine that," Dick said to Slick. "The little lady is asking our advice."

"The cute ones always find their way to us," Slick said.

"Is this really necessary?" I asked them.

"Yes," they said in unison. "You're buying the coffee?"

"Sure, why not," I said. "Let's go."

The spring snow was falling like bullets, so we took the tunnel from the Grain Exchange to the federal courthouse, then walked up to the cafeteria on the first floor, where we chose a table next to the huge windows. They each ordered a grande, of course. I kept the receipt to put on my expense report.

"Where are the feds on their report about the bombing?" I asked.

"Still working on it," Slick said. "But almost done."

"What's it going to say?"

"That it was bombed," Dick replied with a wink.

"Funny," I said. "How do the feds go about investigating?

This is my first bombing story."

"You know, Skeeter, I like you," Dick said. "But I also know that Leona said to keep us out of the loop. So why are you coming to us?"

"Because you guys have experience with this kind of thing," I said.

"Just so you remember that," Slick said.

"What do you want to know?" Dick asked.

"How's an investigation usually run?"

"First, they mark off the bomb site with string, cutting it into a grid, like an archeological site. Then they begin the big sift. They go through every particle, taking everything back to the lab."

"Where are they going to get a lab big enough to put all those pieces together?"

"That's why the Feds do it, not the local guys. They take it back to a hangar in Fort Snelling, which is on federal land," Slick said. "It takes a long time, but sooner or later, all the pieces are reassembled. Everything is photographed and marked. Then the DNA guys move in looking for blood, spit, tissue, whatever they can find to study and put into the federal data base."

"How are they coming along on that part?" I asked.

"Almost done." Dick said the words, but his eyes were following an attractive young woman who was bringing her lunch to the table next to us.

"Careful there," I said. "I'd hate see you get whiplash."

I turned to Slick. "Any preliminary information on the investigation?"

"They think the bomb was detonated by a remote device. Not that hard to do. The bad guy gets on the train with a backpack or suitcase full of C4 plastic explosive. Gets off the train without it. Stands on the platform as it moves away. Pushes some buttons on a cell phone and KABOOM! Just like those bastards at the Boston Marathon."

"The Feds know which bombs are used by which groups. They know which are favored by, say, the Somalis, or the Taliban," Slick said.

"What about a rogue nutcase? Or an old-fashioned organized

criminal?" I asked.

"Yeah, but Al Capone and his boys were run out of town back in the forties, so I don't think it's them," Dick said.

"And what about the mayor?" I asked.

"What about her?" Slick said.

"Was she the bomber's target?"

"You know we aren't going to talk about that," Dick said. "For Leona's eyes and ears only."

"Come on guys," I said. "Give me a hint. Dick: If Rachel was the target, scratch your left ear."

They both just laughed, which made me angry, which they knew, which made them laugh all the more.

"Thanks, guys," I said, doing my best to sound sarcastic. "You've helped me a lot."

We bussed our dishes, with Dick almost tripping over his own feet as he ogled the woman next to us. The snow shower had let up, so we walked back across Fourth Street to the ancient Grain Exchange Building.

"I'm going to buy a lottery ticket," I said, pointing to the little shop just inside the door. "You guys go on ahead."

I heard Dick telling Slick about his fantasy with the young woman in the coffee shop as the elevator doors opened. It looked like the conversation was pretty intense.

Then I heard a yell.

I rushed to the elevator. The outer doors had opened but there was no elevator car there, just the cables. I peeked over the edge. Dick was unconscious and piled on the top of the elevator car in the building's sub-basement. Judging by the twist of his leg, it would be a while before he chased any more women.

Slick peered over the edge. "A buyout would have been a preferable way to get rid of him."

CHAPTER THIRTY-SEVEN

Even though Slick and Dick were the newsroom parody of a long-gone time, people were deeply saddened by the elevator accident. Plans for a fund-raiser began immediately to cover what the newspaper's stingy benefits would not. But his fall didn't stop the bad newsroom jokes.

As I made my way to Dex's work area later, I overheard the breaking news editor say, "Anybody got any news for me, or do I have to sacrifice an intern?"

"Better duck, Dex, or hope news happens soon," I said.

He turned to me. "Hey, Skeeter. What's up?"

"Just thought I'd check in on you, see how you're doing. Any new notes from your ex?"

He had a line of Post-it notes stuck to his computer screen, like trophies. Each had the same all-caps handwriting in red, as though they had been written by an architect.

"What's she do again, the ex?" I asked.

"Graphics artist for Target," he said, snatching one of the notes. "Here's the latest."

CLEAN YOUR ICKY WHISKERS FROM THE SINK BEFORE YOU LEAVE IN THE MORNING.

"Ouch," I said. "Sounds like you have some lingering issues."

"Let's just say we have different ideas of what neat and clean means," he said.

Ah, the trials and tribulations of being a twenty-something fallen out of love. "Can't you get out of your lease and end this misery?"

"Neither of us can afford to live alone. That's one of the reasons why we moved in together."

"Well, I've got a job for you that will definitely keep you away from home for a while." I explained the story I had been told by Sherman Heraty, aka Mr. Ponytail.

"I need you to check it out," I said.

An hour later I sent him an email. Whatcha got for me?

Minutes later he was standing next to my desk.

"I ran Steve Bridgewater and your Mr. Ponytail, Sherman Heraty, through every data base we've got. Looks like at least some of what he said is true. They were in the Navy at the same time, stationed at the same place. They're both listed as members of half a dozen computer-geek clubs."

"So they at least know each other?" I asked.

"True. It even looks like they worked for the bank at the same time in 1999. Bridgewater was quoted in a piece we did about Y2K. So that checks out."

"I'm hearing a 'but' in your voice," I said.

"But Bridgewater looks like a straight shooter, not the type of guy who would take the bank for several mil, then blow up a train," he said.

"How so?"

"He's boring," Dex said. "Owns a nice neat bungalow in southwest Minneapolis. Mortgage is half paid. Doesn't appear to have any big debts. Never even got a parking ticket. Sounds like a computer guy who operates on pure logic."

"He's not in Antigua with a hot honey?"

"I don't know that. But his mortgage payment is always on time. He never lets his Visa balance go over $1,000. Voter registration has him down as independent."

Maybe I should have married him, I thought.

"You are a master at digging up this stuff," I said. "How'd you do it?"

"You don't want to know."

"And what of Mr. Ponytail?"

Dex said he was harder to track. Didn't show up on voter lists, didn't own a home or a credit card. His bank balance fluctuated between one hundred fifty dollars and a grand.

"He looks like he's a renter who could definitely use two and a half million bucks," Dex said.

"Got time to take a little field trip?" I asked.

Sunshine was breaking through two-day-old clouds as Dex and I pulled up in front of Steve Bridgewater's southwest Minneapolis home. A light spring snow had covered the city the night before. Someone had already shoveled Bridgewater's front walk, but not the path to his front door. Perfectly trimmed Japanese yews stood guard at either side of the front door, the soft green shoots popping nicely against the dark brick. If Bridgewater's one-story house was like most others in the neighborhood, it would have three bedrooms, a small kitchen in the back, and a living room behind the picture window at the front. No one had driven on the new snow.

"Looks like no one's home," Dex said as I turned off the key in the ignition.

I nodded while opening the driver's side door. "Let's go see."

We walked up the steps and knocked on the door. Rang the bell and knocked again. No answer. I peeked in the mailbox and behind the bushes. "No snail mail, or even junk mail. He hasn't been gone long. Let's go see if there's a car in the garage."

I didn't want neighbors to see us cut through the gate to the backyard, so we returned to the car and drove around the block to the alley behind the houses. The driveway off the alley to the two-car garage was as neatly shoveled as the front walk. We pulled into the drive, got out, and peeked in the garage window. No cars. No oil spill on the concrete floor. A couple of bikes were hung upside down from the ceiling.

"Are you the people who want to buy or rent?" A twenty-something woman was standing behind us, leaning on a snow shovel. Her red mittens matched her hat and down vest.

"Were you expecting us?" I asked. Dex stood beside me, expressionless. "Looks like you did a fine job shoveling here."

"I try," she said. "Steve always keeps it so neat and clean. I really appreciate that in a neighbor, especially next door. So when he sent me the email asking me to shovel, I was happy to help. We just moved in here a year ago and I like my neighbors. Plus, I have to keep up some exercise so this guy doesn't make me too big."

She pulled open her vest to show us her belly. "He's about half way here. My doctor says shoveling light snow is good for both of us."

"Congratulations," I said. "You're in for many great years. I assume this is your first?"

"How'd you guess?" she giggled.

"So Steve's on winter vacation?" I asked.

"Antigua," she said. "Sounds awesome."

"So do you want to buy or rent the place?" she asked. "Steve said somebody would be stopping over."

"Not sure. We're just here for a real quick look-see. We gotta go now." I headed back toward the car while Dex went around to the passenger side.

"Oh, okay. Bye, then," she said, looking puzzled. "Have a good one."

"Well, looks like Mr. Ponytail was right about Antigua," Dex said.

"Yep."

"Can I ask a question?"

"Sure."

"I thought reporters always have to be honest about who they are. Why didn't you tell her why we were there?"

"I didn't lie to her," I said.

"But you didn't tell her we were from the newspaper, either," he said.

"No. I didn't want her to email Bridgewater and tell him The Citizen is snooping around. When I have all my questions together, I'll contact him and the bank."

Dex didn't say anything for a few minutes. Just fiddled with the radio.

"What's Mr. Ponytail's address again?" I asked. "We seem to be on a roll. Let's check out Sherman Heraty's place."

Mr. Ponytail, aka Sherman Heraty, lived in the Elliot Park neighborhood of Minneapolis, just south of the Mississippi River. Dex's research showed that Heraty had been renting since the early 1980s when the Metrodome football stadium landed there like a Martian spaceship that irradiated everything around it for blocks.

Rents stayed low until recently, when the new Vikings Stadium was built on the same site, causing a renaissance, or gentrification, depending on your point of view. As we parked on the street in front of Heraty's red stone hundred-year-old apartment building, I wondered how the down economy was treating him. We looked for a buzzer to be let in the building, but the hole in the wall where it was supposed to be left the impression we could walk right in.

As we climbed the narrow stairs to the fourth floor, I asked Dex if he'd gotten any more Post-it notes from his ex that he hadn't told me about. I loved hearing about them.

"Yesterday's note said, STOP USING MY HAND TOWELS. GET YOUR OWN."

"I don't think this breakup is going well," I said as I knocked on unit 4D.

"Yeah?" shouted someone from inside. "Who is it?"

"Skeeter Hughes from *The Citizen*," I said. "Can we talk?"

He opened the door a crack to take a peek at us. "Well, I'll be," he said. "You found me."

"Can we come in?" I asked.

"Sure." He swung the door wide open and we stepped in, skirting what looked like an Irish wolfhound asleep on half the ratty rug that covered the floor. His place had huge bay windows that were covered in dust and dog nose prints about halfway up.

"That's Riley," he said. "Been with me fifteen years now. Sleeps most of the time."

Heraty's decor was early computer. There were shelves across every wall stacked with computers that had to be at least twenty years old. I spotted an old Apple IIe just like the one I had in college.

"I repair 'em," he said. "Sometimes I hold on to the older ones. Figure they'll be worth something someday. How'd you find me?"

"This is Dex," I said. "He works for the paper. He has magical detective skills. Your name is Sherman Heraty?"

"Guilty as charged," he said. "Would you like some water or pop? I'm outta coffee."

"I'm good," I said. "Can we sit down? I've got a few questions for you."

He motioned us toward a couch covered in dog hair, then plopped in an overstuffed chair across from us. "What did you find out about my buddy Bridgewater?"

"We stopped by his house earlier today," I said. "Looks like he's in Antigua."

"Told you." He turned his head and looked me straight in the eye.

"Dex is new to the newspaper, and I'm trying to show him the ropes. Can you repeat your story about Bridgewater so Dex can hear it?"

I wanted an opportunity to watch Heraty without the distraction of writing down what he was saying. Dex pulled a pen and a long, skinny spiral-topped notebook from his back pocket and began to take notes. Heraty told the tale about the heist almost word-for-word as he had told it to me, his feet flat on the floor, hip-distance apart, his upper body leaning toward Dex and his notebook.

"So Bridgewater found out you were on to him, right?" I asked.

"Yep."

"How?"

"I don't know," he said, turning toward me. "But I know he did it, because he began to follow me after I told the bank investigator about him."

"You told the bank about the heist?" I asked. "You didn't tell me about that when last we met."

"Guess I forgot," Heraty said. "This investigator guy came here a couple of weeks ago asking if I knew Steve or anything about him. It frosts me that he would get away with something like that, so I squealed."

"I don't recall hearing about a million dollars gone missing," I said.

Heraty said the bank would have kept that quiet out of embarrassment. "Besides, it happens all the time. A million dollars is chump change for a big bank."

Heraty moved his gaze to the bay windows. "Steve sat out there in his car for hours, watching in here."

"How do you know it was him?" I asked.

Heraty scratched his right ear and looked down at the floor

before turning his head back to me. "Because I saw him. And he was with his new honey."

"Dex hasn't heard about how he followed you on the light rail," I said.

Heraty repeated the same story, his face passive as though he were reciting a long poem from memory, his left foot turned away from both Dex and me.

"Mr. Heraty. Sherman—can I call you Sherman?" Dex asked.

"Sherm. My friends call me Sherm."

"Ok, Sherm. I don't understand how Bridgewater could have blown up the train. Do you have any idea?"

"Lots of ways. Remote control. Cell phone," he said, with a swish of his long hair that wasn't held back in a ponytail. "I don't know. I just know he did it."

Several of the computer screens on the shelf blinked the time. Two or three sounded an alert.

"Look, folks, I've got a client coming by in about fifteen minutes. I'd rather he didn't know I was talking to the press, so, can you go now?"

Dex closed his notebook and returned it to his hip pocket. I picked up my purse. "Thanks for your time," I said.

"Are you going to put this in the newspaper?" Heraty said. "People need to know what a son of a bitch Bridgwater is."

"We've got some more checking to do first," I said.

"Well, hurry up," Heraty said as we were heading down the stairs. "I went to you first, but I've got friends at the TV station who would also like to get the story."

We got in the car and I turned to Dex before I turned on the ignition. "He's lying about at least part of that story."

"How can you tell?"

"Body language. It's all in the body language," I said.

But still, I wasn't any closer to figuring out who bombed the train.

CHAPTER THIRTY-EIGHT

I was in the kitchen, finishing up the dishes, wishing I could be smoking a cigarette, or at least eating an entire seventy-percent cocoa Ghirardelli chocolate bar. It had been that kind of day.

"Mom?" Rebecca, who was supposed to be in her room doing her homework, shouted from her room. "Did you smoke weed with Rachel?"

"What?" I asked. "Where did that question come from?"

"Look at this," she said.

I dried my hands with a dirty dishtowel—no time to do laundry—and made my way down the hall to Rebecca's room. She was sitting at the desk we had bought at Paint It Place and finished together. She appeared to be fascinated by something on Rachel's computer.

"What are you looking at?" I asked.

"You and Rachel smoking weed," she said with a laugh.

Busted. I knew it would happen some day.

"I thought Sam had deleted everything on that computer before he gave it to us," I said.

"There's no such thing as total delete, Mom." Rachel rolled her eyes.

I leaned over her shoulder and looked at the images in iPhoto. The particular shot that so intrigued her had been taken when Rachel and I rented a cabin on Potato Lake, just outside Park Rapids in slightly northern Minnesota, with half a dozen other friends from the paper. As I looked at that pic, the memory of that weekend played through my head. It was August in what had been a particularly hot summer. We water-skied, swam, and played Queen of the

Mountain on the dock in the deepest part of the lake. The lake was cool, refreshing and warm, all at the same time.

At night we built a bonfire on the beach, listened to the call of the loons, and watched the aurora borealis finger the sky in blues and greens and oranges we seldom see in the city. Of course, the marijuana had intensified the experience. The only problem with hanging out with newspaper people is they're usually pretty good at making photos of whatever is going on. Hence the evidence of my illegal activity.

"Do what I say, not what I do," I said to Rebecca.

Rachel and I had had one of our famous debates that night at the lake. The topic was global warming.

"I've been coming to this lake since I was a kid," I remembered telling Rachel. "I tell you, it's warmer this year than any other. The cow leeches I used to catch are gone. The shore is growing like Fred's forehead. It's global warming."

"Hey, enough about my hairline," Fred said to raucous laughter.

"You liberals are all alike," Rachel said. "You see one change and make it into some huge catastrophic event that's going to kill us if we don't all go back to eating nuts and twigs and trade in our cars for bikes."

We had gone back and forth like that most of the night.

Now I recalled how much I had enjoyed debating anything, everything, with Rachel. Especially now that I had been proven right about global warming.

Becky clicked through more pics. There was Rachel holding Suzy the day she was born, Rachel pouring beer over Michael's head at his thirty-fifth birthday, Rachel cutting into a sheet cake to serve sixty the day she resigned from the paper. In classic Rachel fashion, every event was carefully labeled.

"Rachel looks a lot younger in these, Mom," Becky said.

"She was. We both were."

"But look at these." Becky clicked on the file in Rachel's iPhoto file. Up popped a shot she had taken of the three of us with her iPhone in the bar just before she left. Fred had his arm on my shoulder and I had mine around Rachel. We were hoisting our beers in a salute to the camera, which Rachel was holding at arm's length. We have huge grins on our faces. I had forgotten she had taken that shot. The time stamp on it was 5:37 p.m. the day she died.

I stared at it for a long time. It was the last time the three of us would ever be together. We looked so…happy. Our eyes were bright, our grins big. I looked closely at Rachel. Her jet-black hair was pulled back in a ponytail. Rachel seldom wore much makeup. With her big brown eyes, bushy eyebrows, and long lashes, she didn't need much. Any lipstick she had applied was long washed off with beer.

Rachel, Rachel, I thought. Why did you have to leave us so soon? Who was the son of a bitch who took your life, and so many other lives? How can I find him or her? Why did it happen? Why bomb a light-rail train?

"How did this get into her computer?" I asked Becky. "She couldn't have had time to upload it."

"You are so behind on the technology front, Mother," Becky said, with another roll of her eyes. "Rachel was probably on the city's internet connection. Her Mac was set to accept streaming. Photos she took with her iPhone automatically copied into her iPhoto file. Hellooo. It's the twenty-first century."

I brushed off her sarcasm with my own roll of eyes. "Click through, see if she took any other shots."

She had. One picture showed her train was packed. Office workers heading home. Moms shushing babies. People dressed in the black-pants-and-white-shirts uniform of the evening shift at the hotels. Looking at the picture was eerie and grotesque at the same time. The time stamp said 6:02 p.m. The cops had said the train blew up at 6:08. *Oh my God.* I was looking at people who had six minutes to live, but didn't know it. I stared hard at the picture. *Get off the train! Get off now!* I wanted to shout, even though I knew it was futile.

There was one last picture on Rachel's computer. It showed people who apparently had just disembarked from the train. A couple of giggling Somali girls covered head to toe in red, purple and orange hijabs. An older white man in a blazer and tie talking to a young Somali man in black pants and a tan zipped jacket. And someone in a gold and maroon University of Minnesota hoodie and jeans.

Becky started to click through that picture.

"Stop," I said. "There's something I need to look at. Zoom in. I need to see their faces. Something here is bothering me."

"Mom, you sound just like some hokey TV show," Becky said.

I swear if that kid rolled her eyes one more time they'd be permanently stuck in the back of her head.

"Do you know one of those Somali girls?" she asked. "Maybe you interviewed one of them."

"No, that's not it," I said. "This picture could be critical in the story I'm working on. It's the last picture Rachel took before the train blew up. "

"Oh my God, really?" Becky asked. "Are you sure?"

"Yes, I'm sure. Look at the time stamp," I said. "Can you zoom in any closer?"

Who was I looking at? Was it the white guy in the blazer or the Somali guy in the tan jacket? I had talked with so many people over the years, seen so many faces, that after a while they all seemed to blend in together. I stared a little longer.

"Zoom in on the hoodie," I said.

I couldn't see all of the face, but something in the body posture was lighting up parts of my memory bank. Then I realized he looked a lot like the war veteran from the town meeting about the LRT.

Rachel's picture of the folks on the platform at Cedar-Riverside just before the train blew up was out of focus and poorly lit. I couldn't be sure the person in the hoodie was the same one I had seen at the neighborhood meeting. But what if it was? Could it be a coincidence that someone who was so opposed to train tracks running through town had been standing on the platform at Cedar-Riverside moments before the train blew up? If so, did that mean anything? It certainly wasn't news, but it was definitely something I should explore. I emailed it to Leona. Subject: *Rachel pic on train just before it blew up.* Message: *Just found this. Talk tomorrow.*

CHAPTER THIRTY-NINE

Leona was headed toward her desk with a box of popcorn in her hand. Her breakfast, I feared. Her desk looked like a trailer park after a tornado. Piles of paper were jammed in one corner next to a heap of notes, books, and newspapers that had long ago toppled. Empty popcorn boxes stuck in dried coffee spills lined the back of her cubicle. Half a dozen pens, the ends chewed, were scattered across the surface like Pick-Up Sticks.

"What's up?" she asked as I plopped in the chair next to her desk.

"I sent you an email with a picture from Rachel's computer last night," I said. "Did you look at it?"

"Not yet. Meetings all morning."

"Look now," I said.

She raised an eyebrow as she opened my email. "What am I looking at? Folks standing on the platform to the Cedar-Riverside Blue Line station. So?"

"Rachel took that minutes before the train blew up," I said. "See the guy in the hoodie? I think he looks a lot like someone I quoted at the light rail meeting the other night."

"You think?" she said.

"I'm not positive. The photo's blurry."

"Take it to the photo guys and see if they can clean it up. Marshal shot that meeting, didn't he? Take it to him."

Marshal was in the back of the newsroom, just in from shooting the St. Patrick's Day parade. He uploaded Rachel's photo and seemed to wave his fingers over the keyboard before giving me the verdict.

"I can't get it much clearer than that, but it does look like that guy from the meeting. See?" He pulled up his out-takes. Same hoodie, same jeans. Still, those hoodies are everywhere."

He looked up at me. "Wish I could help you more, but we don't have the budget to keep up with the good equipment."

"Got any other ideas?"

"Have you tried Target's forensics? They mostly work with law enforcement, but in a case like this they just might help you out. "

"Good thinking," I said. "Dex told me about Target's awesome crime lab. I've been dying to get a chance to do a story about it."

"Now's your chance." Marshal gave me a nod and returned to his work.

I went back to Leona and told her what Marshal had said. She agreed it was a good idea.

"I'll make the call to get you an appointment. Take Dex with you," she said. "He's been working hard and deserves a field trip."

I stopped by Dex's cubical.

"I've got another field trip for you."

"Awesome," he said.

Which is why I found myself walking at a quick clip with Dex—finding parking would have taken too long—to Nicollet Mall on a lovely low-sixties day in March. I've been in California when the temperature was sixty degrees and felt like it was freezing. People were wearing mink jackets, indoors. But the same temperature in downtown Minneapolis brings out shorts and flip-flops for people reveling in the weather.

We headed south on Nicollet, past Macy's and the Barnes & Noble store, until we got to Tenth Street South and the headquarters of Target Corporation.

As we walked over, Dex filled me in on some additional research he had done.

He said Jane Blank, the head of Target security, had begun the job at Target after retiring as an FBI field agent.

"She's told people she likes her new job even more than her days with the FBI," he said.

"How do you know that?" Once again I was impressed with

Dex's skills.

"You're not the only good reporter at the paper," he said with a slight smile. "I have my sources, too."

According to Dex, early in her career with the FBI, Blank had been moved to a different field office every couple of years because the bureau didn't want agents to become too invested in their communities. The FBI thinks agents overly involved in their own communities tend to lose their objectivity, the edge that can make the difference in solving the toughest cases, he said.

"So the job at Target gave her a chance to settle down, maybe get a life?" I said.

"That's what I hear," he said.

We stepped into the open elevator and pushed the button for the second floor. When the doors opened, we walked past red-and-white bull's-eyes to the corporate security department. A Target employee asked for my identification, then Dex's, and took us through password-protected doors to a windowless room crammed with computers and flat-screen monitors. The inside wall was decorated with the badges from the hundreds of law enforcement agencies that Target had helped since the 1990s. I shook hands with Jane Blank.

Blank was tall and thin with blond short-cropped hair starting to gray around her face. "Step into my office," she said.

"I'm Skeeter Hughes, from *The Citizen.*"

"Yes, I know," she said. "Leona called. She's a long-time friend."

"We've got photos taken with an iPhone on the platform at Cedar-Riverside just before the train blew up. Because the train was moving and the light isn't great, we can't see details clearly. We've run them through our labs, but our techs can't clean them up enough. We'd like you to see what you can do."

"I hope we can help you," she said.

I handed her a thumb drive with the file of the photos on it. She took it to a large room where fifty or sixty people, mostly men, sat at computers typing away. She signaled to a young man who sat in the corner.

"He's the best at this type of work," she said, after handing him the file and explaining what she needed.

We followed the man, who looked too young to buy beer, to his station. He popped the thumb drive in his computer, dragged the file, and within seconds the pictures appeared.

"That's the best we could get with our old-school equipment," Dex said to the man, who looked at him with a knowing half-smile. The tech ran his fingers over the keyboard for about another minute until a better picture came into view.

"How's this?" he asked, leaning back in his chair.

We gathered around the screen to peer at the photo of the Somali girls in bright-colored hijabs and the older white man in a blazer and tie talking to the young Somali man in black pants and a tan zipped jacket. Standing next to them was the unknown person wearing the University of Minnesota sweatshirt.

Dex pointed at the last figure, chuckling. "Look at his right hand."

The tech tightened the view on that part of the picture, and with a couple more keystrokes, brought it more closely into focus.

"Looks to me like he's flipping somebody the bird," the tech said.

CHAPTER FORTY

Finally I was getting somewhere. But was it somewhere in the right direction? I now had three possible solutions. Was Abdi the bomber? or Steve Bridgewater? or the person from the community meeting?

Even though I could feel Leona breathing down my neck, I wanted to eliminate two of the suspects. My sense was that Abdi's brother was telling me the truth, but he didn't know the whole story. I needed help. My two best sources on this were my old buddy Sgt. Victoria Olson, and my high school heart throb, FBI Special Agent—er, former special agent—Tim O'Reilly. I decided to go with Sgt. Olson first.

Sgt. Olson and I often do this weird telephone dance where I call her and leave a message, then she calls me back and leaves a message then I call her. I swear she doesn't answer when she sees my name on her caller ID. Actually, I never pick up on the first ring when I see it's her calling. So there.

Anyway, she and I did our two-stepping until finally we connected live—if not in person, at least over the phone.

"Sgt. Olson, how are you on this fine day?" I asked.

"I hear our buddy Dick took a big fall," she said.

"That's true," I said. "Broke his leg in many places. Didn't do so well with his pelvis, either. He's going to be laid up for quite a while. The paper's insurance isn't going to cover half his expenses, so there's a fundraiser for him tomorrow night."

"Where?"

"Grumpy's. Would have been the Little Wagon, but Dick's outlived that watering hole," I said.

"Sounds about right," she said. "So, what do you want?"

"Funny you should ask," I said. "Turns out I need to find a guy. A Somali guy. Whose mother thinks he bombed the train."

I could almost hear Olson raise her bushy eyebrows. I knew she would be interested, because the case had officially been handed over to the FBI, which took all the fun away from Minneapolis's cops. Still, if she could nail the bomber, it would be a big, bright red feather in her cap. No one ever said Sgt. Olson wasn't ambitious.

"Does his name begin with A and end in bdi?" she asked.

"How did you know?"

"I was watching him for a while," she said.

"Really? Why?"

"He was working at a money exchange place in Little Mogadishu," she said. "It looked like he was dealing khat on the side."

"Refresh my memory," I said. "What's khat?"

"It's an illegal stimulant, like amphetamines. Comes from East Africa," she said. "Somali men like to chew the leaves of the khat plant to get high."

"And you think Abdi was dealing?"

"I don't think, I know," she said.

His mother's not going to like this, I thought.

"How do you know?" I asked.

"Because I saw him make a deal," she said.

"Did you arrest him?"

"Yep."

"So....What happened? I ran his name through the data base of arrests and he came up clean."

"His sheet was erased. Suddenly he's out on the street again," she said.

"Over what? How?" I asked.

"Don't know. Wish I did," she said.

"Where's he now?" I asked.

"No idea."

"When did all this happen? Before the train was bombed?" I asked.

"The bust was a few weeks before that," she said. "Next thing I heard he was working at the money exchange on Riverside."

“How did that happen?”

“I don’t know, but it really pissed me off because that was a good, clean bust,” she said.

“Is that why you’re telling me about this? Because you’re pissed?”

“Tell you what? I didn’t tell you anything. You know that, Skeeter. I never tell you anything. In fact, we’ve never met.”

CHAPTER FORTY-ONE

One of the things that newsrooms everywhere do very well is raise money for whatever cause, screwball or not. One pass of the hat can bring in a thousand dollars on a slow afternoon. Dick was looking at big medical expenses so those who love him—and even those who didn't—threw him a fundraiser. Grumpy's, the same dive where I had interviewed Mr. Ponytail, was the perfect setting. With the extra room on the side, it was big enough for all the friends and foes who came to lift a glass. Grumpy's management hung a "private party" sign on the door and hired an extra bouncer, just in case. Management knew the till would be happy for the night.

As I stood in the back of the room, my beer mug sweating. I couldn't help but think about Rachel's funeral not so long ago. Her gathering was classy, filled with important people who said nice things about her in the theatrical setting of the Guthrie. Finger sandwiches and cookies were served.

Although Dick's wasn't a funeral, his event was great in its own way. The tile floor was permanently sticky from so many spilled beers. The click of the pool balls could barely be heard over the laughter that grew more raucous as the night went on. Dick's revelers—mostly journos and cops—couldn't get enough of Grumpy's deep fried tater tots. Too bad Dick missed it because he was still in the hospital.

Slick, who had recovered from his own close call with the Big Deadline, was the master of ceremonies. Grumpy's had agreed to display Dick's picture in the case reserved for trophies from its winning softball and bowling teams next to a silver-plated statuette of the iconic photo of Marilyn Monroe, her skirts blown up from the subway vent on which she stood.

"Dick was always into Marilyn Monroe," Slick said by way of introduction to the evening.

So was Rachel. Thinking back to the Marilyn Monroe portrait hanging in her townhouse, I realized Rachel admired her for an entirely different reason than Dick. Rachel admired Marilyn because she was a smart, hardworking, self-made woman who used men and the motion picture studios to her advantage. Dick merely admired what he thought he saw. Had Rachel been standing there, she would have whispered to me loudly that Dick was "clueless" about Marilyn Monroe.

"You probably all know that Dick and I have been friends for a long time. But you may not know how long. We started as reporters when Minneapolis and St. Paul each had a morning and an afternoon newspaper. Layout editors measured the length of stories in columns with a pica ruler. If a story came up an inch or two short, they would drop in an item that said something like 'There are a lot of cattle in Switzerland' to fill the space. Back then, cut and paste meant, literally, cut with a scissors and paste with glue. Photo editors used a ratio wheel to figure out how to crop a shot, and black and white pictures that weren't exposed properly were fixed with a little white-out or a black magic marker. This was before Watergate, and all the 'gates that continue today.

"Dick worked cops for the morning paper and I had the same beat for the afternoon paper. We never called it 'Public Safety.' Even though the same family owned the morning and afternoon newspapers, management tried to make us think we were competitors. And I guess we were—in our own minds, anyway.

"And then the afternoon paper closed and there were two cops reporters. I remember coming to work the next day and found Dick sitting at my desk. Because I had been at the afternoon paper I normally started at 7 a.m., so I was surprised to see him there. Turns out he had been working all night on a murder-suicide.

"We looked at each other. I know I was wondering which of us would be out of a job. He was probably thinking the same thing. I remember his first words to me were 'This is going to be interesting.'

"Anyway, management must have been expecting a rise in the crime rate because they kept us both on as cops reporters. Now they call it Public Safety."

Slick took a moment to drain his beer. The room was silent but for the sound of everyone else doing the same.

I took the moment to study Slick. Really look at him in a way that I had never done before. In his day, before he had settled into the complacency of reporting only the official news, he was a newsy's newsy. Dick, too. They were the type who believed their job was to comfort the afflicted and afflict the comfortable. In my mind's eye, I put hair back on Slick's head, subtracted fifty pounds, and smoothed out the crow's feet around his eyes.

But after my imaginary vision of Slick dissipated, I saw him for what he was. Sagging from exhaustion. Tired of chasing news. Journalism is a youthful profession. I wondered if I would one day look as tired, be as tired.

My attention returned to Slick as he clanked the side of his mug with a spoon. "To Dick," he said. "Only the good die young, old man."

As the room roared with approval and everyone hoisted a glass, once again I thought of Rachel. Yes, I thought, only the good die young.

My beer was almost gone and I didn't want a third, because I had to drive home. I tipped it back, grabbed my purse and jacket, and made for the door. I'd parked a couple of blocks away. Much to my surprise, my favorite ex-FBI agent was leaning on my car.

"Hello, Tim," I said. "I'm not supposed to still call you agent, am I? What are you doing here? Keeping tabs on me? I know you feds do that sort of thing."

"Can we get into your car?" he said.

"Keeping a low profile?" I got in the driver's side and reached across to unlock the passenger side for him.

Washington Avenue was quiet for a change. Not the usual rush of traffic trying to get to Interstate 94. I took a couple of deep breaths. Good thing I hadn't gone to the third beer, I thought. Wouldn't want to get busted.

"You know, I have a couple of questions for you," I said. "You sent me the advance notice about the press conference. The one about the Mall of America not getting blown up."

"Yes."

The guy does go on, I thought.

"Why so nice?" I asked.

"Because I wanted to demonstrate that I can be trusted," he said.

"Trusted?"

"Yeah, trusted to tell you the truth. I came here tonight to tell you something you may or may not believe. I want you to believe it."

"Go for it," I said.

"Abdi did not blow up the Blue Line," he said.

"And you know that because…?"

"Because I escorted him back to Somalia a month before the bombing," he said. "We flew into Mogadishu, I gave him some money—a lot of money, actually¬—and wished him luck."

"Why did you do that?"

"Because he was my contact who helped us avert the bombing of the Mall," O'Reilly said. "He was the plant in the cell."

"Why are you telling me this?" I asked.

"Because I want you to stop asking questions about him. He's an American hero, but if you keep stirring the pot asking about him, some people might get suspicious. Word could get back to Somalia, and his life could be in danger."

"So, he's in witness protection in East Africa?" I asked.

"You could say that," he replied. "He's a brave young man."

"Who will never see his mother, brother or American friends again," I said.

"That's right," he said. "I can't control what you do, but if you print this information or even talk with anyone about it, Abdi, a good man, will certainly be killed after saving the lives of many other Americans."

He opened the car door to Grumpy's. A blast of cold air filled the car. And then he was gone.

That was a secret I could keep. I was glad that I could finally cross Abdi off the list of possible answers to the question, who bombed the train?

CHAPTER FORTY-TWO

According to my notes from the meeting about the light rail, Hoodie guy's name was Buford—aka Bucky—Fuchs. Because he and his mother, Clara, listed the same address in the meeting registry, I knew they live in Black Duck, a town of about four thousand people, north and west of the Twin Cities. It's the kind of place where residents who live on five acres build a shed for the snow blower, the boat, the rod and reel, and the shotguns. When Minneapolis gets six inches of snow, Black Duck gets sixteen. All the better for snowmobiling.

I tried to get a phone number for the Fuchs household, but there was none. Probably used only cell phones, like most folks these days. If I was going to talk to Hoodie, it would have to be face-to-face.

Assuming I could get to talk to him, what was I going to say? "So, Mr. Hoodie. Why did you blow up the light rail?" I don't think so.

Better to say I was doing a follow-up on the neighborhood meeting about the light rail, which, in a way, was true. If he had been involved in blowing up the Blue Line, the neighborhood meeting would definitely be part of the story. I had to find him or, at least, his mom.

If he was living with his mom, odds were he was unemployed, or at least underemployed, a sad state of affairs for too many vets. I thought about how he might spend his time. Evenings might be at the Cum on Inn, the local watering hole. I could go have a beer and wait for him to show.

But I was trying to be home with my girls as many evenings as I could, so I thought about where I might look for him during daytime hours. When I was a kid, my family vacationed in the area, so I knew Black Duck had a BP gas station where balloons flutter out front, calling customers into the attached gift shop and fast food counter. A couple tables in the back add to the homey feeling. It's the kind of place where guys spend winters playing cards and complaining that they had to haul their fish houses off the lake at the end of February. Damn government intruding on a fisherman's life. I was betting that's where I would find him.

Editors think reporting is a cushy job. You just wait for the phone to ring and take down whatever piece of news the caller is willing to impart. Wrong. I drove to Black Duck, filled up my tank, and headed into the gift shop counter to pay up. I looked around but didn't see anyone who looked at all like Mr. Hoodie. Two or three folks ahead of me in line just wanted to pay for their gas and get out of there, which seemed to be just fine with the plump cashier, her blonde hair pulled back in a tight ponytail and no makeup to cover her acne.

"Busy day, huh?" I said when I got to her register.

"Yep. That'll be $20.21."

"Can't believe the cost of gas these days," I said.

"Me neither. Here's your change," she said with a shy smile.

"I'm looking for a guy who's probably an Iraq or Afghanistan vet," I said.

"Lots of them around here," she said.

"This guy likes to wear a U of M hoodie and jeans," I said. "Name's Bucky Fuchs."

"I went to high school with him," she said.

"He ever come in here?"

"Yeah. He plays cards over at that table Tuesday mornings with another guy—a Vietnam vet. Looks to me like it's some kind of therapy. Jimmy got hit by an IED in Afghanistan. Walks with a limp sometimes. He was a smart guy in high school, but now he talks like his brain isn't always working right."

"Think he'll be in here tomorrow?" I asked.

"Probably. They get here about 9:30. Stay for two hours. I

never charge 'em for the coffee. Seems like the least we can do for our vets."

Driving back to the newsroom in Minneapolis, then home, then back to Black Duck the next morning burned a quarter of a tank of gas. I filled up again at the BP station. When I walked in to pay, the same woman was behind the register. She glanced up at the two guys playing cards at the back table. The guy I figured for a Vietnam vet was thin, balding and about sixty years old. He wore an old sweatshirt and jeans. He was skinny, like a runner.

Bucky had on his usual hoodie and a black cap that said "Afghanistan Freedom" over the visor. He was bigger than I remembered from the meeting. He tapped his left foot continually as he studied his cards as though his life depended on choosing the right one.

I bought a cup of coffee and took a seat at the other table. Mr. Vietnam vet looked up at me first, with a little nod as if to say "I see you," and returned to his cards.

I sipped my coffee then pulled out my iPhone to check my email and the latest news on our website. After about ten minutes, the vets had finished their hand.

"Excuse me," I said looking at Bucky. "Didn't I see you at that neighborhood meeting about the light rail?"

"Who are you?" he asked.

I handed him my business card, which he looked at carefully. Then he turned it over, checked the back, then looked at the front again.

"You're the reporter who wrote that story about the meeting," he said. "You got it wrong."

"Really?" I said. "How?"

"You quoted all the people who wanted it and no one who didn't."

I knew he was off base but let it slide. "I quoted you, didn't I?"

"Yeah, but not my buddy here."

"I wasn't at the meeting, remember, Buck," Mr. Vietnam said.

"Are you against the light rail?" I asked Mr. Vietnam.

"Yes, ma'am," he said. "But I didn't say anything at the meeting because I wasn't there."

"Tell me why you don't like the light rail, Bucky," I said.

"Because it's going to wreck Black Duck. All those people are going to come here and we won't even be able to get a table to play cards," he said. "There will be Somalis everywhere, taking jobs. One of them is gonna blow up Black Duck just like they did in Minneapolis. These people, they blow up their own, you know."

His voice got louder and his foot tapped harder as he talked. His face was getting red.

"Settle down," Mr. Vietnam said. But Bucky wasn't having it. He threw his cards down on the table, pushed back his chair so hard that it fell over, and stomped out of the café.

"He has PTSD," his card-playing partner said. "I had the same problems when I came back from 'Nam. Takes a very long time for it to go away. Sometimes it never does."

"Is he unstable?" I asked.

"Yeah, given his reaction just now, I'd say so," he said.

"No. I mean really unstable."

"Meaning?"

"Meaning, could he do something violent?" I asked.

"I'm not a shrink, so how can I say? I'm just a vet who volunteers to play cards with another vet once a week."

"But you seem to know him fairly well." Outside the window Bucky was sucking on a cigarette, its tip burning bright red.

"We've been hanging together for a long time—since he came back, in fact," he said. "Could he do something violent? He's done plenty of things that are violent, killed even, all in the service of Uncle Sam, and you and me. What are you driving at?"

"Could he bomb the light rail train?"

"Ahh," he said. "Now I see where you're headed. Buck is a gentle man. He wouldn't hurt a fly. Except when he isn't."

"Have you ever seen him with explosives?" I asked.

"You're serious?" he said. "Am I going to be quoted?"

"No. I'm just asking questions at this point. If I'm going to write a story I may come back to you, on the record. You can respond, or not. Have you ever seen him with explosives or talk about it?"

"His job in Afghanistan was dismantling bombs, so yes, I've

heard him talk about it."

"What's he said?"

"He's talked about how tedious it can be—until something blows up," he said. "But have I seen him with dynamite or something that would blow up? No."

CHAPTER FORTY-THREE

I glanced out the window and watched Bucky tamp out one cigarette with the heel of his boot, then light another, all the while scanning the landscape of the BP parking lot, as though he were afraid someone was about to attack him. His feet were shoulder-length apart, with his weight balancing on the balls of his feet. His posture was classic fight or flight.

"I'm going to go talk to Bucky," I said to Mr. Vietnam, who gave me a slight nod.

The door squeaked when I opened it. The smell of wet March air mixed with cigarette smoke. For a brief second I flashed on my childhood and my brother, George. He was the bad boy among us, and my favorite.

Bucky squinted one eye as he looked down at me. He was not much taller than I but at least seventy-five pounds heavier.

"What's your story?" he asked.

"I was just wondering the same thing about you," I said.

"You reporters are all alike," he said. "Lots of questions, no answers."

"What other reporters do you know?" I asked.

"There was a chick I knew in Afghanistan. Looked great in camos and t-shirt. She worked for one of the biggies, New York Times or some shit."

"What did you do over there?" I asked.

"Took bombs apart."

"Sounds scary."

"It was."

He moved so his back was to the brick wall, then he scanned

the parking lot again.

"Any blow up?"

"Yeah," he said taking a long draw on his cigarette. "The last one."

"What happened?"

"I'd been out for three days, shuttin' down IEDs. Worked perfect every time. Figure I saved a bunch of guys' lives. When our work was done, we headed into Kabul. Figured there was a beer in my future. Heetal Hotel there had a great bar and that's where foreigners, 'specially Americans, hung out. Buncha security and high walls around there, so we always figured it was safe."

"And it wasn't?"

"We're sittin' on this patio when this lady comes up to us. She looks like a nun with the whole long dress and headscarf thing. She's carrying a box of somethin' she's selling. Flowers or spices or somethin'. I'm thinking it's not quite right. The look in her eye was dead, you know? Like the lights had been turned out. I get up and stepped toward her, thinkin', hopin' I'm wrong."

"Wrong about what?" I asked.

"That she was a suicide bomber," he said.

He took another drag on his cigarette and scanned the parking lot, again, squinting, not looking at me as he spoke. "Before I could do anything she blew up herself and a bunch of other people. Glass was flying everywhere. Eight people died. Another forty or so were hurt, including me."

He took off his cap and pointed to an inch-deep dent in his head.

"I'm sorry," I said. He nodded in response.

"But those were Afghans, not Somalis," I said.

"Doesn't matter," he said. "I don't trust ladies in long dresses. Who knows what they're hiding under there."

"You could say that about anybody in a long coat," I said. "Like that lady."

I pointed to a forty-something white woman hefting herself out of her car. She wore a black coat that brushed the tops of her boots.

"Think she's packing?" I asked.

"What's your story?" he asked me again, moisture from his breath billowing with the smoke from his cigarette around him. His teeth were stained the same color as the fingers that held his cigarette.

"You working for the newspaper or the light rail folks? Seems to me you're pushing pretty hard."

"Really?" I asked.

"Yeah, really. Listen to me, Sweetheart," he said. "I'm a vet who's not quite right in the head some days. I—"

Suddenly there was a loud pop. Bucky grabbed me around my neck, and with his other arm jammed my arm up behind my back. It happened so fast I had no time to react, not that I could have stopped him because he was very strong. He squatted down to the ground, slamming my face into the sidewalk, which hurt as much as when my brothers used to use the same move when we were kids. In an instant he had his knee on my neck. I could see from the corner of my eye that he scanned the parking lot again, this time sniffing like a dog searching out trouble.

After a minute or two, I could feel his taut muscles go slack. Maybe he realized one of the balloons had popped and he wasn't really in danger. When he stepped back and pulled me to my feet his face was ashen.

When I was in journalism school, we learned how to prepare for an interview, how to conduct an interview, how to write a story. There were classes on fact-checking, classes on covering government, classes on writing for the digital age. There was no class on what to do when a source gets surly. For that I had to fall back on my upbringing in a large unruly household where I was the only sister. I looked him dead in the eye.

"No, you remember this: If you ever touch me again, ever think of thinking of touching me again, you will regret it. I don't care how big you are, or the status of your brain. I promise you, you will regret it."

All his fury dissipated as quickly as it had come. When he hung his head, a tear dripped to the ground. By the time Mr. Vietnam reached us, it was over.

"What's the problem?" he asked. "Buck?"

"He had a little outburst is all," I said, rubbing the bump on my forehead. "A balloon popped and he was back in action. It won't happen again, right, Buck?"

He nodded and Mr. Vietnam clapped him on the back. "C'mon. We got a card game to finish."

CHAPTER FORTY-FOUR

"What do you know about post-traumatic stress disorder?" I asked Leona over lunch.

"Only what I know from being in a newsroom all these years," she said. "But the traumatic stress is current, not post."

"No. I mean really," I said.

"I know what I've read in the paper. Why?"

"Because I'm wondering if I've found the bomber," I said.

"Go on." She pulled her hands away from her keyboard and stared at me straight on. I had her full attention, something that's hard to come by in the newsroom.

I told her about my experience with Bucky. She was taken aback when I told her he had pinned me to the sidewalk, but impressed with how I had handled it.

"Is that where you got the scrape on your cheek? Maybe we should start including self-defense along with how to fill out a timecard in our new employee training," she said.

"Yeah, maybe." I didn't want to talk about the assault. I wanted to talk about the assaulter.

"He knows explosives," I said. "He's frightened by a Muslim woman in a hijab. We've got a picture of him standing on the Cedar-Riverside platform just before the train blew. Cedar-Riverside is packed with Muslim women. He appears to be flipping someone off. What if he was saluting because he knew the train was about to blow up?"

"I can see the headline: 'Gesture Links Vet to Light-Rail Bomb'." Leona is at her best when she's sarcastic.

"Point taken," I said. "But my gut tells me there's something here."

"Always follow your gut," she said as she turned to her ringing phone.

I decided it was worth putting some more time into Bucky, so I ran a data query on him. If he had a few run-ins with the law as a youngster, there was no record, since juvenile files are closed. He did manage to graduate from high school, although without any honors attached to his name. Looked like he joined the army at eighteen, then, after training in explosives was shipped off to Iraq, where he did two tours, then Afghanistan, where he did a couple more, until the last explosion. He had a slew of awards and commendations, including, of course, a purple heart. Didn't sound like a bomber to me.

Still, my gut was telling me something. I just couldn't figure out what. I hate it when my gut doesn't use words. Maybe I was looking at him wrong. But how? I've learned that I think better when I get up and move around, like a kindergartener, so I decided to go get a cup of coffee while I thought about it. Twenty minutes later I was back at my computer, nicely caffeinated but no further along on my problem. I wished there had been a reporter, someone I could call, in his neighborhood back then. It would have been much easier to see what kind of trouble he had been into. Did he have siblings who might have been written about? Did he even have siblings? All I knew was that he lived with his mother. That led me to wonder about his home life. Google provided a telling picture of his home from last fall.

It appeared to be a modest home on a down-on-its-luck street. The wide clapboard was painted aqua, the trim peeling white. It had an attached one-car garage. The grass apparently hadn't been mowed all summer. A huge crack in a picture window, which I guessed lit the living room, appeared to be taped. The only attribute in good repair was the crisp American flag displayed at the front door. I zoomed in a little closer, trying to see what was in the garage, but Google Earth didn't provide that much detail. Maybe next year.

The look of his house got me to wondering about Bucky's mother. I leafed through my notes from the meeting until I found her name. Clara. Clara Fuchs. I got about a thousand hits on her common name among Minnesotans of German heritage. To narrow the offering, I added her address in the search. That afforded about twenty items. This was a lady with a history.

The meeting I covered was not Clara Fuchs's first, it appeared. She was quoted in half a dozen articles, always protesting some form of development in her area. She seemed to be especially opposed to new growth that involved government spending. Plans for a senior citizen home? She didn't want "all those doddering old folks pushing their walkers with yellow tennis balls on the legs up and down the sidewalk." Mass transit would just give the devil a lift to town so he could expand on his evil doing. She was even opposed to a Head Start program for preschoolers. How can anybody find something wrong with Head Start?

I scrolled down until I found an op-ed piece she had written for our paper a year ago. She sounded like a raving lunatic, who writes well.

Her diatribe was titled "Not a Penny More to Government." Basically, it said that if all Americans totaled all the money they had paid in taxes over all of their lives, it would add up to an amount unimaginable. Had to agree with her on that point.

"We've given away enough of our hard-earned money," she wrote. "If we just stopped paying taxes today, we would all live like kings and queens."

This was a lady I wanted to meet.

CHAPTER FORTY-FIVE

Where you goin'?" Slick asked, as I grabbed my coat. "It's not quittin' time for girls, is it?"

"I'm off to talk to a nutcase," I said over my shoulder. Jeez, I hoped Slick wasn't filling in for Dick on the obnoxious-comments rotation.

I took a company car and scooted on the federal highway, built with federal taxpayers' money, and drove out to Grey Duck. With state and county tax, I figured the paper paid about three dollars and thirty-nine cents, plus the cost of gas, for me to drive out to see Clara. Maybe she had a point. Of course, without a good highway, my drive time would have been much longer.

Clara's house looked exactly as it had in the Google picture, except that her out-of-control green grass was now covered with dirty snow. My grandmother lived in a house just like Clara's. The kitchen is behind the living room and the stairs to the basement are right behind the kitchen. When I was a kid I played a game with my cousins where we would hide across the street at night and watched what the grownups were doing. We loved to spy, even though we were just looking at Grandma and Grandpa.

Clara's walkways had been trampled, not shoveled, into icy paths. I pulled onto the gravel drive and parked in front of her garage. I opened the driver side door and put one booted foot in the icy gray snow, then swung my other foot out, using the door handle to steady myself.

As I carefully walked the twenty feet to her front porch, I prayed I would stay upright. If I fell and broke an arm or hand I'd be truly screwed, work- and life-wise. I'm beginning to sound like my mother, I muttered to myself as I climbed her porch steps.

"What'd you say about a mother?" Clara said as she opened her door. Her tone was not amused. She must have seen me coming up the walk. "Who are you?"

I got a better look at her. My first impression was that she looked exactly like Bucky—or rather he looked exactly like her. They were the same height, give or take an inch, the same rounded body, same dirty reddish clown hair. Only difference I could tell was she had breasts under her sweatshirt...although, as I thought about it, so did he. She even smelled of the same cigarettes through the screen door.

"I'm Skeeter Hughes," I said, handing her my card.

"You wrote the story about the meeting?" she asked.

"I did."

"Why you here?"

"I've read your articles in the paper," I said. I wanted her to know I was familiar with her work, but I didn't have to tell her I thought she was nuts. "I wanted to talk with you about the proposed light rail through town."

"Come in," she said. Just as she opened the screen door, a gust of wind blew it all the way open to bang on the front of the house. Apparently whoever had not put in the storm windows for the season had also failed to fix the chain intended to keep it from banging open. The divot in the aqua siding indicated this wasn't the first time.

"Take a load off," she said. "Coffee?"

"That would be great." I took a seat on the couch covered with a throw that had cigarette holes burned in it. A feral-looking cat jumped on the couch next to me and sauntered across my lap. I ran my hand down her back.

"You like cats?" Clara asked.

"Love 'em." Journalism 101: if the source likes cats, you like cats, even if they look like they have fleas. One can never go too far to establish rapport, although this was stretching it a bit.

"What's the cat's name?" I called to her as she stepped into the kitchen.

"Bachmann," she said. She returned quickly. Too quickly. I

took a sip and realized it was instant coffee. Yuck. I set the cup on a scratched side table.

"So, what do you want to know?" she said.

"I was interested in why you went to the meeting about light rail coming to town."

"I went because I want to be heard," she said.

"Heard saying what, exactly?"

"Was that intentionally sarcastic?" she asked.

"Sorry. That's not what I intended," I said. "Let me try again, please. You spoke at the meeting. I was wondering if you had any other thoughts on the topic. I might be writing a follow-up story about it."

I pulled out my reporter's notebook and noticed it was almost full with my notes. Damn, I'd have to flip it over and write on the other side of the pages. Clara eyed the notebook, with a slight smile. Some people love to see their names in the paper, some don't. I was guessing that Clara was one of the former.

"That's better," she said. "I don't believe in a government that takes our money and puts it into mechanisms that are designed to ruin the environment. Laying tracks way out here on the prairie does nothing but destroy the grasses and flowers and wildlife that are meant to be left alone, to do what God intended them to do."

"Others would argue that the light rail is good for the environment because it would cut down on the number of cars that pollute the air and burn gasoline that is not replaceable," I said. "What would you tell them?"

"I'd say that they need to stay put in the city where they can breathe poison air and keep away from the prairie," she said.

Oh, the irony, I thought.

"But you're living here," I asked. "How come you get to be here and others don't?"

"If someone wants to live here at peace with the land, I say fine," she said. "But really, it's the government I object to."

"I talked with your son, Bucky," I said.

"He told me," Clara snapped. "Why?"

Because I'm wondering if he bombed the train, I thought, but didn't say. "I wanted to hear his opinion on the light rail train," I said, which was true.

That seemed to settle Clara down. Bachmann, the cat, jumped on Clara's lap, leaving a cloud of fur in the air behind her. Although I don't think I'm allergic to cat fur, my nose began to itch.

"He's an Afghanistan vet," I continued. "He volunteered to work for the government when he joined the Army. How do you feel about that?"

She dug in the pocket of her sweatshirt, pulled out cigarettes, and lit up, blowing a lung full of smoke in my direction before answering. I recalled, not for the first time, that I really liked to smoke, back in the day before I had kids. Her hand twitched a bit as she blew out the match and tossed it into an empty cat food can on her coffee table.

"My Bucky is a good boy," she said. "He's learned a lot since he volunteered. Big mistake."

"What was his mistake?" The cat jumped down from her lap.

"Enlisting," she said, after deep inhalation and more smoke in the air.

"What did he learn?" I asked.

"Learned the hypocrisy of the American government," she said. "Did you know that Timothy McVeigh was an Iraq war veteran?"

None of this was making sense to me. But then I wasn't here looking for logic. My eyes started to water. Was it because the smoke in her house was getting so thick I should file for workers compensation from the effects? Or was it the cat? If ever I needed a cure from smoking, this was it.

"How is the American government hypocritical by putting a train line from the cities to your home?" I asked.

"Because it takes my money, then spends it on things I don't want," she said.

"Such as?"

"War. Do you know that between 2001 and 2013, the United States spent $1.4 trillion on war? That's trillion, with a T," she said.

I couldn't help but think she sounded just like Rachel, who railed all the time about where her tax dollars went.

"And that was just in Iraq and Afghanistan," she said. "Why

did the government spend that kind of money on a war nobody wants?"

Again, I had to agree with her. But I wasn't there to talk government spending with her. I was there to find out if her son had bombed the train.

"Look, I've got to go to work, so you've got to go," Clara said.

"Where do you work?" I asked.

"Target," she said. "With lots of them Muslim women who take our jobs. Do you know they have their own special prayer room? Nobody ever built no prayer room for us Christians."

"Tell me about Bucky," I said, hoping she wouldn't notice the shift in the conversation.

"Why?" she asked. "I don't know if I should talk to you about Bucky."

That was the point of my visit. I needed to get her to talk about Bucky. What mother doesn't want to talk about her kids?

"When you mentioned him a minute ago I sensed you had more thoughts about him," I said. "I'm a mom, too. Sometimes talking about my kids to someone else helps me figure them out."

"What do you want to know about Bucky?" she asked.

"What was he like when he was little?" If I could get her reminiscing, she might slip into telling me more about him.

Her face transformed from the harsh critic of moments ago. She gazed off in the distance like any mother would, with a Mona Lisa smile, followed by a frown. "He was a wonderful baby, such a good sleeper."

By the time he was two months old, she was pregnant again, she said. The second baby was born premature. That child, a second son, didn't do well. He was hospitalized for the first six months of his life. Then, when he was a year old, he died.

"It was a difficult pregnancy, then I was so upset about his brother that I guess Bucky didn't get much of me when he was little," she said. "Plus his daddy was busy a lot with his mission, and I had my jobs to do."

"Who took care of him when you two were working?" I asked.

"One of the other girls," she said. "Why are you asking me about Bucky? What does this have to do with the train comin' here?"

How to phrase this? We had been dancing around way too long. I had to get closer to the point with Clara. It was a calculated risk, but when I write a story about the picture taken on the platform just before the train blew up, I'd tell Bucky about it anyway to give him a chance to comment.

"There's a photo of people standing on the Cedar-Riverside platform just before the Blue Line blew up," I said. "One of them looks a lot like Bucky."

For a heavy woman, she jumped out of her chair very quickly and ran in the kitchen. Before I knew what was going on, she had a shotgun pointed at me.

"You think my Bucky bombed the train?" she screamed.

My heart started pounding and my mouth suddenly went dry. I could hear my blood rushing.

"Whoa," I said, putting my hands up, as if they would stop a bullet. "I didn't accuse anybody of anything."

"Get out of my house." She said it quietly, which scared me even more.

I grabbed my purse and began to back out, my eyes on her shotgun the whole time. "I'm leaving. Okay?"

My focus was so tight I saw every pore in her face, every hair on her chin, the weave of the fabric in her sweatshirt. But I just couldn't resist one last question as I felt behind my back and grabbed the door handle.

"Do you think Bucky bombed the train?"

"No, he did not," she said through clenched teeth. "Now get out."

CHAPTER FORTY-SIX

I spent a few days trying to figure out how I was going to keep the secret that Abdi was a hero who had saved many lives, yet keep my promise to Fortun to help her find him.

Send her an anonymous note? No, too much risk that someone else would get hold of it. I couldn't call her or send her an email or even a text, given the National Security Agency's tendency to snoop around those sorts of things.

I knew that Fortun volunteered sporadically at the Somali Resource Center Riverside Plaza, home to many immigrants. Because she traveled to all her jobs by bus and her schedule was unpredictable, I decided it would be best to just swing by there and see if I could catch her. It took me three tries, but finally she was there one afternoon as I dropped by.

"Somali Resource Center," Fortun answered the phone with her perfect English while giving me a big smile as I stepped to the counter. She raised her pointer finger to indicate she would be with me as soon as she finished the call.

While she spoke with the caller in Somali, I looked around. There are enough Somalis living in Little Mogadishu to keep two centers busy day and night. Fortun worked in the smaller one, which comprised three rooms. One was stocked with long narrow tables where older-model computers were available to anyone who wanted to use them. Another was a small classroom where immigrants learned English as a second language. A sample sentence was written on the blackboard: "The shower is leaking. Call the manager."

Fortun hung up the phone. "Skeeter, I haven't seen you in a

while."

"Sorry it's been so long," I said. "When are you done working here today?"

She said she had about ten minutes left. While I waited for her outside in the parking lot of broken blacktop within full view of the Minneapolis skyline, I thought through how I was going to do this. It wasn't going to be easy.

"Let's go for a walk," I said when I saw she was wearing running shoes.

It was late in the day, starting to get dark. In another few days, once daylight savings time kicked in, we'd have another hour of sunlight. But for the time being, the twilight emboldened the colors of her red, blue, purple and green. Once again I thought about what a beautiful woman she was.

"Have you heard anything about Abdi?" she asked as we walked through Little Mogadishu.

"That's what I wanted to talk with you about," I said. "Has Mohamed told you anything about Abdi?"

"He said I should quit worrying about him," Fortun said. "But it's difficult."

Hmmm, I thought. Does that mean Mohamed knows where Abdi is?

"Are Mohamed and Abdi close as brothers?" I asked.

"I thought so," she said. "At least when they were boys they were. Are they close as men? I don't know. What does that have to do with Abdi?"

I told her I had spoken with both Mohameds, her son and the Mohamed who runs the cash transfer.

"Your son Mohamed is right," I said. "You shouldn't worry about Abdi anymore."

We had reached Seven Corners by then, the place on the edge of the University of Minnesota West Bank where streets converge to create seven corners, with bars on every one, the most famous being Sgt. Preston's, where Bob Dylan played during his misspent youth.

"Why shouldn't I worry about Abdi?" she asked in a soft voice. I looked at her. Her eyes were getting misty.

"Because I know he is all right," I said. "I know you should be proud of him."

As a mother, I knew what was in her heart. Motherhood is a universal lifetime license to worry, even if you know your kids are just fine. To hear someone say you should be proud of your child is to know, if only briefly, that all the sweat and tears you've put into raising that child was worth it.

"And I suspect Mohamed knows the same thing," I said.

"Thank you," she said. Her tears were flowing freely now. She gave me a hug that communicated her gratitude in the purest form.

"Can you tell me any more?" she asked. "Will I ever see him again?"

"No, I can't tell you more," I said. "It's likely you'll never see him again. But know he is alive and well. And he's a good man, wherever he is."

CHAPTER FORTY-SEVEN

"I'm sorry." There. I said it.

It took a great deal of convincing but I finally got Michael to return to Wilde Roast where we had tried to have dinner when the FBI so rudely interrupted us with a press conference.

"I said a few things I shouldn't have," I said.

"Yeah, you did," he said. "Which are you apologizing for? The part where you said I'm not making enough money to support my family? Or when you implied I've lost my professionalism?"

The same server who took our orders the last time was tableside again. I took that as a good sign that we could pick up where we had left off. "Have you had a chance to look over the menu?" he asked.

"No," Michael said, churlishly.

"I'll give you a little time." He turned with a huff and wrote something on his notepad as he stepped away. Yep, same guy.

"If I said either of those things, I didn't mean them," I said.

"If? That's what you said."

I could feel my heart start to beat in a rhythm that told me I was getting angry all over again. This had not been my intent for this evening. I had wanted to make peace between us. And I wanted to do it in a neutral setting where the girls wouldn't hear us. But first we had to clear the air.

"And you said I needed to know my place as a woman," I hissed through clenched teeth. "Something about wearing a hijab."

"That may have been a mistake," he said.

"*May have? May have been a mistake?*" I said. "You're kidding me right now, right? Because if you're not, our problems are even bigger than I had feared."

He peered into his beer mug as though the answer were printed on the bottom. When he looked up at my eyes, he gave me that funny little half smile that I fell in love with so many years ago.

"I guess," he said.

"Michael, if we are going to make this marriage work, we've got to be on the same website," I said.

"Website?"

"You know, on the same page, only in the twenty-first century. The same URL," I said.

"God, are you that deep into it?" he asked. "Do we have to go off the grid to get any peace? How are we going to do that? Throw the iPhone, iPad, Macbook Pro, iPod, even the Nano in the river?"

"Now I know you're kidding," I said.

This time he gave me his full smile, the one with the dimples. The crow's feet in the corners of his eyes deepened. He loves his techno gear as much as I love mine. It was the first time in a long time that he had warmed my heart with that smile. When I saw it I knew he was listening.

"We've got a lot going for us," I said. "Two beautiful daughters, a nice place to live, lots of friends in a spectacular city, much of the time."

"You didn't mention work that we love," he said.

No, I hadn't. It was the one huge stain in our lives. And I didn't see it getting better. He'd already been laid off. I was finding it increasingly difficult to enjoy what I did. There was constant pressure to give online readers news immediately, before I had time to figure out what it was. The paper had fired all the copy editors so there was no one backing me up in case I misspelled something, or dropped a word, or God forbid, had a fact wrong. Meanwhile, photographers were not being replaced, so there were times when I had to take pictures, ask questions, listen to the answers, then sit down with my laptop and write the story as it was happening.

On the other hand, the pay was not bad, and the job did come with pretty good benefits, all thanks to the work of the union. It was usually sit-down, indoors work. Better than wearing a hairnet and yanking the guts out of chickens while standing on an assembly line, although I've always thought enticing some sources to talk is like gutting chickens.

"Your job is wearing you down," he said. "You barely make it home in time for the girls and me. And when you are home you're asleep. You're not a wife and mother anymore. You're a roommate."

Ouch. It was like he stabbed me in the eye with his fork. Was he right? Had I lost touch with my family so much that I had reduced myself to roommate? To someone who just lived in the same house? Was this job costing me my family?

I've always told myself that doing my job right makes a difference. If I could figure out who bombed the train, I might even save people's lives.

"Made any decisions?" It was the server again.

"We're still thinking." This time I was churlish.

"What I do is important," I said. "I care deeply about my work."

"Unlike everyone else?" he asked.

Another zinger. He was on a roll.

"You've changed, Michael," I said. "You used to be as passionate about your work as I am."

"Okay, what'll it be?" The server was back.

"I'll have a burger and fries, and another beer," Michael said.

"Make mine the ham-and-cheese quiche, and more coffee," I said. We handed the server our menus without looking at him.

"Getting laid off changed my perspective," he said.

"That reminds me, how many more resumes have you sent out?"

He shook his head then took a deep slug of his beer. "You're still not hearing me, Skeeter, or else you just don't get it. I'm done with newspapers."

"Are you done with journalism?" I asked. "Because I'm not."

We both looked out the window at the cityscape of downtown Minneapolis. Lights were just coming on as twilight descended, turning most of the buildings gold. We watched the Mississippi rushing by, the spring water fast and hard at the first falls on the river.

"I love living here," he said. "I don't want to move. But there are no jobs here for an experienced journalist."

That broke my heart, because he was, is, a fine journalist. I thought back to when we first met, working together. He was smart, hard-driving, fearless. I valued his opinion, on everything, and he took serious consideration of mine. We were yin and yang, hand and glove, Lois and Clark. How had we lost that?

"Okay," I said. "I get it. You and the girls want me home, paying attention more. I promise I will do that. But you've got to let me just get this story done. I've got to find out who bombed the train. For Rachel, if for no one else."

"I'm holding you to that promise, Skeeter. Because if you are around any less, I may as well leave for good," he said.

As our food came, I debated with myself whether to tell him about my almost tryst with Sam. I heard Rachel's voice in my head: "Are you insane? That's a little secret between you and Sam."

"I think you're right," I heard myself say.

"What?" Michael asked.

"I think you're right that we should have dessert."

"I hadn't said anything about dessert."

"But you were going to."

"You know me too well," Michael said. "But that's not what you were going to say."

Well, here goes, I thought.

"Rumor has it the paper is going to offer buyouts," I said.

"And ..." he replied. "You're thinking about taking it?"

"Depending on the offer, yes," I said. "I want to make this marriage work. I want to spend more time, some time, with you and the girls."

He didn't say anything for a couple of minutes, until, "That would put a serious dent in our finances. It's not going to be long until the girls are in college. How are we going to pay for that?"

"Make up your mind, Michael," I said. "One minute you want me home more so you can do more serious work, the next you want me earning a salary bigger than yours. What's it going to be?"

"What about that Pulitzer you were going to win?" he asked with a half-smile.

"The awards for this year don't come out until next spring," I said. "Who knows? Maybe I'll win on the light rail stories. Plus, there's nothing that says freelancers can't win Pulitzers."

"Name one who has."

I thought a while. "I'll get back to you on that."

"Seymour Hersh," he said.

"What?"

"Hersh was a freelancer in Vietnam when he sold the story about the massacre at My Lai to the Dispatch News Service. It won him a Pulitzer in 1970."

"How do you know that? We weren't even born then."

"I don't know how I know it," he said. "I just do."

"Look," I said. "Journalism is nothing like it was when you and I started in the business. Now it's all about online. We don't need paper, literally. We can work for online pubs. We could work together again. From home. Get some balance into our lives."

"And less money," he said.

"What's it going to be, Michael?" I said. "Me or my salary?"

CHAPTER FORTY-EIGHT

After my story ran, all the other media found Harriet Lansing, the train driver, making it even harder to get to see her after she was sprung and returned home. Reporters almost had to take a number. Of course, Harriet loved the attention. With her eyebrows growing back and the scabs on her cheeks healing, not to mention her charming irascibility, the TV folks liked having her on the screen. As a symbol of hope and survival in the face of tragedy, she was a gift from the god of ratings.

I just liked her, so I decided to pay her a visit to see how she was doing.

"Skeeter," she said with joy in her voice when I called. "Long time no see."

"Feeling better?" I asked.

"Yep. I loved the mystery book you left for me. Got me seriously into reading mysteries. Have you found that bookstore, Once Upon a Crime on twenty-sixth and Lyndale in Minneapolis? They're the best people. They know it's hard for me to get around so they mail books to me. Isn't that special?"

"They're great folks," I agreed. "Say, I'd like to come to your house and see you."

"Let me grab my calendar," she said. "It has been busy, busy, busy."

She found time the next afternoon. When I pulled up to her house in Northeast Minneapolis, I was not surprised that it was unassuming. Avenues in Northeast are named after presidents. Hers was on Polk. It was set on a steep hill up half a dozen concrete steps. I wondered how she managed to cut the grass in the summer.

I couldn't see her hiring someone else for that job.

"Come on in," she shouted from inside when I rang her bell. "It's not locked."

I pushed my way in, kicked off my boots, threw my jacket on a chair, and made my way to the kitchen, where she was sitting at a small round drop-leaf table next to the window, drinking tea.

"Just in time, dear," she said. "I was just sitting down to take all my pills. I've got more pills than dollars, I can tell you that."

She gestured at the chair across from her. "Take a load off, honey."

I inquired about her health—"Fine, just fine"—and whether she was in any pain—"Just a little."

"So tell me, honey, how is it going for you?" she asked. "You know I thought you did a real fine job on that story you wrote about me. Got all your facts right. Of course, I suspect the FBI was none too happy about it, but that's their problem. Now, is that newspaper treating you right?"

"The paper's okay," I said. "But I'm really missing my husband and girls. It feels like I never see them because I'm working so much. If I'm lucky, I get a few minutes with them before they go to school, but they're in bed by the time I get home at night. All I do is work. The paper is really on me to find the bomber."

Why was I telling her all this? I never bare my soul to a source. It's so unprofessional. But there was something about Harriet that felt nice—Minnesota nice.

"So your husband is taking care of the girls? How many daughters do you have?"

"Two—Rebecca, who's fourteen, and Suzy, who's eleven," I said. "They're good girls, doing well in school. I just wish I could spend more time with them. Michael's a good father, so they're fine. I'm the one who's missing out."

"Does Michael have a job?"

"He did. Was a reporter for the St. Paul paper, but he took a buyout last month. They were going to lay him off soon, anyway. Now he works from home, freelancing, which is why I can work longer hours, even though I don't want to."

She grabbed a Kleenex from the box next to her chair and

coughed into it. I worried that there was something even more seriously wrong with her than the burns, but she said she just had a tickle in her throat, probably the start of cold.

"Your face changed a bit, got a little pinched, I guess, when you mentioned Michael," she said, touching the back of my hand. "Is there some tension between you two?"

I could only laugh. "You would make an excellent reporter, Harriet."

She gave me a cute little half-smile, a nod of her head, and one arched eyebrow.

I wasn't prepared to discuss my marriage with her, so I changed the subject.

"Do you know whether the cops have figured out who bombed the train?" I asked.

"Not a word. Of course, they aren't going to share that with me. Who am I? Just the driver, that's all."

I dug into my purse and pulled out my iPhone to show her the picture Rachel had taken of the folks on the platform just before the explosion. "Anybody here look familiar?"

"Get me my glasses, will you, honey?" she asked waving in the general direction of her kitchen counter.

"Would you like a glass of water, too?" I asked. She nodded yes, so I stepped into her kitchen, searched the cupboards until I found a glass, and brought it to her, full of cold water, along with her glasses. She balanced them on the end of her nose and gave the picture her careful attention.

"These Somali girls look like all the others that ride the train," she said. "Same with the Somali guy in the brown jacket. I swear every Somali cab driver in Minneapolis has a jacket like that. And they all listen to MPR, too. Ever notice that? Of course, I don't take a cab ride all that often. They've gotten so expensive. Now the guy in the suit? I don't know him. But this one in the red hoodie looks familiar."

That had to be Bucky. My heart started to beat faster and I could feel my mouth going a little dry. "How does he look familiar?"

"He? That's not a 'he'. That's a 'she.' She rode the train three times a week for six months. Always wore the same hoodie and baggy jeans. At first I thought she was going to work. But she got off at a different stop every time."

She handed me my iPhone. I looked more closely.

It was Clara. Bucky 's mother. "Are you sure?" I asked. Judging from her reaction, I must have sounded incredulous.

"Yes, I'm sure," she said. "I'm a judge of people. Driving train gives me the opportunity to study people. This lady rode the train a lot."

"Did you tell the FBI about her?" I asked.

"If they had brought me a picture like this, I would have," she said. "But they didn't."

"Did you notice any other regulars?" I asked.

"Of course," she said. "There were probably half a dozen people who rode the train like she did. Some of them were a little odd, like the huge guy with the gray beard who would just sit and knit, getting on one train going one way then getting on the next train going the other way."

"Did they make you nervous?"

"Oh, no. They were harmless. People who are odd aren't necessarily dangerous. Why are you asking me about this one in the hoodie?"

I told her about Clara, the illogical militant anti-government environmentalist.

"Do you think she bombed the train?" Harriet asked.

"Don't know," I said. "Could be."

"Are you going to write a story about me recognizing her?" Harriet asked.

"That's likely," I said. "How do you feel about that?"

Harriet took a sip of her water and looked me dead in the eye. "Well, honey, fact is fact," she said. "You're a journalist. Now you just go do what you've got to do."

Sometimes I'm so deep in thought while I'm driving that I arrive at my destination with no recollection of how I got there. Very scary. That's what happened as I returned from visiting Harriet. My return to the newsroom felt like teleportation.

I kept turning the story over in my head. At first I had feared that Abdi was the bomber, but then FBI Special Agent Tim O'Reilly convinced me he was not. Then I thought it might be Bucky in the hoodie, until Harriet said it was his mother, Clara. I sure hadn't seen that one coming.

Now I was left with the embezzler or Clara, neither a sure bet. There was no hard evidence about the computer guy—only an allegation from someone who was probably lying. And just because Clara was standing on the platform didn't mean she bombed the train, even if she was nuts and flipping the bird at God-knew-who. By the time I pulled into the newspaper's parking lot my brain was totally muddled. I had to talk to Leona.

Newsroom rhythm beats to the cadence of deadlines. At our paper, mornings are languid, editors and reporters reading papers or online, talking softly on the phone, drinking coffee. Midday the newsroom can be pretty much empty as people go to lunch. The pace picks up by midafternoon. Voices get louder, people move faster. By four o'clock, when blood-sugar levels drop, reporters on deadline need an extra boost to keep them going. Some make a quick run for the candy machine, others just get crabbier. As the six o'clock deadline looms, fingers are flying on keyboards and phones are ringing. When reporters are done writing their stories, they push a key and send it to their editor. Editors who supervise half a dozen or more reporters can suddenly have a handful of stories to edit, all at the same time. That was the reality Leona was facing as I cruised up to her desk in hopes of getting her take on this new twist on the story that consumed me.

"Ah…Leona?"

"Not now, Skeeter," she said. "Come back in an hour."

"Got it," I said and made my way toward the newsroom coffeepot. On the way, I passed an editor who was saying to no one in particular, "If I'd known this is what four years of college would get me, I would've gone ahead with that eight-week dog grooming course instead."

I'd reached the candy machine when I ran into Dex.

"What's the latest from the ex, Dex?"

"You into rhyming now?" he asked as he pulled the silver handle that caused a stale Mars bar to drop into the tray.

"A candy bar for dinner?" I asked him.

"Yes, MOM," he said with a roll of his eyes. Just like Rebecca. "How's the story coming?"

I told him about Harriet's identification of Clara in the picture.

"Now what?" he asked.

That was exactly what I was wondering.

"A story that says the driver of the train identified a woman who was standing on the Cedar-Riverside platform just before it blew up is a pretty good story," I said. "But it's not the whole story. I hate telling readers only part of the story."

"What's her house like?" Dex asked.

I described the Fuchs' house, including the cracked picture window.

"Maybe we should go out there when she's not expecting us," he said. "We might see something through that front room window."

"What do you mean 'we'?" I asked.

"You're going to need a getaway driver," he said with a hint of a smile.

I looked at him closely. Tall, skinny, still fighting acne. One earring that created a hole in his earlobe the size of a nickel.

"How'd you get that big hole in your ear?" I asked.

"Gradually," he said.

"And you want to be my driver? I thought you were a computer geek."

"I am," he said. "That's why I'm just the driver. Plus, you have a cool car."

Ahhh, now I get it, I thought. It's not me, it's my car he likes.

"You old enough to drive?" I asked.

He rolled his eyes, again.

"Well, I can't talk to Leona for a while, anyway," I said. "Let's go."

CHAPTER FORTY-NINE

I only had to tell Dex to slow down once as we drove to Black Duck.

"You know this is a bad idea, right?" I said to Dex. "I'm not supposed to be teaching you these kinds of tactics."

"I'm not doing this, you are," he said. "I'm just the young impressionable computer-geek driver."

I thought more about our plan to surprise Clara with a visit. Maybe he was right. This was exactly the sort of thing I would have done when I was a young reporter, Dex's age.

I remembered when Michael and I were working together on a story that didn't win a Pulitzer. We were nominated, however, even though all it takes to be nominated is fifty dollars—credit card only—and someone who will fill out a form. That's why I often chuckle when I hear someone say they were nominated for a Pulitzer. Hell, we were nominated. The big deal is to be a nominated finalist for a Pulitzer. That's almost as good as winning, although it doesn't come with a $10,000 prize and all the hoopla.

We were working together on the newspaper in Rochester. The story involved a lot of document research, which was his job, and dumpster diving, which was mine. It had been years since I had swung a leg over the side of a dumpster. Why had that slipped away from me? The more I thought about it, the more I was glad that Dex had suggested a little look-see on Clara.

Darkness was falling as Dex parked the car a quarter-mile from Clara's house. We watched lights go on in kitchens, living rooms and basements as we walked down the dirt road.

"The plan here is to just peek in her windows," I said to Dex. I spoke quietly because sound carries across rural fields. "None of this is going in any story. This is just background research."

The memory of that night playing laser tag with Rachel and the girls filled me with warmth as I walked down the dirt road to Clara's with Dex. Maybe it gave me a false sense of security because we weren't playing with real guns. Whatever the reason, I knew window peeping was a mistake, but I couldn't turn back. My gut told me I was getting closer to the truth.

We were two hundred feet from the Fuchs' house when I saw Clara, dressed in a gray sweatshirt and sweatpants, walk through the living room and turn on a light. No drapes on the cracked picture window, which made sense to me. I had never figured Clara for the kind of woman who would spend time fussing over window treatments.

Dex and I froze behind a gnarly bush, then jumped into the ditch once she had passed.

"That her?" Dex whispered.

"That's her," I said. "Does she look like the person in the picture to you?"

"If she had on a hoodie and jeans, yeah," he said.

A moment later we saw a light flick on in the kitchen. We saw Bucky open the fridge, grab a beer can, pop the lid, and chug the whole thing down in one gulp, then grab another and shut the door. He wore the requisite hoodie and jeans.

"What about him?" I asked. "That's Bucky. Does he look like the person on the platform?"

"Yeah, he does," Dex said. "His shape is the same as hers. He's even got man-boobs."

"So which one was in the picture on Rachel's computer? Clara or Bucky ?"

"I don't know," Dex said.

"Let's wait a bit and see if there's anything more besides a quick couple of beers," I said.

We hunkered down in the ditch. Pretty soon the snow was seeping into my jeans. Dex was probably feeling the same icy creep. After about twenty minutes my knees began to ache. I was just about to say it was time to go when the front door opened. Out came Bucky.

"Jeeeezuuuuss, Ma," he shouted back into the house. "Get a grip. There's nobody out here."

He stumbled along the icy rut from the front door to the garage, opened the door, and backed out a rusted Toyota. Dex and I crouched down even further until we were practically prone when Bucky's headlights scraped the edge of the ditch. My heart was pounding. I heard Dex taking quick shallow breaths. Bucky was well down the road before we felt safe enough to raise our heads. I took a deep breath.

"That was close," I said.

"Remind me why we came out here." I was soaked with melted snow. The romance of journalistic endeavors was dissipating with my every shiver.

"To find the bomber," he said. We whispered about going back to town for dry, warm clothes when Clara walked through the living room, then disappeared in the back of the kitchen. Seconds later a light went on in the basement.

"Told ya," he said.

Without a word, we crept to the back of the house to peek in her basement window.

The Fuchs' basement was a mess. Old chairs with the stuffing hanging out, a rusted refrigerator, concrete laundry tubs. Half a dozen shotguns, much like the one Clara had pointed at me, leaned up against a back wall. A naked incandescent light bulb hung from the ceiling. She was in the back of the basement bent over a workbench doing something with a pair of pliers and a screw driver. She was so wide I couldn't tell what she was working on.

BOOM! The explosion was so strong that it blew me back twenty feet.

CHAPTER FIFTY

It must have knocked me out because I woke lying on my back with smoldering debris everywhere. The pieces that fell on me sizzled in my wet jeans and sweatshirt. My hearing was muffled as though I were under water. I couldn't raise my head, which hurt like hell. Flames from the back half of the Fuchs house spiked into the sky.

I opened my eyes to Dex standing over me. "You okay?" he asked. His face was smudged. A red lump was growing on his forehead. Pieces of glass glinted in his hair.

I slowly moved my arms and legs, then finally my head. My side hurt when I tried to sit up.

"I guess. Where's Clara?"

"Don't know," Dex said.

"I'll find her," I said. "You call 911. Then call the news desk."

Dex pulled out his phone. When he couldn't get a signal he ran for the road.

The acrid smell of burning plastic, wood, plaster, insulation and God-knows-what-else filled the air. Suddenly my brain swirled back to the explosion on the light rail. What I was feeling was probably nothing compared to the stark terror Rachel and the others felt, caught in the deathtrap. There's scary in the movies, but it's nothing like the scary of a real explosion.

Would there be a second explosion? Were there more explosives in the house, ready to go? What about the garage? Likely there were flammables in there. Would sparks from the house fire ignite something in the garage?

It took me a moment to force my legs to move, but I managed.

"Clara," I shouted.

No response. "Clara!"

"Over here." The voice was coming from the back of the basement. "Can't move."

I ran as fast as I could to where the back of the house had been. Clara was lying at the bottom of the charred staircase. I looked around for Dex, but couldn't see him. I knew I had to get Clara out fast before something else blew her to the heavens.

The wooden staircase was charred on the edges. I had no idea whether it was stable. I did know I had to get Clara out of there. There wasn't time to find Dex to help me, or wait for the fire engines.

"I'm coming," I shouted to her.

I put one foot on the top step, and then carefully touched the second step with my toe, testing how well it would hold my weight. It felt solid, so I gingerly took another step, then counted how many more there were. Eight. Eight steps to get to Clara. Assuming I made it to the bottom that meant there would be eleven steps to get her out.

Another step. Another. Halfway.

Craaaaack. I felt the center of the step give way. Time to either go back up and wait for help, or keep going to get Clara now.

"Clara," I said. "I'm coming. Try to relax. Everything's going to be fine."

I ran down the remaining steps, figuring that stopping just put more of my weight on each step. When I hit the last one all the others gave way, throwing me forward, where I landed on Clara.

"Oh my God," she moaned in pain.

I rolled to my side, then sat up to get a better look at her. Her leg was bent the wrong way, just as Dick's had been. A bone was sticking out, creating a bump in her sweatpants. Definitely broken. There was blood all over her face, in her hair. Her hands were burned black. Her sweatshirt was in tatters.

What was worse, the stairs I had just descended were smashed to smithereens.

I looked up through the burned ceiling to see a beautiful country night. Stars were sparkling. The Big Dipper shone so bright in the early spring sky it felt like I could reach out and touch it. I wondered if it would be the last thing I saw before I died.

"What are you doing here?" Clara asked.

"Long story," I said. "We've got to get out."

I looked around the basement. Concrete floor. More stuff than a five-family garage sale. In the corner opposite from us stood three red plastic jugs, with handles and spouts.

"Is that gasoline?" I asked Clara.

She nodded.

Shit. This is it. I'm going to die. I thought about Michael, Rebecca and Suzy. I didn't want to leave them. I hadn't had enough marriage, or motherhood. They needed me and I needed them. I still had plenty more living to do. It wasn't fair, I thought. I was too young to die, had still too many more things to do.

I heard the wail of sirens getting closer. Dex must have gotten a signal for his phone. As the sparks from the fire danced on the wood around us getting closer and closer to the gasoline, I knew we couldn't wait for the fire trucks to arrive. We had to get out that very minute.

Clara had passed out again from what had to be excruciating pain. I shook her, which probably hurt a lot, but she rallied.

"Is there another way out of here?" I asked.

"Bomb shelter," she said.

"What?" I asked.

"We've got a bomb shelter. For when we're invaded. Government," she said.

Of course Clara and Bucky had a bomb shelter. If our situation hadn't been so dire, I'd have laughed right out loud.

"Got drinking water and canned food. Has a sort of cellar door to the outside. Bucky built it when he came back from Afghanistan. Faces south. He planted pumpkins over it so the soldiers wouldn't be able to find it."

"Where is it?"

She pointed to a wall behind an old refrigerator. "Bucky didn't want anybody to find it from the inside, either," she said.

Great, I thought. Now I've got to move a refrigerator. And fast. The flames were getting closer to the gas can.

I pushed my way past cardboard boxes full of newspapers and old clothes, moved a pile of storm windows and doors, including one that probably went on the front entrance to the house. That left the old refrigerator about as tall as I am. I opened the fridge door. At least it's empty, I thought.

I dumped a bunch of clothes from one of the boxes looking for something, anything, that would help me move the fridge. I was thinking of some kind of belt, but then I spotted an old rag rug. I lifted one corner of the fridge, then another and stuffed the rug under its feet. I dug in the box more and found a sweatshirt that I stuffed under the other two feet of the refrigerator making it easier to slide along the tile floor. Then, bracing my back on a perpendicular wall I pushed with my legs as hard as I could. The fridge moved just enough to expose the door to Bucky 's bomb shelter.

"Ok, Clara," I said. "I'm afraid this is going to hurt, but I've got to get us out of here."

I grabbed her under her armpits. She screamed "Oh my God," and I dragged her about six feet to the door. She was so heavy I had to stop and get a better grip on her before I could take her any further. As I got her closer I realized I hadn't left a passage big enough to accommodate her size. I left Clara on the cement floor while I went back to repeat my effort to move the fridge several more inches. Geez, Clara, I thought, couldn't you have lost a little weight?

By this time I heard a cacophony of sirens outside. I've become inured to the wail of sirens, but when they stop abruptly near me, I pay attention. That's what happened as each piece of emergency equipment arrived on the scene. Radios were crackling with instructions as the first responders set to work.

I pulled her through, then grabbed at the door Bucky had built to the shelter and closed it. If those gas containers blew the rest of the house, I didn't want any debris coming through the opening. I stopped a second to catch my breath and look around. Food, water, and a whole arsenal of weapons decorated one wall. On the opposite wall, a set of clear glass canisters labeled flour, sugar, coffee and tea filled a shelf. But they didn't contain foodstuffs. They were full of coins. Gold coins.

CHAPTER FIFTY-ONE

This was not the time to ogle gold, although I must admit I was sorely tempted. Clara had passed out again, which was just as well from my perspective. I needed to focus on getting us out.

I didn't know how long ago Bucky had built the shelter, but the roots from the pumpkins were curling around the wooden door, which was rotted on one corner. I also didn't know how much dirt he had piled on top of it. I guessed it was a lot. Damn him. All that dirt was sure to muffle any sound I could make to try to alert the first responders.

No use in spending time cursing Bucky. I looked around to see if I could fashion a way out of this mess.

Bucky had built four wooden steps to the door, so I could reach it easily enough. Good for you, Bucky. I looked around and spotted a gardening claw and a small trowel. I had no idea why they would be in a shelter, but it didn't matter. Could I break through the door and dig my way out?

I grabbed the claw and started to work on the rotted corner of door. Unfortunately, it was stronger than it looked. Minutes later, minutes I didn't think we had, I was still trying to pry the corner open.

"What're you doing?" Clara had revived.

"Trying to get us out of here," I said while I continued to work.

"With a garden claw?" she asked.

"You got a better idea?"

She didn't respond.

"You bombed the train, didn't you?" I asked as I worked. "Did Bucky help you?"

"My boy had nothing to do with it," she said.

"Why? Why kill all those men, women and children?"

"The government's done worse. Do you know Timothy McVeigh was a soldier in Iraq?"

"Yes, you already told me that. How is that justification for killing people just riding the Blue Line?"

"The government put him to death for being a patriot," she said.

"Timothy McVeigh was executed for bombing a federal building in Oklahoma. He killed men, women and children. Just like you did." I pulled a piece of wood with my bare hand, and in the process shot a huge splinter under my thumbnail. Shit. Now I knew why shoving tooth picks under fingernails is a favored method of torture.

The air was getting thick with dust. Clara began to cough and I began to sneeze. Shakes from coughing must have hurt Clara's broken leg because she began to moan.

"Water," she said.

I grabbed a gallon jug of water from a top shelf and held it to her mouth. Then I took a swig of my own. Beer would have been better. I was surprised Bucky didn't have at least a six pack stashed somewhere. Clara settled down a bit.

"That was after the government killed seventy-five people in Waco. We were just people who were trying to follow our leader, David Koresh," she said.

I was trying to focus on what I was doing instead of feeling the pain in my thumb. I couldn't quite remember what happened in Waco, or when, but I had a vague recollection that the feds had screwed up a raid in Texas.

"Nineteen ninety-three. The federal government killed everyone," she said. "Except me."

Now she had my attention. I stopped my digging. The story was suddenly coming back to me. "You were a member of the Branch Davidian cult?"

"Wasn't a cult. A following. David was our savior. He was going to set us free."

I thought everyone was killed in that fiasco, but my memory

was a little foggy.

"How'd you get out?"

"I was pregnant with Bucky," she said. "We had an outhouse on the back of the property. I was peeing when I saw the ATF launch their bombs on the compound. I ran."

"So, how is that related to bombing the Blue Line train?"

"Oklahoma City was payback to the Feds for killing David and the other followers," she said. "I bombed the train to show the Feds they were wrong when they killed Timothy on June 11, 2001."

Oh my god, I thought. I'm trapped underground with a whack job. I got back to digging. "Why did you kill all those innocent people on the train?" I was indignant. "Some weren't born when that happened. Others weren't Americans."

"I wanted the government to take responsibility for killing Bucky's father," Clara said.

"One of the people you murdered was my best friend," I shouted, turning to face her.

She didn't react. Just looked at me impassively. Was she in so much pain that she didn't care how many people she had killed? Or was there something else?

"Whoa," I said, 'For killing Bucky's father?' Who was Bucky's father?"

"Why, David, of course," she said. "He was father to many of the children the feds killed. Bucky is the only one of his descendants who lives."

If I get out of this alive, I'll have an incredible story for the "I can't make this stuff up" file.

CHAPTER FIFTY-TWO

Clara moaned again, then passed out. Unfortunately, I couldn't quiz her any more.

The air was getting so dusty I was afraid we were both going to suffocate. Above us I could hear the firefighters calling for us. I tried repeatedly to respond, but every time, I began to cough uncontrollably. I thought I even heard Sergeant Olson calling my name.

My digging wasn't going to work in time. I had to come up with a different idea. I looked around the shelter. Ancient, rusted cans of baked beans weren't going to free us. Same for back issues of Playboy. Leave it to Bucky to make sure he had reading material just in case he had to stay in the shelter for a long time. Then I spied the guns on the wall.

I don't do guns. I'm a firm believer in the pen being mightier than the sword. But I watch television. Surely I had seen something that would guide me in using a gun.

I grabbed the shotgun from the wall, checked to see if it was loaded. It wasn't. Point one for Bucky and Clara. Now, how to load it? It can't be that hard. I found the safety and pushed it to on, then found a box of shells on the shelf. I grabbed two, then I braced the gun against my hip and turned it upside down with the magazine tube facing me. Then I slid two shells into the magazine tube and turned the gun over.

I stuck it through the hole I had managed to carve out of the wooden door and pushed it as hard as I could until it slipped through. My plan was to hopefully shoot into the inky black sky, to draw attention to us. Please, God, I thought, don't let me shoot anybody.

I closed my eyes and pulled the trigger. Nothing. No bang. Nothing. Then I remembered the safety. I pulled the gun back out, turned the safety to "off," and shoved it through the hole again. Once again, I squeezed my eyes shut and pulled the trigger. The shotgun jumped back like a horse kicking out a barn door as the shot went off.

I could hear the people above us moving about and shouting. "What was that? A gun shot? Where did it come from?"

"Skeeter. Skeeter. Where are you?" That was Dex.

I pulled the trigger again, releasing the second round. Again a bang and a kickback. This time I heard Dex right above me.

"Skeeter?" he shouted. He pulled on the barrel of the shotgun. I pulled back and shouted, "Dex."

"Found her." Apparently he was calling to the others.

"Don't shoot, Skeeter. We got ya." He was definitely talking to me.

"Get us out of here." Don't know if he heard me, but I figured he knew where I was because there was a scraping noise coming from the dirt above the door.

In moments, three or four people pulled up the hatch-like door. I looked up to the sky to see stars, the kind you don't see in the city. Then I took a deep breath, filling my lungs with clean country air. Dex, Sergeant Olson, and a couple other faces I didn't recognize were peering into our underground lair.

"Bilbo Baggins, at your service," I said.

CHAPTER FIFTY-THREE

April 1

Dear Rachel,

It's so hard for me to find peace with your death. I think of you all the time, wondering what your opinion might be on my new purse or Suzy's latest remark. As you know, I always think better when my fingers are running over the computer keyboard, so I decided I would write you an occasional email just to check in.

You're gonna love this. When I was digging in the box looking for something to stuff under the refrigerator in Clara's shelter, I apparently found the sweatshirt she wore when she blew up the train. The feds matched her DNA with the DNA on the sweatshirt and residue from the same bomb she used on the train.

They arrested her and charged her with bombing the train. Every time I think of all those poor people she killed, especially you, it makes me sick. She's pled guilty but there will still be a sentencing hearing. Minnesota abolished the death penalty in 1911, but because this is a federal crime she may face the same fate as her hero Timothy McVeigh.

My story about her arrest and her child with the leader of the Branch Dividians ran today, exactly a month after you died on your birthday. Ironic, isn't it? The higher-ups at the paper ran the story first as "an exclusive" in the print version before running it online. They also increased the print run by twenty-five percent in hopes readers would be enticed to subscribe again. It felt like the old days. I've attached a link to the piece.

The story about Clara was picked up by lots of bloggers, who each had a different take on what had happened. My personal favorite was the guy who wrote that Clara clearly was right to stash away all those gold coins as a hedge against the inevitable decline of the American dollar.

Apparently Steve Bridgewater, the guy who got away with robbing a bank, saw the story because I got an email from him. He said he was living happily in Antigua where he heard Mr. Ponytail was spreading ugly rumors about him. Bridgewater's exact quote: "Heraty always was a self-centered son of a bitch who thought everything was about him."

Fortun has not heard a word from Abdi. She misses him desperately but she's proud of him. To compensate for his absence, she insisted Mohamed spend more time with her. At the very least, I'm betting Mohamed thinks Abdi owes him. I'm hoping Mohamed knows enough about Abdi to fill her in.

It will come as no surprise to you that Slick and Dick, before he fell down the elevator shaft, turned up no connection between you and the bombing. Of course, they did their usual stellar reporting, which is to say they called the public relations folks for most of the developers and other big businesses in town and asked them if they had heard about anybody who was out to get you. Of course, they came up with zilch.

I know this sounds odd, but I'm glad you weren't the cause of the bombing. I know you would never want all those people to die because someone had it in for you.

April will likely be a slushy mix of rain and snow. As you know, April is probably the worst month in Minnesota, when the rest of the country enjoys the first really warm days of spring, and we do not. Always makes me feel like a kid with my nose pressed up against the window at someone else's birthday party.

All right, I can hear you saying "Get over it, Hughes, or move to Florida." Definitely not moving. Minnesota is in my DNA.

Looking back, I now see that my lucky escapes from the elevator were a sign that it's time to leave the newspaper. I will miss all the smart funny people who make up the fabric of journalism. There's no more entertaining place to work than a newsroom. But I just can't do it anymore. I've been gone from home too much. I miss the time with the girls, and even Michael. The buyout was just too attractive to pass up.

Michael and I are heading to IKEA this afternoon to get me a desk and some bookshelves for my new home office. Here's hoping our working relationship is as good as it was when we were kids in our first newspaper jobs. What do you think?

More to come.
Love ya,
Skeeter

The End